Courting
Samira

Courting Samira

A Novel

AMAL AWAD

HARPERVIA

An Imprint of HarperCollinsPublishers

HarperCollins books may be purchased for educational, business, or sales promotional use. For information, please email the Special Markets Department at SPsales@harpercollins.com.

Originally published as *Courting Samira* in Australia in 2021 by Pantera Press Pty Limited.

FIRST HARPERVIA EDITION PUBLISHED IN 2023

Designed by Ralph Fowler

Library of Congress Cataloging-in-Publication Data has been applied for.

ISBN 978-0-06-331767-3

23 24 25 26 27 LBC 5 4 3 2 1

For my parents, Samia and Mahmud Awad,
with love and gratitude

But when a young lady is to be a heroine,
the perverseness of forty surrounding families
cannot prevent her. Something must and will
happen to throw a hero in her way.

—Jane Austen, *Northanger Abbey*

Courting Samira

Chapter 1

When I was in kindergarten, my class's end-of-year presentation was *The Nutcracker Suite*. Being slightly plump, rosy cheeked, and all golden curls, I'd been chosen by my teacher to play one of the sugarplum fairies—no small honor. There were playground fights over the sugarplum fairy roles.

My costume was composed of my sports leotard (a vibrant fire-engine red covered in silver tinsel), tights, and a wooden spoon wrapped in aluminium foil with a homemade star at the top.

I sparkled. People talked about it for days. Admittedly, that was mainly because a boy named Matty had run out mid-performance in tears. Still, Mum told me later that a little boy in the audience had pointed me out to his mother during my performance and said I was his favorite. Unfortunately, we'd lacked the foresight to take down his contact details, but as it was unlikely he was Muslim, that was probably for the best.

The memory played on my mind as I sat in front of my latest suitor. His name was, not surprisingly, Mohammed. He wore a sour, bored expression and didn't seem interested in even glancing at me. Not even in a mildly curious How-can-I-look-at-her-without-making-it-obvious-that-I'm-looking-at-her sort of way.

I couldn't take my eyes off his hairstyle—gelled-back black hair, like a manga character. I half expected him to leap from his seat and speak out of sync. I actually began hoping he would, to be honest. It would have made for an exciting turn of events.

I looked over at my mother, who was engaged in conversation with Manga Boy's mother. Our fathers were also deeply engrossed in a discussion punctuated by occasional guffaws. Any moment they could be high-fiving, such was the frivolity.

Well. At least they were all having fun.

Manga Boy tilted his head slightly to the side, perching his cheekbone on his index finger. The sourness swelled to *Zoolander* proportions. Truth was, I was starting to feel a little sorry for him. Clearly, he was here against his will. He didn't seem at all interested in assessing me beyond a cursory glance when I'd entered the room an hour ago.

And not because he was the pious, shy type who was lowering his gaze. He was evidently the bored, simpering type who was thinking one month's army training in the bush was preferable to a Saturday night door-knock appeal.

In my universe, instead of boyfriends there were only potential husbands.

Wasn't it every girl's dream to get proposed to? Well, try being proposed to no less than seventeen times—including twice by one particularly overzealous suitor—since the age of eighteen. And they weren't sweeping, romantic *Will-you-marry-me?*-written-in-the-sky types of proposals. Like any courtship ritual, door-knock appeals had clear procedures.

After the all-important first visit, a suitor would call if he liked me (or his mum told him he liked me), or we wouldn't hear back at all. It was rather like a first date with no obligation to call again no matter how well you thought it went.

Out of all the suitors, four or five had never called after our meeting. And I'd been through this enough times to realize Manga Boy's family certainly wasn't going to call. [Insert confident, woman-of-the-world laugh of indifference.]

Still, dud factor notwithstanding, the majority had called. They hadn't seen enough to be turned off, or they'd seen enough to be keenly interested.

I was living my very own Victorian-era-style courtship. The only things missing were the fancy costumes and calling cards, and we didn't have a butler or a posh name for our house like Wyndham Cottage. But aside from that, the similarities were rather eerie.

The minutes ticked by, and I realized I'd been playing a scene from *Gladiator* in my mind: the one where Maximus takes on the gladiators' ring by himself, then yells rather dramatically, "Are you not entertained?"

I loved that movie. But naturally this wasn't the best of signs.

I directed my thoughts back to my stint as a sugarplum fairy. I remembered how the tinsel on my leotard had crinkled throughout the performance. I'd been so shiny and new. My moment in the spotlight. I'd held so much promise. The future had stretched before me in all its glory. And, as it had been kindy, the boys had boy germs and the girls had been all feminine and precious. As with warring gangs, the playground had observed strict boundaries: male versus female. *West Side Story* for tots, minus the tragic ending.

Although, I couldn't say I'd ever forgotten my first crush—also Muslim, also named Mohammed. He'd broken my heart when he wouldn't share his mortadella sandwich with me. I hadn't invited him to my birthday party by way of revenge. Seeing as Mum didn't let me invite any boys, it hadn't been quite as sweet as I would have liked.

Point was, there'd been very neat and logical divisions. Nobody had breached those boundaries. The rules had been strictly enforced (note earlier observation on respective boy–girl germs). Not at all like this. Giving up a perfectly nice Saturday evening to be ignored. I would've much preferred to waste a Wednesday night being ignored.

But moving on. I noticed that Manga Boy's hair had flopped a little to the side, and I found myself studying it closely. It must have been a science in itself, really. Ensuring the right amount of gel was applied to achieve maximum density. Getting the flip just right. Allowing the hair to *tumble* as opposed to *fall* over his forehead.

I'd never seen it in real life before. The manga look, that is. A feat of engineering.

Oh God, it had come to this. I'd had my share of dud suitors, but I'd never, ever resorted to critiquing a man's hairstyle in such detail. So long as it wasn't a nod to Flock of Seagulls, the door-knocker's hair was of little importance. Honestly. I didn't usually pay much attention to that sort of thing. I generally knew what to expect by now, even if Manga Boy did bring something new to the whole awkward setup.

And, well, it wasn't as though I was expecting him to be an Arab-warrior type—my preferred choice. I knew a suitor wasn't going to burst into our house astride a magnificent horse, wielding a sword. It would have been totally brilliant if one did, though. I'd have definitely considered him.

Mum always told me to leave if I wasn't interested, but I'd

never had the courage to do that. Let *him* leave, thought I. That, and it felt a bit rude. I hated to be rude.

But really, door-knock appeals were like paint by numbers with only minor variations on the theme. Like whether the suitor was homegrown or FOB (fresh off the boat). There was always an assessor (mum/sister/relative). We always offered snacks and beverages. We stopped short of offering in-flight entertainment.

At least there were biscuits, so the meetings weren't total write-offs. And Mum always put out the fancy chocolate ones, not the plain shortbread she'd buy for us ordinarily.

I rose from my seat without a nod or a smile and disappeared down the hall to my bedroom. Sitting on my bed, I checked my phone. No new messages. I considered venting to my cousin Lara. She would understand. Single herself, with no plans to get married, she was prepared for the possibility that, unable to outwit fate, she might end up hitched with some obnoxious kids (her words) before intended.

I began composing a message—anything to delay my return to Mohammed's hairdo and his engaging company. My life seemed to be turning into a really bad episode of *The Price Is Right*, but instead of a car and home appliances, I was the prize and the contestants were all potential suitors.

Lara and I had joked about this before.

I could just imagine my parents standing on a stage, microphones in hand, cracking million-dollar smiles while crazy lights flashed around them. And then the voice-over man (one of my uncles) would boom out, "Suitor number 534, come on *down*!" in Arabic and English. The trademark music would play as the suitor jumped his way down to the stage, everyone cheering and calling out in-jokes, and the voice-over man (well, my uncle) would make me sound like a bargain, which I guessed I shouldn't sniff at.

"Samira Abdel-Aziz is twenty-seven years old! She has never been married, graduated with a communications degree, and currently works as an editorial assistant at *Bridal Bazaar* magazine! In her spare time, she likes to read books and watch movies. She is also proficient at burning salads."

Yes, I had a communications degree. It was a continuing source of distress to my relatives that I had "studied" (and some of them actually used the air quotes) communications at uni. A series of substandard media jobs had followed. A dreary trajectory made worse by the API (Arab Price Index). Case in point: My cousin Zahra had excelled by becoming a lawyer; I was the "dumb" one. Her stocks rocketed once she graduated; mine suffered a loss.

However, when I'd gotten the assistant's role at the magazine, I'd enjoyed a minor bump in market value. My newfound success had pleased my entire family, mainly because they'd thought it would help when it came to my own big day. Not sure how, really. But when the words *Bridal Bazaar* magazine" became my get-out-of-jail-free card, I'd learned to invoke it shamelessly as needed.

As fortune would have it, just as I came to terms with returning to the sitting room, my mobile phone rang. I'd been intending to go right back to being ignored, God's honest truth. But someone was calling me, and it would be rude not to answer.

Zahra. Shit. My aforementioned cousin Zahra lawyer-beat-communications-grad.

But . . . what if this was important? The guests would just have to wait.

"Samira."

"Hi, Zahra."

"Are you busy?"

"Erm, sort of."

"Really? It's just that you're usually at home on Saturday watching TV or whatever. If you're busy, I can call back another time."

Oh God. She was so good at that. A Jedi master of putdowns. "Wow, black really does slim people down!" was one for the history books. "It's just that you don't really have any hobbies, so why would you be busy?" was another fave.

My family in Australia was actually quite small by Arab standards, meaning I still had a whole bunch of relatives I'd never met who lived in the Arab world (and Chicago). But in Sydney there was just one aunt on Mum's side and two uncles on Dad's.

Still, my family tree wasn't so much a tree as a forest, or even a jungle, teeming with weird and wonderful species. And like all jungles, there were the predators, the prey, and the pure.

My cousin Zahra—twenty-six, lawyer in a top-tier firm, single, and evil—fell squarely within the predator category.

"That's okay, Zahra," I said calmly. "What's the problem?"

"You watch too much TV, Samira."

"You're calling to tell me I watch too much TV?"

"No. I'm just saying it now since it came up."

"I don't ask you how you spend your time, Zahra." Besides, so what if my idea of a decent Saturday night was to stay in wearing my Betty Boop pj's, with a packet of fun-size Snickers and a movie? I only needed me for that, and I got along well with me.

"That's because you already know I don't have time for silly things," she explained.

"Oh, right. Well, in that case, it's none of your business," I said, looking toward the door. Manga Boy was suddenly feeling like a more preferable option.

"Sorry, I guess some people just can't handle honesty."

Another not terribly subtle put-down.

"I can handle honesty, Zahra." Totally calm. Thinking of meadows and rainbows and chocolate and other lovely things.

"Well, I'm just saying one thing and look at how defensive you're getting."

I'd stopped trying to get along with her years ago. By now, I was like *Kill Bill*'s Uma Thurman to her Lucy Liu, sans funky yellow jumpsuit and assorted weaponry.

"Zahra, what do you want?"

"My mum asked me to find out when you can come by to get the olives."

"What olives?"

Zahra sighed. "Samira," she sang. "My mum marinated some olives for your mum. You need to pick them up," she said, enunciating every syllable.

"I am not an idiot," I enunciated back.

"Look, just come by whenever. Later."

I hung up, thankful she'd spared me the career speech: the one where she'd point out how "lucky" I was because I "don't have a proper career to worry about."

Oh, and how I just wasn't "motivated like that."

Agitated, I put down my phone and finally went back out to the guests, a sacrificial air about me. As I sat down in the sitting room, I glanced over at Manga Boy and noted his look of desperation, his eyes pleading with his mother to end the torture.

It was actually kind of amusing. Although, it occurred to me that I should have been insulted. Here we'd put out the nice Cadbury biscuits, and all evening I'd been dutiful and obliging and everything. Yet all Manga Boy could do was sit there and pout.

Some people are simply ungrateful.

Chapter 2

The following Monday afternoon, I was in the middle of drafting an email to Lara when Marcus began hovering. Marcus was head designer at the magazine and, despite being extremely annoying, was rather clever at his job. He'd won a bunch of awards last year.

The staff were planning afternoon drinks. They would usually go out for drinks on Fridays, but the sales team had exceeded budget, so they were in celebration mode. Or, as Cate explained, "Any excuse for a piss up."

Respect for me among members of the sales team had increased greatly the moment they found out I didn't drink my weight in liquor. Somehow it meant more for them. They had been, however, somewhat perturbed to discover that I didn't drink at all, and at the first work function I attended, a small semicircle of watchers had gathered around me. Our finance manager, Tim, had raised an eyebrow and said, "You know, I don't think I've ever known a Muslim."

That sort of comment would have normally pissed me off, because it wasn't as though we were a bloody species one had to familiarize oneself with. Like a David Attenborough doco, but instead of animals and plants, there'd be a man geared up in a safari suit on the lookout for Muslims. "By golly! There's another one. This one's white!" Then he'd approach ever so slowly and continue to narrate in soothing tones: "Here we have a bona fide Muslim who doesn't drink! We shan't get too close yet, though, as we're not sure if it's easily provoked!"

But Tim was nice enough, so I kept my thoughts to myself.

While everyone at work understood why I never attended drinks, Marcus would still come by every week to try to shame me into going with them.

"How about no?" I said, still typing. I actually had a ton of work to do and I'd spent the last hour looking at bags online. I wouldn't ordinarily do that, but I was still feeling a little disillusioned after Manga Boy's visit. Only two things gave me comfort in times of distress: prayer (which I attempted to do five times a day) and shopping (which, rather unoriginally, I wished I could do five times a day). Both were capable of inspiring the same warm, fuzzy feelings of comfort and joy within me.

Marcus laughed. Oh God, the hyena laugh.

Cate groaned. "Marcus, shut up! Is he hassling you again, Samira? She doesn't friggin' drink!"

"She can have orange juice!" Marcus said with a smirk.

This was his cause; getting me to Friday drinks sat just below anti-whaling but beat out obtaining subsidized vending machines for the office kitchen. We were all behind him on that one, though.

"I don't go into pubs, Marcus," I said in my maternal voice—the one I reserved for my nieces. I'd only told him this several hundred times before.

Marcus pouted in response, much like my nieces when I refused them a second helping of chocolate. "I can't believe you won't even have an OJ with us," he said.

"Get used to disappointment," I replied distractedly, finally sending off my email. I'd stolen that line from *The Princess Bride*, my absolute all-time favorite comfort-food movie.

I looked up from my screen and waited for one of Marcus's stunning one-liners. He always had them ready for swift deployment. Cate suspected that he had a list of them written down, catalogued for different occasions, like Mr. Collins in *Pride and Prejudice* (Cate's ultimate comfort-food movie).

"Marcus, did you reflow that feature layout yet?" said Cate, coming to my rescue.

"The system crashed and I had to start again from scratch," he said, still leaning against my cubicle.

"What was the problem?"

"A bug," said Marcus. "But nothing I couldn't fix with a crucifix and some holy water."

The hyena laugh again.

He looked at me, and I nodded and smiled. *Yes, just nod and smile.* It was only Monday.

When Marcus finally turned away, I put my head in my hands and massaged my temples. I truly believed in God's mercy, and right then I prayed wholeheartedly for it to be showered down upon me.

I was the first to admit that *Bridal Bazaar* magazine was a vast improvement on my previous place of employment—an accounting firm called Pachowski and Pachowski, where I'd been secretary to three chain-smoking men with potty mouths, including a recently arrived Indian Hindu who had wished he could "propose me." And in actuality, there was only one Pachowski. When I'd asked the boss why there were two in the name, he'd said in his strong Eastern European accent, "Looks better. When can you start?"

Vast, vast improvement.

At least the magazine was one of those trendy workplaces where everyone called each other by cool nicknames, and at regular intervals a game of cricket or a round of Hula-Hooping would begin. So far, Cate was reigning champion in the latter.

There was Timbo (Tim), Bazza (Barry), and Mickey (Michael) and Ollie (Oliver) and Shazza (Sharon). You get the idea. Incidentally, my "nickname" was Mira. Samira became Mira, which was preferable to Sammy, or Sazza, now that I thought about it.

We even found the time to circulate emails that contained links to immensely profound and revealing tests like "Which Care Bear Are You?" In the interest of full disclosure, I was Tenderheart Bear, which meant I was a keeper of the peace, a thinker, I was organized, and people listened to me. I didn't say it was necessarily accurate.

"I really like your headscarf today, Samira," Marcus said, turning back to face me. He leaned his forearms against my cubicle wall again, evidently settling in for the morning.

"Thanks, Marcus." I typed away at an email, this one work related.

"You're all matching."

"Yes." I continued typing. Marcus didn't move.

"Is it hard to find headscarves to match your clothes?" he said a few seconds later.

"Not really. You just look for variety." I looked up and gave him the smile I'd give to the Mormon boys who stood on the street corner near my building and yelled, "Assalamu alaykum!" to me as I walked past. Cheeky buggers.

"Samina! Coffee, please," demanded Jeff, the publisher, as he walked past my desk.

Despite the fact that I was his editorial assistant, a year later he still didn't have my name right.

I smiled at Marcus apologetically and pushed myself away from the desk. Marcus walked off as I went in the direction of the kitchen.

Despite a reasonable amount of office space, there was a shortage of meeting rooms and the kitchen was tiny. Which was a pity, as it could have doubled as a meeting room. The kitchen was, however, a substantial improvement from the insect-ridden one at Pachowski and Pachowski. At least here we had utilities and appliances, and occupational health and safety rules.

There was a small microwave, which no one but me ever bothered to clean. We also had a toaster, a hot water tank beside the sink, and a fridge that had seen better days. Rounding out the benefits were unlimited supplies of instant coffee, tea, Milo, five different varieties of milk, sugar, and stirrers. Which naturally made the workday all the more tolerable. I wasn't sure I'd be able to face it without stirrers.

And we had never, I repeat *never*, misused the significant stirrers supply to build a castle. Nor had it gotten knocked down by a random cricket ball while Marcus yelled, "Incoming!"

Just as I was finishing Jeff's coffee, he boomed out from across the hall. "Samina! Where's my bloody coffee?"

I jumped, spilling the contents of the mug all over the kitchen counter.

Bugger. I cleaned up the mess as quickly as possible before pouring a fresh cup. It was the instant kind, so it wasn't really coffee, but Jeff seemed to like it. He'd told me once that it helped to calm his nerves. I wasn't exactly in a rage to find out what he would be like without his fix.

Cate flew into the kitchen just as I was leaving it, giving me a shock and causing me to spill the second cup of coffee. This time I was the lucky recipient of the contents.

"I'm so sorry!" Cate said, her eyes wide. She grabbed the roll of paper towels and ripped some off. "Does it burn?"

"No, it's okay." I put the mug down on the counter. "Just feels hot and soggy." I inspected the damage. "I'm wearing black at least."

Cate turned on the tap and wet a paper towel, then began fussing over me to sponge off the damp spots.

"I'm going to smell like instant coffee now," I whimpered.

"Oh, honey, I'm so sorry," Cate said again.

"Don't worry. But I can tell it's going to be one of those weeks." I sighed.

"Well, that's why I came in. I forgot to tell you that Jeff wants you to attend the bridal convention with me."

I was about to reply when Marcus walked by and then circled back to the kitchen door. He assessed us for a moment, Cate still mid-clean. He smiled, then winked, cocking a finger in our direction before taking off.

Cate shook her head sadly once he was gone. "Such a shame. He's so *pretty*," she said, tossing away the damp paper towels.

"Too much information, Cate," I said, washing Jeff's mug so that I could make him a third cup of instant's finest.

"I'm just saying the man is good-looking."

"Uh-huh," I said, scooping in some coffee. I supposed Marcus wasn't bad looking, although I couldn't be sure because I tried never to look directly at him. That, I surmised, would have the effect of drawing him in, the way an unsuspecting tourist might provoke a dangerous animal while on safari in Africa.

"Anyways," she said more brightly. "The convention. Freebies galore, baby!"

"Great," I replied with a tragic sigh. "That's just what I need right now." More samples of crap I was unlikely to get any use out of. But perhaps there'd be chocolate and cake pops, I realized hopefully.

"You can write something up," said Cate, completely oblivious to my sarcasm. She grabbed the mug off me and poured in some hot water.

"Sure," I said as I grabbed a stirrer. "Tell me, is this convention by any chance run by Arabs?"

Cate laughed. "No. But it'll be a nice change from the office. And from making coffees," she assured me, handing back the mug.

"I suppose so."

"What's with all the sweets?" She pointed at the tray of baklawa I'd brought in that morning. Manga Boy's family had given it to us, but because we weren't likely to finish it all at home, Mum had told me to bring the surplus in to work. This was always a good idea, since just about the only thing *Bridal Bazaar* staff were united in—besides discontent—was food. Group emails were ignored unless they contained an internet quiz or an alert for cake when someone was celebrating a birthday or leaving.

"A door-knocker brought them," I said as Cate dug into a piece of baklawa and commended Manga Boy's generosity.

"Another dud?" she said with a sympathetic smile. "What number are we up to? Twenty?"

Twenty-three, actually, but I didn't correct her.

Cate knew all about the duds, and to her credit, she was generally an attentive listener, as I was to her when she'd had the date from hell and was trying to cleanse herself of the memory.

"So, what happened?" inquired Cate.

"He looked like a manga character."

We were both quiet for a moment. I was cradling Jeff's mug, and Cate was looking as though she was trying to figure out a complex equation.

"Huh," said Cate eventually, nodding slowly. "A manga character. Did he sound like one too?"

"I don't know. He didn't say a word to me."

"Ouch. Well, obviously there's something wrong with *him*. You're gorgeous. Those blue eyes of yours? What isn't there to like?"

"You have to say things like that because you're my friend."

"Oh, come on, Samira. You just said he looked like a manga character. There could be trauma there. God knows what's going through that boy's gelled head," she said, and I bowed to her knowledge.

That afternoon, after what was perhaps an ill-advised double-shot coffee break, I logged on to Facebook. I was planning to do some intense work, of course, but I just needed to get settled in for the afternoon. I didn't do this every day. Just some days, and everyone did it on occasion. It was practically an unwritten rule that we'd spend an hour or so at work doing other things. In fact, I was pretty sure I'd read something about that somewhere.

Within a few moments a chat window popped up on my screen. I looked around to check no one was about, feeling a bit like a renegade. Not surprisingly, it was Hakeem, a childhood friend with whom I had almost daily contact.

Hakeem: "The most perfidious way of harming a cause
   consists of defending it deliberately with faulty
   arguments."

Hakeem: ?

Samira: Brad Pitt?

Hakeem: Lovely, Samira. It's good to see you're not
   expanding your mind with trash.

Samira: That stings. Brad does a lot of good for humanity.
   He's adopted, like, a hundred kids, and he builds houses
   and stuff.

Hakeem: I'll get you a book that requires thinking.

Samira: No need. I just picked up some Mills & Boon
   hot-doctors-in-the-desert romances. I'm all set.

Hakeem: Right. Hours of introspection to follow, no doubt.

Samira: There are so many levels to them.

Hakeem: I saw your parents the other night at Westfield.
   They were arguing over a book.

Samira: Perfect. No doubt they drew a crowd.

Hakeem: Your mother was saying your father didn't need an
   encyclopedia on botany. It was actually quite funny. Have
   you ever noticed how your parents fight but don't really
   fight?

Yes. The smallest things could set them off. A casual observation, a simple statement about the weather. It was unbeliev-
ably embarrassing when it happened in public, especially in
shopping centers, because people around us would start staring. And God knew what they thought, what with the headscarves and Dad exclaiming, "Don't abbrehensive me!"

Dad had yet to master the letter *p*, because it doesn't exist
in the Arabic alphabet, nor did he have a handle on verbs—no

matter how many times I've told him "apprehensive" isn't a verb, he'd still say, "Don't abbrehensive me," whenever he got upset.

Samira: I'm sorry you had to witness that.

Hakeem: They made up, don't worry.

Samira: Gawd. That doesn't make it better!

Hakeem: Now, don't be like that. That's marriage. Understanding, compromise.

Samira: I'll have to get back to you on that one. I'm having enough trouble with the pre-marriage part. But for the record, I've no doubt I'll be a perfectly lovely, compromising wife if I ever get married.

Hakeem: Indeed. You think you have it hard, but did you ever think about what the poor guy is going through when he comes for a visit?

Samira: I'll have you know that I am the very essence of hospitality. The very essence.

Hakeem: I don't doubt it. But are you just ignoring what I'm saying?

Samira: Of course not. I'm copying all of this down as you type.

Hakeem: I hope you're not like this when guys come to visit.

Samira: Bad?

Hakeem: Allahu akbar.

Samira: Just saying. So anyway, you still looking at the moment?

Hakeem: Not really.

Samira: You should get a move on.

Hakeem: True. I do have four positions to fill.

Samira: Ah, those polygamy jokes never get old.

Hakeem: Shouldn't you be at work?

Samira: I am at work.

Hakeem: And Facebook falls into your job description how exactly?

Samira: Is that a trick question?

Hakeem: It's Friedrich Nietzsche, by the way. The quote.

Samira: Oh yeah. Didn't he invent the light bulb or something?

Hakeem: I'm confiscating your magazines.

I knew who Nietzsche was, of course (even if I hadn't known he'd said that quote). Obviously, being a humanities grad, I was a voracious reader. But I tended to filter out things that weren't relevant to my life. Working at *Bridal Bazaar* didn't require Nietzsche. It required shoes and dresses—even if they were all white—and that was something I could always relate to, no matter what else was happening in my life.

Samira: Is it from *The Gay Science*?

Hakeem: I'm impressed.

(Lucky guess.)

Samira: You really do read a lot for a scientist. Ordinarily scientists lack imagination.

Hakeem: I'm an engineer.

Samira: What's your point?

Hakeem: You don't remember what I do, do you?

Samira: Not true! You're an engineer. Taking creativity to new levels.

Educated Arab men were almost always either engineers or IT specialists. Medicine was also a valued profession. Law was yet to make a solid impression. I'd no idea why, though I suspected it was because Arabs once ruled the world of science and invented mathematical equations.

> Hakeem: OK. What kind of engineer am I?
> Samira: You told me once but you know, halfway, zzzzzzzz.
> Hakeem: I don't think your work stimulates you enough. Find something that challenges you more.
> Samira: Just last week there was a breaking story on warring models at an expo!
> Hakeem: Really?
> Samira: No. But it could happen.
> Hakeem: No doubt Zahra will be tapping into your knowledge of weddings soon.
> Samira: Why's that?
> Hakeem: Because she's getting engaged.
> Samira: Are you joking?
> Hakeem: You didn't know?

No, I didn't bloody know. I'd just spoken to her on Saturday and she hadn't mentioned a thing. I would've remembered a detail like that.

My heart plummeted into my stomach. I mean, really? Zahra getting engaged? Evil cousin, successful-lawyer-with-career, has-everything-but-it's-never-enough Zahra was *getting engaged*? Zahra, who used to mock anyone who expressed a desire to get married?

I was rather surprised I was finding out this way, despite

knowing full well I was the last person Zahra would talk to about a guy.

> Samira: I didn't know.
> Hakeem: OK, well, it's this weekend, inshallah.

My face grew warm. Then I felt shaky inside, and I remembered why I avoided double-shot coffees. There'd been an incident once involving some slight hand tremors. And, well, me actually yelling at Marcus. (I still felt rather awful about that.) Although, in my defense, Cate had said that my outburst against Marcus was in response to a silly question about the length of a Muslim man's beard, which followed a query about the Islamic version of Catholic confession (there isn't one).

> Samira: I have to go.

I didn't even wait for Hakeem to reply before I logged off and messaged Lara.

Chapter 3

A couple of hours and multiple work distractions later, Jeff appeared at my desk.

"Ethnic weddings."

"Excuse me?"

"We want to do a story on ethnic weddings. Diversity's all the rage," he said, like he'd just discovered an elixir for eternal youth. "I'm telling you because I want you to work on this story. Yeah? It will be a writing opportunity for you, Samina. You'll have insight Cate doesn't." He indicated my headscarf. "Any relatives of yours getting married?"

He waited.

I was about to say no when I realized that I apparently *did* have a relative (evilness notwithstanding) getting married. Zahra was getting engaged, which would eventually lead to marriage and naturally a wedding of some sort.

I wasn't about to mention this to Jeff, though, otherwise I'd end up having to cover evil Zahra's wedding. Wouldn't that just have been the icing on the wedding cake?

"Don't forget to send out a reminder about the team-building exercise," continued Jeff, not even waiting for an answer to his previous question. "Did you check the advertisements for the cadetships? I may make changes to the photographer ad—

they keep bloody getting it wrong. Get me some coffee, please. Now, please."

Jeff walked off and my mind went into *Oh-crap* mode. I'd forgotten all about the team-building exercise. I had no desire to bond with anyone, let alone my coworkers, and I'd been dreading it ever since it was first proposed a couple of months ago—hence my lack of organization. It was scheduled for this Friday and was meant to be a Bridge Climb, but I hadn't confirmed the booking. I doubted I'd be able to secure enough spots at such short notice.

I was used to being kicked when I was down. In my family it was survival of the fittest, none of this "We're a team" business. If we did that exercise where you fall back onto a crowd of people standing behind you, we'd all go splat. This would be followed by a lecture on why we went splat, and by the end we'd be acknowledging that it was indeed our own fault for going splat. (Arab Guilt in all its glory.)

Images of me tripping and dangling off Harbour Bridge attached to Marcus also haunted me. I'd be on the evening news, and everyone would talk about me being seen with a boy. My reputation would be in tatters. I'd never be able to show my face in polite society again, even though I wasn't exactly sure who constituted polite society. I was fearful of being shunned from it all the same.

Half an hour later, Lara finally appeared online.

> Lara: Baby face!
> Samira: Lara! Where the hell have you been?
> Lara: Ah, ghastly work! It's killing me.

Samira: Working overtime?

Lara: Yessssssss. And the commute is KILLING ME.

Samira: You only live half an hour away from work.

Lara: I don't have a caaaaaaar.

Samira: I've seen you behind the wheel. Let's be grateful.

Lara: Why did I think I could be a nurse? Today a patient
vomited on me.

Samira: Only six more months of your placement. And TMI. I
have news. Bet you can't guess.

Lara: Who's getting married?

Samira: Zahra.

Lara: Nooooooooooooooooooooooooo!!!!!!! I don't believe it!

I looked up nervously and saw Jeff hovering nearby. I alerted
Lara and jumped up to go and call her on her mobile before
Jeff could bark another order at me. Or catch me on Facebook.
Either-or, really.

"What poor victim has she convinced to marry her?"
shrieked Lara when she answered my call.

"Come on, you know that Zahra is only selectively evil. She's
actually nice to people who don't give a crap about her."

"True. I give it a month. Seriously, who *is* the poor sod?"

"I don't know anything yet." I'd know more soon enough,
though, because information spread through the family network as smoothly and efficiently as machine parts on a factory
assembly line. The key was to make sure you didn't look like
you wanted to know the information. Make it seem like the
info was but a minor piece of news and you would be showered
with juicy tidbits. Otherwise, Mum would purse her lips and
change the subject to tomorrow night's dinner. By that point
the cause was lost and retreat was your only option.

"I want details!" Lara demanded.

"I promise I'll tell you as soon as I know."

"When's the engagement?"

"This weekend."

"Bloody hell! That's a bit unexpected!" gasped Lara.

"I know. She called me on Saturday and didn't mention a thing."

"Samira, I know you, and I know what's going through your head. Do not be upset by this. She is evil, and in no way is this a reflection of her value."

Lara was a good person, really, but she actively disliked Zahra. Any mention of her was like pressing a bruise. And in any case, she was completely right. Zahra's engagement wasn't an indication of her worth. So she had found someone. Except I did wonder what sort of person she'd be getting engaged to. She really was a difficult person. "Smug" was the word, actually. That and she used to mock me for entertaining suitors, like she was allergic to marriage.

"Well, anyway, I think I need to get my life in order," I said as I crouched in the stairwell.

"Honey, you'll be fine so long as you remember that all boys suck."

The biggest way they sucked, Lara once told me, was in the control they had over our emotions, a power the really sneaky ones were completely aware of. She likened them to bulls in a china shop. "The more they realize they're screwing things up, the more they panic and buck about, which of course does even more damage, which then messes with our heads," she'd said.

"I think I might lose it if one more dud comes through our door," I grumbled. "Is it too much to ask for someone without an obvious complex?"

"Um, yes! We *are* Arab, Samira. What did you expect? This is why I don't do the door-knock thing."

"I know," I said with a dejected sigh. "I guess it's just been a bit of an ordinary year so far."

"Have you been watching soppy romantic comedies?"

"No! It just hasn't been going very well."

"Remember to always be grateful anyway," advised Lara in a moment of seriousness. "Things could always be worse. You could be Zahra, for example."

A very brief moment of seriousness.

Still, she had a point. I should have been thankful that I wasn't jobless or stuck in an unhappy marriage.

"Anyway," Lara continued. "Just start getting more selective about who you allow into your house. You're going to have to revise the screening process, methinks."

"I think I have to stop doing them," I said, realizing I was more than happy to call a moratorium on the whole door-knock-appeal process altogether.

"Do it. Seriously. The further you are away from all that negative stuff, like the conveyor belt of loser suitors, the better you'll feel."

"Yes."

"Look, I have to get going. Do you have enough ice cream at home to last you?"

I thought for a moment. "I don't know actually."

Lara and I had a rule that we weren't allowed to overindulge in self-pity. But we were allowed to eat tubs of ice cream because that was what girls always did on those American TV shows whenever they were down. We weren't sure why. But personally, I couldn't see any downside to a plan that involved sugar.

"Look, what lies within us is nothing in comparison to what we've done and what we'll do," offered Lara profoundly, trying to quote a bookmark I'd once given her.

"Don't you mean 'What lies behind us and what lies before us are tiny matters compared to what lies within us'?" I said. Attributed to Emerson, but almost definitely not him.

"Same diff. Look, will you just do as I say? Otherwise, you'll end up considering another loser like The Boy. Oh Lord, babes, I have to go," whispered Lara. "I promise we'll chat soon, yeah?"

"Sure."

"Bye, sweetie. Mwah!"

The Boy. He was a bad memory. Lara and I never used his real name in conversation: he was always referred to as The Boy, The Loser, or He Who Shall Not Be Named. Only Lara knew about him, and she cyber-pinkie swore she wouldn't breathe a syllable about it to anyone. Not that she needed to: she was a bit excitable (in an endearing way, of course, which she put down to being three-quarters Arab and one-quarter Libyan), but she would lie down in traffic for me.

Literally. She'd done it once when we were younger. I was nine and she was ten. She'd only gotten up when we'd heard her mum's shrill voice crying, "Allahu akbar! Lara!" Admittedly she'd done it on our quiet street, and there'd been no cars, but it was the thought that counted.

Anyway, Muslim or not, sometimes we had choices outside of the traditional *Price Is Right* format. And Lara and I had had our share of dud prospects come our way by these other means—especially Lara. We'd never done anything inappropriate, of course. We just never explicitly told our parents about them because that would involve explanation and possibly having to manipulate the truth, which *I* avoided because I didn't like lying and wasn't very good at it.

I often wondered about Lara, though. The most she'd ever admitted to were some "cheeky" kisses ("pashing, not petting"), but that could have meant a whole heap of things. I didn't judge, but I was curious.

Chapter 4

All right, I can do this. It's easy. I'm not afraid of heights. Or plummeting spectacularly to my death.

Actually, I was afraid of heights. I obviously hadn't thought this through properly before booking. As I'd anticipated, we'd lost our booking for the Bridge Climb since I'd forgotten to confirm it in time. So that was how I ended up standing on a platform at one end of a flying fox rigid with fear and questioning the value of my own existence.

Okay, so I'd dropped the ball. But I'd been understandably distracted. And the most recent distraction still loomed: Zahra's engagement. Most of me didn't care an ounce that she was getting engaged. But part of me was, well, *something.* I had no idea what. Maybe it was as Lara had diagnosed. I couldn't understand why so many great things seemed to happen for Zahra when she was such a horrible person. Either way, the feeling was on a par with ripping open a wound and pouring a box of Saxa salt on it.

On Monday afternoon, as I'd frantically searched online for team-building exercises that would cater to us at such short notice, Zahra had called me up just as I was on the verge of wanting to hurt myself.

"What's wrong?" she inquired, a little taken aback at the panic in my tone.

"I am in so much trouble right now," I whispered, although I wasn't sure why I bothered; everyone in the office knew by then. "I was supposed to organize a team-building thing, but I didn't book the Bridge Climb early enough."

"You're doing the Bridge Climb?"

"No, not anymore."

"Oh, you should. It's so much fun," she said languidly. "If you can handle that sort of thing. You're not afraid of heights, right?"

I pictured the *Kill Bill* moment again but snapped back into focus.

"Someone mentioned a team-building place the other day," Zahra continued. "It sounded pretty good, but it involved sporty activities," she offered a little grudgingly.

"Where? What's it called?" Hope surged through me as I prayed for a solution, *any* solution. I'd have agreed to line dancing at that point.

"Can't remember the name, but I know it's in Picton. Just Google it. So anyway, I have some news," she said perkily.

As if I hadn't heard. The crew of the starship *Enterprise* probably knew. She'd already changed her Facebook relationship status to "In a relationship," no doubt a precursor to the almighty "Engaged."

"I heard. Congratulations, Zahra." She may be evil, but she was entitled to that at least.

After hanging up, I'd quickly drafted an email to the team, and a separate, strictly businesslike one for Jeff.

> Subject: Changes to team-building exercise
> Due to unforeseen circumstances, there has been a slight
> change of plans for Friday's team-building exercise. We're

now going to the True Blue Team Building Center in Picton,
not doing a Bridge Climb (which I hear is highly overrated).

Please be here by 7 a.m. sharp, as we're traveling by bus
and cannot wait for stragglers.

Samira

Picton ended up being much farther away than I'd anticipated. On the bus on the way there, I scanned the program the
instructor had emailed me. In my rush to fix my big stuff-up, I
hadn't stopped to consider what we would actually be doing at
True Blue, and as I examined the list of activities, I felt my face
heat up. Flying fox, abseiling, trust exercises.

Outward Bound flashbacks came flooding in. Year nine,
facing nature's challenges with people I didn't like because we
needed to "get to know each other." I'd been in the same group
as Sahar and our schoolmate Jennifer. We never fought, but
for some reason on Outward Bound, we argued all the time;
it was practically *Lord of the Flies*. Lara wasn't around at the
time; by then, she'd moved to London with her parents. She
didn't come back to Sydney until the last year of high school.
Anyway, we were so excited about the camp because we'd
convinced Sahar's uber-strict Muslim parents to let her come
along. We went to an all-girls school and there would be no
men about. They eventually agreed after much cajoling and
well-timed conversations with my parents.

But it rained most of the time, Sahar cried every other day,
and Jennifer kept trying to take my fruit—the only edible thing
we were given each day.

Events were especially marred by the rock-climbing incident. I
got stuck on "rock two" and only emerged, bloody and scraped,
after forty-five minutes of coaxing from my camp instructor.

Sahar's crying didn't help. She stood at the bottom of the little mountain, reciting verses of the Quran, and by the end of it I hadn't known what made me more panic-stricken: the thought of the instructor having to inform my parents their daughter would now be living in a mountain crevice or the state of Sahar's health as she quietly but frantically prayed for my life.

There was no rock climbing at True Blue, at least. But now, facing my own mortality on the flying fox, I glanced down to see Cate standing at the bottom, one hand shading her eyes from the sunshine despite a pair of monster sunglasses.

The weather was great, everyone was having a good time, but I was standing at the top, paralyzed. I realized it wasn't a fear of heights stopping me; it was a fear of something snapping and me falling like a heap onto the unforgiving ground below, my headscarf billowing dramatically under my helmet as I did so.

"Come on, Samira, you'll be fine!" Cate yelled. She jumped up and down and did a little clap as though this might help.

I could hear my own unnaturally heavy breathing.

What if the end of my headscarf got caught in something?

What if the equipment was faulty?

What if I was too heavy?

Oh God. I wondered if this was what people meant when talking about their lives flashing before their eyes. My thoughts went to my family and friends. My nieces and their giggly greetings. Lara and her giggly greetings. Sahar and her culinary treats; she was probably baking something delicious right now. Hakeem, one of my oldest childhood family friends. And then Zahra. Evil cousin Zahra, who was getting engaged tomorrow.

I closed my eyes and tried to shut out the voices. No, wait, the instructor was telling me something.

"Samira, you can come down or you can face your fears. You are in control. Do you want to be defeated?" she called.

I suspected the correct answer was "No," but I nodded anyway, a slight whimper escaping me.

"Your team is waiting for you at the end of that wire, Samira. They've all been through this too. They're waiting to congratulate you. This is a trust exercise, Samira. Do you trust your team?" she persevered.

I wasn't sure if I trusted my team. I trusted Cate at least. Trustworthy or not, what was my team going to do if I fell flat on my face? Help the True Blue crew scoop up my broken remains?

Adding insult to injury, it wasn't just my team waiting at the bottom. There was also a group from another company. Cate told me they were actually from the same building as us, or maybe they were just from a nearby building. I hadn't really been paying attention because all I could think about was the fact that I'd be humiliating myself in front of more people. Worse, they were people I was likely to run into again.

Of course, I'd probably passed them a million times and they'd never blinked. After today they'd know me, though. It wasn't every day you saw a hijabi at the top of a flying fox, holding everyone up while her lackluster life flashed before her eyes. Nevertheless, I couldn't stay up here all day—I realized that. So I nodded, still unable to speak, my eyes shut so tight you'd need a crowbar to pry them open.

"I'm going to count to three, Samira, and after three I want you to shed your fears and fly," commanded the instructor.

Was this woman serious? Shed my fears and fly?

Oh, bismillah, bismillah, bismillah. I was suddenly penitent, faithful, making promises to God I had every intention of keeping but knew I was unlikely to follow through with should I live.

Then, as another life-playback of random meaningless moments began, I heard the instructor yell, "Three!"

Without thinking, I went for it, and before I knew it, I was flying. It was kind of . . . exhilarating! It sort of hurt but at the same time felt wonderful.

"Woo hoo!" came the cheers—well, cheer—from Cate when I tumbled onto the grass a few moments later.

Despite my momentary excitement, I felt a little disappointed. It was over so quickly. All of that agony and fear for just a few moments of adrenaline hardly seemed fair.

Cate strode toward me and enveloped me in a bear hug. "Fun, wasn't it?"

I laughed. "Yes!"

When she released me, I looked around proudly, ready for my applause, but my team were scattered about, not even paying attention.

Cate put her arm around me and we began walking to the next obstacle. As we trotted along, I noticed a few people from the other office standing to the side, waiting for their turns on the flying fox. They hadn't been paying attention to me either, for which I was grateful. I was about to turn away when I noticed a man among them who was paying attention. He was looking directly at me, his expression serious, but there was an element of amusement there too.

Cate followed my gaze and raised her eyebrows. "Someone's looking at you," she said.

I stopped walking, my cheeks burning, and turned to Cate. "How rude. Did I look that ridiculous up there?"

"Not at all. You looked kind of cute, actually. I didn't know it was possible for someone to close their eyes that tight."

"You couldn't see that! Could you?" I said, humiliated.

Cate smiled. "Honey, he's not making fun of you. Trust me on this. I know looks."

I did trust Cate on this. Looks were one of her many specialties. Years of barhopping had beefed up her expertise in assessing whether a guy was a sleaze, megalomaniac, loser, or all of the above—or on the flip side of the coin, whether he was a decent sort and genuinely interested. There were generally more of the former, but nonetheless Cate knew her stuff. So I yielded to her expertise and we kept walking.

I glanced back one last time to see if the man was still looking. He was chatting to one of his colleagues, but he caught my glance and smiled a little bashfully. He didn't look so amused this time.

Maybe Cate was right. Still, I was feeling a little flummoxed. Why was he staring at me like that at all? Was he surprised or amused to see a hijabi doing high-action sports? (All right, fine: medium-action sports.) My initial instinct was that he must be Arab and/or Muslim, but he didn't appear to be either. He was dark blond, almost European looking.

I shook off the discomfort and reverted to the infinitely more pleasant, pumped-up feeling I'd experienced at the end of the flying fox. I could have cried. I'd felt so full of energy, as though I truly had been flying.

Admittedly it hadn't been terribly poetic in my mind at the time, as I'd also been scared crapless. But I knew that I wasn't afraid of heights. I simply had a fear of falling. Or maybe it was flying.

Chapter 5

We crunched our way through the trees to the abseiling cliff, chattering about how this topped a day in the office. I was still feeling a bit pumped; I would have agreed to try just about any sporting activity.

Skydiving? Easy. White-water rafting? Yes, please.

Had I been in the office right now, I would have been doing something terribly dull and boring, not soaring meters above the earth. Shedding my fears! Staring into the face of—

Oh my God, was *that* the abseiling cliff?

It was a rather steep cliff face. Quite high. Were they always this high? This was a beginner's cliff, wasn't it? Maybe I should check, as coordinator, whether or not this was the right cliff face. I could have sworn we'd passed another one along the way. I was about to advise Cate as such when she gave me a look. We were starting to lag behind the rest of the team. Poor thing. She should have paired up with someone more athletic.

The cliff face looked a little daunting, that was all, with its dark spotty surface and several ominous-looking plants spilling out of the crevices.

"Come on," said Cate, pulling me toward the cliff. "It'll be great."

When it was finally my turn—because there was no one else left to let through ahead of me—the instructor clicked me into my gear. It all looked rather complicated.

I tried to pay attention to what the instructor was saying, but Cate was standing next to me, getting into her gear and chatting away.

"I mean, do we have to question every little thing we do?" said Cate. She looked at me expectantly, but I hadn't heard half of what she'd said.

"Well, do we?" repeated Cate. "I mean, it's not like it's such a big deal if I do one thing I wouldn't ordinarily do."

I was starting to feel a little light-headed as I nodded slowly at her, still not sure what she was talking about. I was too preoccupied with making sure the equipment was going to hold me.

"Okay, ladies, now you're going to position your feet like so," the instructor said, pointing at her own feet. "Do not look behind you. Just hold on to the rope and lean back."

"What's going on, Cate?" I asked, trying to distract myself from the sheer drop looming directly behind me. I could feel my face taking on that familiar panic-stricken sheen.

Cate, however, seemed unperturbed, as she easily leaned back. "Nothing's going on," she replied.

"Samira, concentrate. Lean back, take your time," said the instructor. My stomach throbbed with anxiety. Easy for the instructor to say; she'd probably done this a thousand times. I knew she was doing her best to make me feel at ease, but this was rapidly morphing into a mammoth task. So I kept talking, hoping it would assist in allaying my fears. And stop me from looking down so much. Why was I doing that?

"No, really, Cate. I can tell something's up. You look guilty," I said, leaning back another millimeter.

"I'm just being thoughtful and meditative," she said with a gasp.

We were slowly starting to make our way down the cliff face. I wasn't as sure-footed as Cate. She was obviously proficient at this, something she'd neglected to mention before I'd agreed to be her partner. I made tiny movements, inching my way down ever so slowly.

"You can jump out a bit, ladies!" yelled the instructor. "This cliff is not your base! Jump away from your fears!"

Not this again. Cate jumped out with ease and swung back to the cliff face again. I attempted it but lost my nerve and ended up swinging from the rope instead. I tried to stop true panic from making an impromptu appearance.

Still swinging, I looked down and saw Jeff in a retro tracksuit. He had his hands clasped at the small of his back. At least the strange blond man from the other office wasn't with him. That was the last thing I needed about now. Although, it seemed a bit silly to say that given, out of all of the things in the world that could happen, no doubt there would be a million other things less appealing. For example, I'd hardly want to be in the dentist's chair about now. Or working in a bottle factory. Or—

"Samina. Keep moving! Concentrate!" yelled Jeff.

Perfect.

All of a sudden, blond man and co. were back. Wonderful, an audience.

This was much worse than that mortifying embarrassment you feel when you're running late for the bus and you make a mad sprint for it before it pulls out from the curb—knowing all the while that the passengers are watching, entranced, mentally wagering whether or not you'll make it.

"Okay, I'm going out for dinner with someone," said Cate, who had stopped abseiling and was waiting for me half a meter below.

I could hear birds. It also felt a little humid. Or was that just my panic? No, the sky had turned a foreboding gray. It was likely to begin raining at any moment.

"So? What's the big deal about a dinner?" I said, slightly out of breath.

I tried to get back into position, pushing the thought of the spectators below firmly from my mind. The instructor was calmly imparting instructions while Jeff looked up at us and yelled again, "Con-cen-trate!"

"No big deal," said Cate.

I knew it was difficult for her to comprehend my lifestyle sometimes. Dating was such an integral part of her life; she couldn't imagine not doing it. But even though people lived that way all around me, I just never had, which was why I was always willing to listen to her experiences. It was very educational. Although Lara's guidance ("Boys suck") was useful, I'd gained some useful insights into the opposite sex through Cate's dealings with men.

"Never look too anxious for them to call," she had advised after one particular failed relationship. "If he doesn't, don't send him a text message, then pretend it was meant for someone else. Don't accidentally call him, then pretend you meant to dial your mum."

I was actually glad I never really had to worry about that kind of thing, because even when I got to know someone myself, it was never proper dating.

Despite a few similarities, I figured I had the better deal. Awkwardness was minimal with Austen-era-style courtship. There were rules and behaviors. Better still, everyone involved knew and understood them. Dating wasn't so clear-cut.

"Who are you having dinner with?" I said, finally back in place against the rocky cliff face. I certainly wasn't going to attempt more fancy jumps.

"Nobody," said Cate.

"Good work, Samira!" said the instructor. "Just take your time, and remember, this is a trust and releasing exercise. We're purging!" She pumped her fist in a gesture of victory.

"Cate?" I said, looking sideways at her while trying to maintain my balance. I was not letting go of that rope for anything. I was more than willing to hold everyone up too. *And let them all stare,* I thought a little radically.

They were probably all laughing at me. Heartless jerks.

Whatever. At this point my primary objective was to make it to the bottom in one piece, and I considered it a fairly important objective.

"Who is it, Cate?" I asked again when she still hadn't replied.

"Marcus," said Cate eventually.

"Who's Marcus?"

Cate let go of her rope and put her head in her hands and whimpered.

"Oh. Oh! *Marcus* Marcus?" I lost my balance again and started swinging.

Cate nodded into her hands, not even bothered that she wasn't holding on to her rope. "Don't judge me," she mumbled.

I looked down. Jeff was still standing at ease. God, that tracksuit.

"I won't. But why are you doing this exactly?" I was still

swinging. Thank God no one was filming this, or I'd end up on YouTube for sure.

"He asked me," said Cate.

"Okay, but there's that part where you can say no. Like when I get proposed to and I don't see a future, I say *no*." I heaved my way back to the cliff face.

"I know he's annoying, but he's actually kind of nice, and he buys me chocolates every so often. It's not like we're getting *married*," Cate pointed out. She repositioned herself before easily completing the abseil down.

I'd had enough. I'd purged enough. I'd faced my fears. Now I just wanted to be standing on solid ground. I couldn't be bothered to do it properly, so I shimmied the rest of the way down.

"Well done, Samira!" the instructor called over the edge, relief marking her features. I assumed there was always one like me in the group: the one who got stuck at the top of the flying fox, and the one who shimmied her way down the cliff face rather than abseiled.

"Okay, Cate." I unclasped my helmet and passed it to one of the instructors on the ground.

"He's just so *pretty*," she gushed.

In a twisted sort of way, it made sense—he would probably be an improvement on the guys Cate usually dated. Marcus, despite his annoying tendencies (and we all had them), was a gentleman. He opened doors for the girls at work. He offered to buy coffees for everyone when he was going out to buy one for himself. He stayed behind without complaint to help Cate when she was running late for a deadline, and she was always late.

"Well, I hope it goes well," I said.

"I'll let you know. But it's just dinner, not a date!" Cate assured me.

"Okay. Keep repeating that to yourself and it might become true."

"Cate. Samina. Well done," said Jeff as we walked past.

"Thanks, Jeff," we sang in unison.

I looked ahead at the group from the other office, and sure enough, the blond man was there and he was looking in my direction. As we approached, one of the men in the group recognized Cate, so we stopped.

I waited a couple of meters to the side while she chatted with him, feeling a little embarrassed, my arms folded, my face still a deep red from the abseiling exertion. There really should be warning labels on the ropes and helmets or something. CAUTION: STRENUOUS ACTIVITY AHEAD; POTENTIAL HUMILIATION. WARNING: THIS IS WHY A GYM MEMBERSHIP SHOULD BE COMPULSORY. Things like that.

I pretended to be concentrating, although I wasn't exactly sure what I was supposed to be concentrating on. Just playing it cool. Blond man didn't exist. He hadn't been looking at me earlier and I hadn't seen him not looking at me.

Except that he did exist and I could tell he was still sort of looking at me, and it was a touch unnerving. I looked around, feigning interest in the trees. They were fairly remarkable. Very tall. I assumed rather old.

"Assalamu alaykum."

Startled, I stopped pretending to concentrate and looked up to locate the person behind the voice.

Blond man. Huh.

"Wa'alaykum assalam," I said, doing my best not to look surprised.

He must have Muslim friends, I thought. It wasn't unusual to have non-Muslims sending out a salam on occasion.

As if reading my thoughts, the man said, "I *am* Muslim." He was looking slightly amused again. The cheek. Well, how was I supposed to know? I must have looked taken aback because he added hastily, "I didn't want you to think I was mocking you or something."

"I wouldn't have thought that." It hadn't occurred to me that he could have been taking the mickey at all; I just assumed he was being nice.

"Okay, good," he said. After a beat, he added, "I wasn't expecting to see a girl in hijab here."

"Yes, well, I wasn't expecting to meet a blond Muslim man here," I said. Not that his blondness ruled out Muslimness.

"That wasn't an insult," he clarified.

"That's all right. I didn't take it that way."

"Where are you from?"

"Would it be a really obvious joke if I said Sydney?"

"Definitely."

"I'm Palestinian. How about you?"

By now we were standing apart from the rest of the group, even though I didn't think we had actually moved. Cate was a couple of meters away, still chatting to her friend.

"Lebanese," he said.

That did surprise me. I hadn't expected him to be Arab. He could have easily passed for European of some kind. He was nice looking. Clean-cut. No beard. He wouldn't have looked out of place in a period film.

"Do you have a name?" he said.

"No, my parents never gave me one. Caused a lot of trauma."
Then, remembering myself, I said, more formally, "My name
is Samira."

"Nice," he said, a glimmer of amusement in his eyes, a hint
of a smile forming.

"Well, I gave you mine," I said, cheeks burning. "Are you
going to give me yours?"

"Menem," he replied.

"That's not a very common name." I'd never even heard
of it.

"You can thank my parents," he told me. "I've struggled to
be ordinary."

"I feel for you. So are you extraordinary then?"

"Depends what you consider extraordinary," said Menem
sensibly.

"Well, are we talking superhuman abilities or terrifying
hang-ups that eventually lead to a life of crime?"

He laughed. "Neither. I'm very ordinary, actually."

"So am I."

"I'm sure you're not," said Menem. "And you did well, by
the way. Abseiling isn't as easy as it looks."

I'd just been thinking that myself! But, oh God, he hadn't
seen me, had he?

"I couldn't see you properly—don't worry," he said, once
again reading my mind.

I relaxed. "Well, I made it down, although I don't think it
was exactly the right way."

Menem raised his eyebrows.

"I improvised," I added.

He grinned. "Shimmying can work."

How did he know?

"You did have a little trouble on the flying fox, though," he said, eyes twinkling.

"Well, I wouldn't call it trouble per se," I mumbled, blushing profusely.

"True," said Menem. "You did it in the end. That's what's important."

But I realized he wasn't being nasty; he truly seemed to mean it. Nevertheless, I was still blushing. "Yeah, I guess. Did you go up as well?"

"Yes, I'm pretty sporty in general," he said, glancing up at the cliff.

I was tempted to tell Menem that I hadn't always been this unfit and non-sporty, but I didn't think mentioning I was a champion runner in the sixth grade would count for much.

"So where do you work?" said Menem.

I hesitated. He could find out easily enough, but instilled in me were the stranger-danger rules: Don't accept lollies from strangers. Don't get into a car with people you don't know. Don't give dark-blond Arab Muslim men your work details.

Okay, yes, I made that last one up.

"I see we have trust issues," said Menem after I'd paused for too long.

"It began in the third grade when my best friend became BFFs with another girl."

"BFFs?"

"Best friends forever."

"Would you want a best friend who would betray you so easily?"

"True. I'm not quite sure I ever recovered."

"There's help available for that sort of thing," he said.

He had my attention, but I was saved from giving him my

work information when Cate called out to me and waved me over.

"It was nice meeting you," I said, a little torn because a part of me wanted to make sure he could find me.

"Hopefully I'll see you around," he called out as I turned to walk away, and I couldn't ignore the murmur of excitement in my belly.

Chapter 6

The next day Mum woke me up at 8:30. I was feeling the consequences of Friday's team-building exercises. My body wasn't just sore, it was crying. I whimpered as I stretched. I was cozy in bed, and my body was begging me not to get up.

Rising for sunrise prayer a couple of hours earlier had proven exceptionally difficult. I hadn't quite made it.

"Zahra's mother needs our help today," Mum said. "You have to pick up some things."

I curled up under my covers and whimpered again. Today was going to hurt on so many levels.

"Yallah, Samira, quick. We have a lot to do," Mum said, then she yanked the covers off me.

"Mum!"

Not surprisingly, Mum gave me The Look. Feeling empowered after the flying fox, I stared back with a courageous I'm-twenty-seven-now-so-I'm-not-afraid-of-you look. Mum still won, though.

"Go to Zahra's house first," she instructed in Arabic. "Do whatever your aunt Shaimaa asks. Quickly."

When she'd finally left my room, I grabbed the covers and pulled them back over me. I wasn't going to get out of helping

Zahra today, but right now I just wanted ten more minutes of rest. I closed my eyes and thought of door locks.

An hour later I was driving to Zahra's place, which was about twenty minutes from my house. We'd all lived in the same sub-urb for most of our lives, but Zahra's family had moved a few years ago.

My recently acquired sense of empowerment had been short-lived, as I was already in a sullen mood, unable to contemplate a day of errands when even pushing down on the accelerator was an effort for my muscles. I hadn't realized how unfit I was.

Note to self: go to gym.

Further note to self: invest in actual gym membership.

After all, getting fit in winter was the thing to do, especially when you worked in the central business district and every five meters a gym junkie handed you a flyer to join up.

As I drove, I found myself contemplating the previous day's team-building exercises.

And thinking about Menem.

It wasn't outside the realm of possibility that I might see him around in the city. It was also quite conceivable that I wouldn't. We hadn't even left the conversation anywhere in particular. He'd made fun of my sporting abilities, then I'd had to go.

But I couldn't seem to get him out of my head. It had been such a strange meeting; it wasn't every day you met a Muslim man in the workplace. And for our teams to be at the same team-building center on the same day was just a bit of a coin-cidence.

And he'd seemed rather nice. And normal! The value of which was never to be underestimated. For those very reasons, I concluded that I'd never run into him again.

When I reached Zahra's house, I parked in the driveway. The air was a little humid, and the smell of freshly mowed grass hit me as soon as I stepped out of the car.

Zahra's mother opened the door and smiled.

"Assalamu alaykum, Khaltou," I said as she ushered me inside.

"Wa'alaykum assalam, Samira," she replied ever so softly.

I spoke in Arabic to her. "Congratulations on Zahra. This was unexpected."

I knew what was coming next, and as if I was in a slow-motion scene of terror, I wanted to scream, "Nooooo!" but it would've been too late. Aunt Shaimaa responded with the Arabic phrase feared by Muslim singletons everywhere: "O'balik." One loathed expression contained in just a few syllables, meaning, "May it be your turn next."

I smiled weakly in response and said, "Insha'Allah." God willing. It didn't sound desperate when you said that to an elder. Oh well, I was going to hear it all night anyway. I suspected some people even took pleasure in saying it, searching for singletons in order to rib them about their marital status.

I wished a blanket regulation could be enforced at all social functions: "Attention, guests! Welcome. Please beware the singletons in the room. For your own safety, do not approach them. Do not offer them wishes that it be their turn next. We thank you for your sensitivity in this matter."

Zahra appeared in the hallway. "Samira!" She met me

halfway and we kissed each other on the cheek. As usual, she didn't kiss me properly; she just pressed her face against mine.

"How can I help you, Khaltou?" I said, turning back to Zahra's mother.

"You're such a good girl to help us," she said.

Aunt Shaimaa pulled out a sheet of paper with a list of things to do scrawled on it. A rapid scan of the list told me I could get it all done in a couple of hours.

"I have my mobile if you remember anything else," I told them.

An hour and a half later, after picking up the dress from a seamstress, I was off to my final stop: the sweet shop. The smell of pistachio and syrup hit me as soon as I entered the store. *Perhaps there was time for a quick snack,* I thought as I eyed the fresh kanafeh. But an assistant broke my gaze by asking if he could help me. It was probably best to forgo the kanafeh given my rude fitness reminder.

Just as I was directing one of the assistants at the sweet shop to my car, several trays of pastries and cakes between us, my phone rang. Holding the boot open and balancing two boxes and the phone all at once, I answered.

"Samira!" It was Lara. "Heya, gorgeous!"

"Lara!" I said, relieved to hear her voice.

I smiled gratefully at the assistant when he'd finished loading the boxes, and he left with a polite smile. Leaning against my car, I turned my attention back to Lara.

"I can't talk much. I'm designated pick-up person today."

"I bet she wrote a list for you," said Lara in disgust.

"Yep. Numbered it too." She'd even underlined a couple of things.

Lara unleashed a torrent of commentary that I only half understood because a bus rushed by midway. But I did pick up the words "evil," "spawn," and "karma."

"Just don't say 'O'balik,' Lara," I said.

"Puh-lease! I want you to have a shot at happiness in this life," she replied. "Anyway, guess what? I'm not coming to the engagement!"

"What? No! You can't desert me."

"Sorry, hun. Work. I *want* to come to be with you, but I'm in a bit of a bother at the hospital, so I have to be here tonight."

"Okay," I said, deciding it was better not to ask.

"Did you find out more about the fiancé?"

"Just that he works in the same building as her or something. Turns out they didn't know they were both Muslim until they met at some fundraiser."

Zahra didn't wear the hijab, so the story made sense. Although, I was pretty sure this was the diluted, parent-friendly version. It was more likely they'd been emailing each other and "accidentally" running into each other around town.

I knew it. Lara knew it. Their parents probably knew it deep down, in places they cared not to acknowledge. Had the boy in the sweet shop been brought up to speed on Zahra's engagement, he'd know it too. Sometimes these matters, understandably, progressed outside of the parental zone.

Remembering the time, I looked at my watch. I had to keep moving because the engagement started at six o'clock and I didn't even know what I was going to wear.

"Sorry, Lara, I have to go."

"Okay, sweetie. I want all the info when you get back. Mwah."

Slightly deflated, I got into my car. My body was still punishing me for yesterday's workout, but I had a long day ahead of me.

While I wasn't exactly in a rage to see Zahra get engaged, it was more the lead-up that was bothering me. There was a reason I hated family functions. Barbecues in the park were the worst, but anything that involved us going out en masse was always a nightmare.

Mum and Dad would always squabble because Dad would insist on taking his beloved Falcon, but Mum knew it could break down on the way because it was a hundred years old. So she'd insist on taking my car, a more reliable Toyota Yaris.

This debate could go on for hours. Dad would milk his hurt for as long as he could, delay everyone, bring up the time twelve years ago when [insert family member's name] didn't do [insert something Dad wanted done]. Then he would later complain to me about it, and somehow the conversation would move on to my older brother, Omar, and how he hadn't visited in three days.

While all of that was going on, I was inspecting my closet for a suitable outfit. I had scarves of several varieties, but clothing was more the problem. I didn't want to wear anything too formal, because it wasn't a huge party, but it wasn't a denim affair either.

I could get away with a plain outfit if I paired it with a flashier headscarf. Something with light glittery threads perhaps.

Or I could dress down a more formal outfit with a plain head-scarf, a soft, simple fabric in a beautiful color.

I toyed briefly with the idea of wearing my headscarf a bit differently for a change. I'd recently had a yearning to change things up—tying my scarf back rather than having it all around my head. That way I could wear gold hoops, because my ears wouldn't be totally covered. I missed wearing jewelry.

Half an hour later, I settled on an ensemble of an ankle-length black chiffon skirt, a dark-blue cashmere top, and a light-blue headscarf in a sheer fabric. I pinned the headscarf up as I usually wore it. I wasn't in the mood to deal with the potentially strained reactions if I tried a modified version.

It was a silly idea, really. It would look stupid.

Just as I'd finished getting ready, Mum slipped her head in my doorway.

"Samira, you're driving us tonight."

"Okay, no worries, Mum," I replied, even though all the arguing had kind of given it away.

"Yallah, Samira. And don't frown. It doesn't look nice." Mum walked off and I let out an earth-shattering sigh. I wasn't frowning; I was just concentrating while pinning my scarf, for goodness' sake.

I shook my head, then quickly applied some kohl and a light lashing of mascara.

I emerged to find Dad sulking by the door while Mum was switching lights on because she never left the house dark, see-ing that as an invitation to be robbed.

"Ready, Baba?" I said cheerfully.

"Hmmph."

I patted him consolingly on the arm.

"Yallah," Mum said.

We got into my car, my father sitting in the front seat still looking affronted. I knew he'd be fine once we got to the party. In fact, it wasn't long before he brightened up, taking out a hanky (he carried one with him everywhere) and wiping my dashboard.

"Don't you clean your car, ya Samira?"

Chapter 7

We were a bit late, but—in line with Arab Standard Time—the party hadn't started yet. Even though I'd brought everything that afternoon, I still hadn't anticipated this many people. There must have been about sixty guests at least, all crammed into my uncle's modest living room.

I spotted Zahra in one corner talking to an older man and woman, who I presumed were her future parents-in-law because she had a plastic smile fixed on her face. But she looked good. She was attractive, although perhaps not beautiful. Lara was always considered the beauty among us—a position she was only too happy to claim.

That didn't stop Zahra from being competitive about it. When I'd put on the hijab six years ago, I knew it had given her some perverse pleasure because she'd thought guys wouldn't look at me. "Much better!" she'd said the first time she saw me in a headscarf. Instead of congratulating me like everyone else, she'd told me covering up was an improvement.

But she did look pretty tonight with her hair straightened and her makeup done nicely. She wore a dusty-pink chiffon dress down to her calves, leafy layers falling neatly over her shoulders.

I looked around to see who I knew in the crowd and only rec-

ognized a few people. I picked out Hakeem and his father sitting
to the side. I walked up to them and greeted Abu Ibrahim first,
exchanging the usual inquiries: "Yes, work is good, thank you
for asking. No, I'm not getting married yet." Then Abu Ibrahim
turned to his neighbor and resumed the discussion he'd been
having before my arrival.

"How are you?" asked Hakeem.

"Good. You?"

"Alhamdulillah. Some turnout," he commented. He looked
bored or unimpressed—perhaps both. He didn't like to attend
parties. A social butterfly Hakeem was not.

"Yeah, I wasn't expecting this many people," I said, survey-
ing the room.

Hakeem took a small bag out of his jacket. "By the way, this
is for you," he said, handing it to me.

"What's this?"

"I told you I was going to bring you a book that required
you to use your intellect, remember?"

"And I told you I have a very good romance book to read,
remember?"

Hakeem gave me a disapproving look, which differed only
slightly from Mum's.

"Okay, well, this is very nice of you. Thank you." I beamed.

"You're very welcome. Make sure you actually read it,
though," said Hakeem, a trace of amusement in his voice.

I opened up the bag to see what was inside, expecting a book
on religion, or perhaps something clichéd like Kahlil Gibran; he
was generally the favorite with these sorts of gifts. Instead, I
found a compilation of short stories I'd never heard of before.
The book had a fancy cover with embossed lettering.

"Thank you," I told Hakeem, just as I heard my mother call out my name. "Sorry, duty calls."

He nodded. "Later."

No sooner than five minutes after that, I was once again a member of the staff. Mum sent me to the kitchen to help. I imagined myself as a Victorian-era servant who spent all of her time in the kitchen and laundry, and slept downstairs in a room the size of a shoebox.

It was customary to assist, and if I was completely honest, I didn't mind terribly, as it saved me from having to deal with people and their invasive inquiries about my life (my marital status), my goals (whether or not I'd consider an import without a visa), and whether I knew so-and-so over there by the door (who, didn't you know, is studying to be an engineer).

I really only minded this time because it was for Zahra.

Zahra, who never made the effort for anyone but herself. Who never lifted a finger to help with dishes or preparation whenever she was over at our house for dinner.

"Thank you again, habibti," said Aunt Shaimaa as she came into the kitchen. She placed her hand at the back of my head and praised Allah to my mother.

My mother smiled at me. I smiled back, basking in her approval since really there weren't enough occasions when my mother could be proud of me.

A moment later, Zahra swung her head through the doorway.

"Mum, where's the camera?"

"You left it on the fridge."

Zahra practically stomped over to it in her stilettos, clearly put out by the effort required.

"Why don't you ask Samira to take some photos?" said Aunt Shaimaa. "She always takes nice pictures."

Zahra looked amused. "It's okay, thanks anyway. Najwa's going to take the photos. She's done a course." With that, she swept out of the room. Najwa was Zahra's best friend, and they did everything together, including law degrees.

Fine by me, I thought as I got to work on the sweets. Mum and Aunt Shaimaa started chatting—domestic talk—so I tuned out immediately. I carefully unwrapped the paper from the Styrofoam trays, attempting to arrange the sweets nicely. When I was on to the second lot, I heard a male voice say, "Coming through!"

I glanced up to see a young man in a blue suit carrying a large tray with a cake on it and wondered if he was the fiancé. At a peek, he didn't seem like Zahra's type. Then again, I couldn't picture any man with a pulse being her type, so I couldn't be sure.

"Thank you, Menem!" Aunt Shaimaa gushed.

The man put down the tray and I saw his face properly. My stomach plummeted a thousand feet and I nearly fell over.

Oh. My. God.

Our eyes met for a split second. I'm sure he recognized me from the team-building day, but he didn't give anything away. With barely a nod, he smiled politely and walked out of the kitchen.

"That's Malek's brother," said Aunt Shaimaa to Mum.

Okay, so he was just the fiancé's brother, but still, how was this even possible? Didn't this sort of thing only happen in movies?

I continued with the sweets. By now I couldn't care less about making them presentable, so I hurriedly finished the arrangement and took two trays out to the sitting room. I was still feeling utterly taken aback and a little ill, but I wasn't sure why.

Although not really the shy type, I felt bashful all of a sudden, as though all eyes in the room were on me. I was also keenly aware that Menem was there somewhere, probably lurking in the shadows. Well, if there had been any shadows in which to lurk.

After I'd set out the trays, I found a small empty space against a wall. A few moments later, I felt someone pinch me and I jumped in fright. Then I breathed a sigh of relief.

"Sahar! You came!"

"Assalamu alaykum!"

We kissed each other's cheeks, and I grabbed her hands. "How are you?" I asked.

"Alhamdulillah. Sorry I'm late. My brother took his time."

Sahar would never have come alone; she was too shy. But her older brother, Salim, didn't mind taking her places whenever she needed. I looked over and saw him chatting with Hakeem.

Salim was as fundy as Sahar, quite possibly more so. I worried they'd be uncomfortable because this was turning out to be the kind of gathering they wouldn't normally attend. The guests looked thirsty for some heavy partying. One woman even had a scarf wrapped around her hips like a belly dancer.

"I'm so sorry, Sahar, I had no idea it was going to be such a party," I said, biting my lip.

"It's okay! We won't be staying long anyway," she replied. "At least there's no dancing," she added, taking a quick look around. Obviously she hadn't seen the belly dancer yet.

"You look beautiful," I told her. Sahar never wore makeup, but she always had a nice glow about her. Her headscarf framed her cherubic face, and she was wearing a stunning black abaya that she'd brought back from Jordan after a recent visit. She'd given me a similar one—it had diamanté across the top half, set in an elaborate pattern, and on the edges of the sleeves.

Sahar blushed. "Don't be silly," she said.

When she'd returned from her holiday in Jordan at the beginning of the year, Sahar had also brought back with her a shiny engagement ring. It had taken all of one week for her to accept her fiancé's proposal.

One week. Imagine that. It could take me longer to decide on a pair of shoes. She talked to him on the telephone, they messaged each other, but she didn't reveal much.

I squeezed her hand and we continued to assess the room.

I saw Menem across the room and watched for a moment as he greeted some guests. He looked up and made eye contact with me again, this time a grin on his face. My stomach continued with its somersaults, but I stood my ground as an odd sensation surged through me.

Before I knew it, he was making his way toward us.

"You must think me very rude," he said as he approached us. He smiled more reservedly, but I could see a trace of the cheekiness he'd displayed at team building.

"Not at all," I said, trying my best to be nonchalant. Meanwhile, Sahar was standing next to me looking at the ground, her face a little red. I really needed to get her out of the house more. Not so she could start making eye contact with boys, mind; more so she wouldn't turn beet red when she encountered *anyone* new.

"I did notice you in the kitchen, but I didn't want to say anything," said Menem.

"That's okay. I didn't expect you to." *Although a brief*

acknowledgment wouldn't have hurt, I thought. Even a nod. A tiny wave.

"Let me start again. I'm Menem. I'm the future groom's brother," he said, now looking a bit flustered. He pointed to everyone behind him by way of indicating who his brother was. "Obviously, I met you yesterday."

"Some coincidence," I said. Had he seemed this dashing yesterday? Probably not. But he hadn't been wearing a suit yesterday.

"Now, I've been advised that Zahra has a cousin who works at a bridal magazine. That's you, right?"

"Um, yeah, that's me," I confirmed slowly.

I looked over at Sahar. The poor thing must have been completely confused by now. Her head was still lowered, and I could tell her eyes were wide. I knew she would be formulating her escape, but I didn't want her to leave me.

"I'm going to get a drink," she said.

Crap. Sahar scurried off, her head still lowered, the swirl of colors in the room contrasting wildly with her black abaya and white headscarf.

"Sorry," said Menem, putting his hand to his chest. "I'm being very forward." If anything, he'd been very forward yesterday, not today. "The truth is, I've seen you in the city before," he continued. "I work at AMD. I'm in IT."

"I work at *Bridal Bazaar* magazine," I said a little awkwardly. And dumbly, wordsmith that I was. He *knew* that already. I looked toward the kitchen door, hoping that Sahar would remember her duties as a friend and come back to rescue me.

"So do you work at the magazine in anticipation of your own big day?" he joked.

Now. Either he was just trying to break the ice with a very blunt knife or this was his very unsubtle way of finding out if I was taken. Or maybe it was both.

I realized a moment later I still hadn't replied. "Yes, that's why I work there. I like to be prepared," I said, mock seriously.

"Sorry, I bet you hear that a lot," he said.

"Actually, I haven't heard it for at least a week."

"Right." Menem took a sip of his drink and looked around. "This is pretty big for an initial engagement, isn't it?"

"Yes!" I said, a little too loudly. "You must have a big family."

"I did mention that I'm Lebanese, didn't I?"

"Yes, you did."

"Look, they're just about to start," said Menem when he saw his father signaling him. He acknowledged his father back, then turned to me. "I'll see you around, then? I owe you a coffee after that rude introduction." He smiled at me as he backed away. Then he turned and walked off.

What was that? Did he just . . . Was he asking me to have a coffee with him?

"He just said he owes me a coffee," I told Sahar in a rush when she finally crept back to me.

Sahar looked immediately disgusted. "You're not going to, of course. The nerve," she said, as though he'd suggested a raunchy night at a hotel. "Samira?" she prompted.

"Hmm, what?"

"You're not going to have coffee with him, are you?"

"Of course not." Maybe.

If I was in a coffee shop and he happened to come in—that wouldn't count, would it?

Sahar looked at me with an earnest expression. "It's times

like this that you have to be especially careful, Samira," she said. Then she began to recite a short hadith by way of example, which I didn't hear a word of, before shaking her head in annoyance. "Coffee with workmates isn't the same," she added, reading my next thought.

"It is kind of," I said.

"No. Unless your workmates are all looking at you the way that guy just did." I could tell Sahar was asking for Allah's forgiveness on his behalf. Sure enough, a few seconds later, I heard her say, "Astaghfir'Allah."

I didn't think it was that big a deal, but maybe she had a point. Menem was obviously not the "strict" type, otherwise he never would have suggested we have coffee together. And so casually too. Maybe he did this all the time: approached girls at engagement parties, abruptly introduced (or reintroduced) himself, then made up for it with a coffee. Was it his shtick?

I wasn't bothered about talking to boys, but I had my limits. Any "secret" meetings thus far had been fairly tame catch-ups, all during workdays—that way I could justify it if someone I knew saw me and told my parents. My parents wouldn't do anything; they would casually mention that so-and-so saw me at such-and-such, before offering me the explanation they gave to so-and-so as to why I was at such-and-such. All very exhausting. Not worth the effort.

Admittedly, the limits were gradually getting stretched over the years, but there were still Don't-go-there zones, a requirement made stricter because I wore hijab. Hard to blend in, or even find people not put off by it. It all depended on the guy I was dealing with, really. If he was uptight and fundy, I'd be sweet, because he would most likely stick to the internet and the occasional text. Someone like Menem, however, was likely to be more outgoing and adventurous, which could complicate things, but did make things infinitely more interesting.

Seeing as I was hardly the essence of piety, I wasn't going to judge Menem and think badly of him. Not yet, anyway. There was plenty of time for disappointment when it came to this sort of thing. Besides, I didn't even know him yet. We'd spoken only twice, on both occasions for less than ten minutes. Hardly enough time to assess his character! And he'd been very polite in any case.

A sudden hush in the room broke my stream of thoughts. Malek's father spoke a few words about his son in Arabic, then said Malek would like to ask for Zahra's hand in marriage. My uncle Hamza, Zahra's father, responded with some kind words about Malek and said his daughter accepted Malek's proposal of marriage.

Following this, Uncle Hamza recited the opening passage of the Quran. This was purely cultural, as Sahar whispered passionately in my ear, and not to be mistaken for the Islamic marriage ceremony that was sometimes done months or even a year in advance of the actual wedding.

This recitation was pretty much all that happened at these initial engagements. No fanfare, no fireworks display. And there were, of course, sweets. Lots and lots of sweets. And if you were very unlucky, a bountiful belly dancer with a scarf wrapped around her hips.

Really, our engagements were the same as Western ones. The main difference was in the timing. Which sounded simple enough, but explaining the intricacies to Cate had proved tricky, particularly given there wasn't a universal way of doing things among Muslims, let alone Arabs.

"Is this an Arab thing or a Muslim thing?" she'd said on the bus on the way back from True Blue. And "What do you mean by an Islamic marriage?" and "Why can't you just date Islamically?" and "But surely there is an Islamic way of dating?"

I'd finally pulled out a piece of paper and drawn a flow chart to clarify the courtship process. No easy task while riding in a bumpy old bus.

> Western courtship
> Dating → moving in together → engagement →
> wedding
>
> Arab-Muslim courtship
> Door-knock appeal → more meetings/chatting
> if mutual interest → engagement → more visits/
> chatting → Islamic marriage ceremony ("nikah")
> before or on wedding day

I hadn't gotten further than that because Cate had confiscated the pen from my hand and motioned for me to stop.

"How . . . ?" she'd said listlessly.

"Everyone's a little different. Some parents don't even like their daughters to go out alone with the guy *after* the marriage ceremony until the actual wedding night because it's still so easy to call the whole thing off."

Lara always snorted at that.

"Why?" Cate's eyes had been wide, her mouth parted awkwardly.

"Well, if it goes too far and they end things, people will gossip about them."

"But they're married!"

"Yes, but no wedding, so no . . . you know. I suppose, technically, they can, but it's not really appropriate. They should have some sort of gathering first."

"But can they do anything?"

"Oh, of course. They'd be intimate."

"You've lost me, Samira," she'd said.

I'd honestly never realized how complex Arab Muslim courtship could be.

As Zahra and Malek exchanged rings, some of the older women let loose with the zaghrouta—ululating, Arab style. The older women moved their tongues frantically, making a high-pitched noise, their hands positioned above their mouths, while one woman sang out poetic good wishes for the couple.

The neighbors would call the police if they kept up for much longer.

Menem walked over to his brother and hugged him. He looked and seemed younger than Malek, who, as far as I could recall, was in his early thirties. Malek, like Menem, was pleasant looking and clean-cut. Neither was the Arab-warrior type. Not that it mattered, of course. Honestly, it was just an observation.

More significant, both seemed confident and easygoing. Neither appeared burdened with complexes or concerns. In other words, refreshingly different from most of the males I knew.

Malek then joined Zahra, careful to keep a respectable distance. This wasn't their nikah; it was the initial still-no-touching engagement, so there were rules. At least in front of the guests.

I maintained my position by the wall as the sound of Arabic music suddenly filled the room. The belly dancer guest—a voluptuous woman clad in an extremely unflattering sparkly outfit—began to drag Zahra into the middle of the room. She had one arm raised, her index finger pointing upward, and as soon as she hit the center, she immediately started doing some rather complicated belly-dancing moves.

The horror. This was a room full of pious men and women (or, at the very least, half full). Zahra, to her credit, looked embarrassed by the exhibition. I suspected the woman was one of Malek's aunts, the kind they only brought out at major functions out of obligation.

As I began my escape, I noticed that almost everyone in the room was busying themselves with something. Suddenly guests were inspecting the Arabic sweets on the tables, or commenting on my uncle's Jerusalem mural, which he'd won at an auction at the local Palestinian club.

The guests were all talking, moving, doing anything but looking at the sparkly belly dancer, who by now had set Zahra free and had been joined by someone who resembled her in looks and clothing.

I found refuge in the empty kitchen, sitting down gratefully at the table. The music was only a little softer from here, the garish melody at odds with the humble, homely surrounds.

Resting my cheek on one hand, I picked at some kanafeh, even though I wasn't hungry.

Mercifully the Arabic music eventually stopped, and when it hadn't resumed a couple of minutes later, I felt it was safe to rejoin the party. I stood at the entrance to the kitchen and leaned against the doorjamb, safe in the knowledge that I could look out at the guests, but no one was looking at me.

Belly-dancer woman and her partner looked flushed but obviously now realized this wasn't the right crowd for their act. They fanned their faces as they returned to their seats, their curly hair now substantially more voluminous.

I couldn't locate my parents so they must have gotten away too. Dancing in and of itself wasn't the problem—it was the overblown belly-dancing moves in such a confined space that would have offended them. Dad loved a good party, but he was painfully innocent.

Hakeem was still sitting beside his father, and his gaze briefly met mine. He was frowning. I raised my eyebrows and smiled in mutual understanding, but he just looked away. Which I found rather strange.

Chapter 8

We got home at midnight, and I immediately commandeered the bathroom to sneak in a shower. I prayed, then sat down on my bed, snug in my pj's. With one hand, I grabbed my phone, while with the other I pulled up a large pillow behind me. I'd promised Lara I'd tell her everything, so despite bone-crushing fatigue, I messaged her on WhatsApp. While I waited for her to reply, I read an article I'd saved a while ago about the money-making industry of weddings—part of my research for a feature Cate and I were going to work on together.

Just as I was on the last paragraph (did you know that in the US weddings cost an average of $30,000?), a message alert sounded.

> Hakeem: You got home OK.
> Samira: Yup.

When Hakeem hadn't said anything a few moments later, I went back to the piece. When I'd finished, another message popped up.

> Hakeem: You were very helpful this evening.
> Samira: As always. At least I was spared clean-up duty.

Something felt wrong, but I couldn't put my finger on what it was exactly. Though I had an inkling. The fact that Hakeem had frowned at me and not even said goodbye at the party might have had something to do with that inkling.

Samira: "Hello. My name is Inigo Montoya. You killed my father. Prepare to die."

Hakeem: ?

Samira: It's a quote. Now guess it.

Hakeem: No idea. I don't watch movies.

Samira: Who said it's from a movie?

Hakeem: Isn't it?

Samira: Maybe.

Hakeem: OK. Well, I don't know the answer.

Samira: *The Princess Bride*. Only the greatest film ever made! Also a book, just FYI.

Hakeem: OK. I'll take your word for it.

Samira: You're grumpy.

Hakeem: No, I'm not.

Samira: Why were you giving me dirty looks at the party?

Hakeem: I wasn't.

Neither of us wrote anything for a minute. I could just imagine him brooding.

Hakeem: Why did that guy come up to you?

Samira: Which guy?

Hakeem: The brother.

Samira: Oh, he recognized me. Apparently he works near me. He's seen me around.

Hakeem: But you don't know him?

Samira: Nope. Actually, well, I did see him yesterday,
  but I didn't know who he was obviously.
Hakeem: At work?
Samira: No, we were at a team-building exercise.
Hakeem: With your workmates?
Samira: Uh-huh.
Hakeem: What was that about?
Samira: Bonding. Flying fox, abseiling . . . that sort
  of thing.
Hakeem: Uh-huh.
Samira: It's not like we were holding hands!

About now I was very glad I hadn't opted for the line dancing. Disapproval all over the place had I done that.

Samira: Anyway, so he recognized me from that.
Hakeem: Just be careful.
Samira: What?
Hakeem: You don't know him.
Samira: What's your point?
Hakeem: Nothing. We just don't know their family well.
Samira: Do you know him at all?
Hakeem: No.
Samira: But you don't have any problem judging him?
Hakeem: Samira, I'm not judging him, I'm telling you
  to use common sense.
Samira: You're also assuming there's a need for me to
  use common sense.
Hakeem: Well, I know what you're like with people.
Samira: Excuse me?
Hakeem: I mean you're too trusting.

Samira: I am not!

Hakeem: OK, you're not.

Samira: What are you suggesting?

Hakeem: For goodness' sake, a blind man could see the guy
is interested.

Well. Perhaps Menem had *appeared* interested. But the conversation had been pretty harmless. Still, it was a little unsettling that Hakeem had noticed enough to think that Menem was interested, enough for him to comment on it.

Samira: I have to go.

Hakeem: Samira, wait. Why are you mad?

Samira: I'm not.

Okay, I was. Hakeem was poised to declare a state of emergency because a guy had shown interest in me. I was twenty-seven, not seventeen. It wasn't as though Menem was the first man to show an interest. There had been a few—even if that was a rocky history.

Hakeem: I'm just looking out for you.

Samira: I don't need you to look out for me.

Hakeem: Samira . . .

Samira: You're not my father or my brother.

I felt guilty saying (well, typing) that, even though it was, technically speaking, true.

Hakeem: I'm sorry if I upset you.

Samira: You didn't. I'm just tired.

My head was spinning as I closed the app. I felt nervous and my face was warm. Hakeem and I fought a lot. But this one felt wrong. It felt yuck.

But I didn't want to be lectured on everything I did. I'd always managed my affairs—maybe with the help of lots of sugar and caffeine, but no one could accuse me of not being proactive and capable.

Despite my irritation, my eyelids were sluggish. Lara had obviously bailed on our conversation and I couldn't be bothered to wait any longer.

I put my phone on sleep mode and got straight into bed. I drowsily recited a prayer, my eyes already closed.

The next day, Lara and I agreed to meet at Centennial Park at three o'clock for a post-engagement debrief. I was feeling human and functional again, but I still needed caffeine. We located an outdoor vendor and bought coffee and chocolate croissants.

As we made our way to the duck pond, Lara regaled me with a work story involving one of the male doctors who had the hots for her. Once we were seated on the grass, she stopped talking and turned to me expectantly.

"Well?"

I proceeded to recap the engagement in microscopic detail while I sipped my coffee. Lara wanted sordid, but I had to disappoint her with the mundane: details about Zahra's dress and descriptions of her fiancé and the guests, including the frightening belly-dancing interlude.

"Sounds like it was boring," said Lara when I was done. She put her empty cup aside, then leaned back on her hands.

She wore black sunglasses that covered half her face, but like Cate's, they suited her. Mine were a more modest light-gold pair that stopped at my cheekbones.

"It wasn't too bad," I told her. As strange an evening as it was, it hadn't been the horrible night I'd envisaged.

"So the fiancé's brother came up to you?" said Lara as she brushed away a loose strand of hair.

"Yeah, his name is Menem."

"Menem?" said Lara, confused.

"I know, it's an odd name."

We were both quiet for a moment as we watched the ducks glide through the water. Some children stood at the edge of the pond with their father and threw chunks of bread into it, laughing and dancing about.

"Last night I was texting with Hakeem for a bit," I told Lara. "We kind of had a fight." I batted away a fly and took another sip of coffee.

"What's new? You guys are always arguing. And not even about interesting things," she said, sounding bored.

"Yes, but this one was different."

"How so?"

"I don't know. It was a proper fight."

Lara straightened up and waited.

"It was weird," I said. Strange and unusual and disconcerting.

"You mean it was an exciting fight?" said Lara, no longer a casual observer. "Because that would be relationshippy!"

"No, no, not relationshippy. I just don't know what happened. And the worst part is, I feel bad about some of the things I said."

"What happened?"

I recounted my conversation with Hakeem as best as I could

remember it, all the while anxiously picking at the grass. When I was done, Lara laughed.

"Well, I'll be damned," she said. She sat back again, her face to the sun.

"What?" I prompted.

"Hakeem's jealous. I always thought he liked you, but I didn't think he'd be so obvious about it." She laughed again.

"Okay, no. *No*," I said, a little mortified. I abandoned the blades of grass and uncrossed my legs, suddenly feeling very uncomfortable.

"Um, yes," insisted Lara. "You've got blinders on if you can't see he's jealous."

"No, he's just doing the brotherly concern thing," I said.

"Right. The brotherly concern thing. Menem didn't even ask you out! Sheesh. He's totally jealous!" Lara concluded, with a little too much glee.

"Well . . ." I bit my thumbnail and looked away awkwardly.

"Wait, he asked you out?" asked Lara.

"Not exactly. He said he owed me a coffee." I felt myself blushing, even though it was just Lara in front of me.

"Does Hakeem know that?"

"No way. He flipped out about him just speaking to me."

"Exactly!" Lara erupted in laughter again. "Oh gawd, this is hilarious."

"I'm glad you're amused," I told her. I didn't think it was very funny.

"Oh, I'm sorry, honey. But come on. Be realistic. If it was just a brotherly thing, why didn't Omar say something? Or your dad? Did he even blink?" Lara looked at me knowingly.

"Omar wasn't there! Ha!"

Lara gave me a look of pity.

"And you know Dad would never tell me off." We were talking about a man who'd cried when he'd watched Paul Potts's audition on *Britain's Got Talent*.

"Fair enough," said Lara, "but I wouldn't say the same about your mum." Then she said a little more gently, "Samira, this is what Hakeem meant by you being too trusting. You're smart and all, but when it comes to your life, you're so naive!"

Honestly, what was wrong with everyone? I wasn't too trusting. I was actually rather cynical most of the time. Of course, that was mainly when it came to general things. The public transport system. Midyear sales. Politicians. Door-knock appeals.

I sighed, suddenly feeling very tired again, and resumed playing with the grass.

"Now, be gentle with Hakeem," warned Lara in mocking tones.

"Very funny. Anyway, you're wrong," I said, this time looking directly at her.

"Sure. Okay. So what's this new guy's deal?" she said, sitting up and dusting off her hands. "Give me deets."

The quiet confidence. Menem had it and it stood out. Then I remembered how he'd looked in his blue suit. Not that I'd paid a great deal of attention to that. It was just a minor observation, really. But the self-confidence was definitely noticeable. It made for a stark difference to many of the men I'd met over the years through door-knock appeals or at social functions.

Hakeem was also a very confident man, but in an intense sort of way. Not that I had anything against shyness, particularly when it was bundled with such a sound level of humility like Hakeem's.

"He's unlike a lot of the guys we generally meet," I summarized.

"What does that mean?"

I shrugged. "I can't explain it. He was confident, but not overly so. And he didn't seem to have any hang-ups."

"You worked all that out in five minutes?"

I shrugged. "I just sensed it about him."

"Are you sure he's Arab?"

"I *know*. But yes. He's Lebanese."

"Well. Your life is certainly getting exciting," observed Lara.

My mind felt uncomfortably full. There was my strange conversation with Menem, Hakeem's reaction to my strange conversation, and now Lara's hypothesis about it all. It was too convoluted for me to comprehend. A little too daytime TV. And I hated daytime TV. There were only so many breakups and people returning from the dead that I could handle on one show.

Anyway, it was all so typical. When it rains it storms. Something about tangled webs being weaved. He who pays the piper calls the tune. Actually, wait—that meant something else. Whatever.

"Come on, let's get some ice cream!" said Lara, interrupting my moment of intellectual pathos. She dragged me by the hand. "My treat."

Chapter 9

When I returned home, Omar's car was parked in the driveway. As soon as I opened the front door, my niece greeted me eagerly.

"Aunty, Aunty!" Layla squealed. I had my arms ready for her, her bouncy curls framing her sweet face. I held her up and gave her a big kiss and a hug.

"Look at my new Barbie!" Layla held up a doll in hijab.

"Wow!" I said. "But, sweetie, are you sure this is a Barbie? I don't think Barbie wears hijab." Last I'd checked, anyway.

Layla nodded emphatically.

"Oh, you're getting heavy!" I said in exaggerated tones. I put her down and examined the doll. The clothing looked legit, not like the makeshift veils Sahar used to put together for her Barbies.

"It's a Fulla," said my sister-in-law, Rabia, as we walked into the sitting room. "It's a doll from overseas for Muslim girls," she explained, plopping down onto the couch with a sigh.

"No kidding," I said, still looking at the doll. Fulla looked exactly like Barbie, from the made-up face to the abnormal body proportions. Well, actually, she was perhaps a little less generously proportioned than her "Western" counterpart. Thank goodness for that. A bit of realism didn't hurt. But this doll was, well, Muslim. A Muslim Barbie doll!

Mum bought me my first Barbie when I was five. She was blond, blue-eyed, ridiculously proportioned, and dressed in a very cool glitter-pants-and-top combo with faux-leather jacket. I would have *loved* a Fulla to go alongside her. I could have set up my own little feminista UN.

Rabia let out a deep breath and looked longingly ahead of her, probably recalling a time when she wasn't carrying around something the size of a tiny watermelon in her belly.

"Are you okay? You look a bit pale," I said, sitting on the armrest beside her.

"I'm all right. This is what we call the joys of pregnancy," she lamented. I was about to offer her some words of comfort when she grabbed my arm and swiveled to face me, a look of desperation on her face. "Listen to me! Stay single as long as you can. It's too late for me, but you can save yourself! I used to have a waist!" she sobbed.

Yikes.

"Morning sickness?" I rubbed her shoulder comfortingly.

Rabia closed her eyes. "Yes. And afternoon sickness and evening sickness. I'm throwing up practically every meal."

It was moments like these when the benefits of being single weren't lost on me. I didn't have to worry about getting home on time to burn dinner. I had only my own dirty laundry to worry about. There was no one to hog the TV. And I certainly didn't have to agonize over the prospect of squeezing out a baby that would spend half the night crying and the rest of it eating. Cute didn't make it any less exhausting.

By now my other niece, Haneen, had joined Layla and was tugging at my dress. She looked up at me, delivering a goofy smile. "I kill you!" she said.

So that was this week's phrase. Last week it was "Party boy!" but it had come out more like "Party *boooy*!" And it had totally pissed off my parents. I could see Mum trying not to get annoyed and Dad trying not to yell. But, you know, rules were different with grandkids.

"Aunty, look at my doll!" she said after a few more I-kill-yous. She also had a Fulla doll, but this one was dressed in hot-pink prayer clothes. In her other hand she clutched a Ken doll.

"Is this her prince?" *Not Muslim*, I wanted to add as a joke.

"No, Aunty! This is her brother!"

"Are you going to marry a prince, Aunty?" demanded Haneen.

Oh God. I wasn't quite sure what to say to that. I wasn't sure I would be marrying anyone at this stage, let alone a prince. And besides, I didn't want to mess with their heads. Looking back, it would have been helpful if someone had pulled me aside when I was a little girl and dispelled that particular fairy-tale myth: "*No*, Samira. A prince is not going to awaken you with a kiss. He needs to be supervised while seeing you until the wedding so there'll be nothing untoward beforehand." Also, consent and all that.

"No, my darlings, I'm not going to marry a prince. I'm going to take up full-time work as a consultant to boys in pain," I said, to which my nieces responded with silly grins and confused expressions on their faces.

"You're funny, Aunty!" said Haneen. "I kill you!"

"This is why I don't ask you to babysit," said Rabia.

"I'm doing them a favor. Would you have them go through what I've gone through?"

Before Rabia could answer, Layla grabbed my face with her pudgy little hands and turned it toward hers. "You look like

Barbie, Aunty!" She then pursed her lips into kiss mode. I cuddled and kissed her, and she giggled insanely.

And before you think me deceptive for not correcting my niece, I should clarify that I was aware I didn't resemble Barbie or any of her counterparts. But who was I to shatter Layla's childhood illusions?

Mum summoned me to the kitchen (designed circa 1985) and pointed to the small, cluttered table in the center. There awaited the ingredients for a salad, as well as a large jar of marinated olives.

"Yallah, Samira, I need your help," said my mother, who was making kibbeh at the kitchen counter.

"Yes, Mum."

She was making two kinds of kibbeh. She'd already prepared some football-shaped patties. They were filled with minced meat, onions, and spices, and covered in a thick shell of crushed wheat germ and ground meat. They would then be deep-fried and come out completely, deliciously fatty. Now Mum was on to the oven-baked version. She patted the mixture of minced meat and wheat germ into a casserole dish, spreading it out so that it covered the entire surface. Then she used her thumb to make little dents across the top.

"Why are you frowning?" said Mum in Arabic.

"I'm not."

"You shouldn't frown."

"Yes, Mum."

"You should always look happy and grateful. You have nothing to frown about." She dimpled the kibbeh efficiently with her thumb.

"I'm just tired, Mum."

My broader understanding of family dinners had been heavily influenced by two things: the setup at my friend Jennifer's place and *The Brady Bunch*. In "normal" families, there would be casual banter and polite inquiries as the family sat down to eat their meal.

"Did you have a good day, son?" the father would ask. "How are you finding the public transport schedule these days?"

"Pass the salt, please," someone would say.

"Here you go, dear," would be the mother's reply.

"Would anyone like the potatoes?" another would offer.

Maybe not in those exact words, but generally that's how it'd been at Jennifer's place whenever I'd gone there for dinner when we were growing up.

The Brady household was like that too, if I recalled correctly. And while it was a comedy, I had found it funny for entirely different reasons to those intended. I had kept waiting for the episode when Jan would get humiliated with an ear pull from Mr. Brady for being half an hour late. Or when Mrs. Brady would chase the boys through the house with a slipper because they had answered back. *Never happened.*

After Maghreb prayer, we were all seated in the dining room. We each quietly said bismillah, then dug in. We had been taught from a very early age to give thanks before the first bite and after the last. That and two very important words: "no" and "haram"—forbidden.

For a few moments, we all ate in silence. Then Omar looked up and turned his attention to me. My trial wasn't going to wait until after dinner, it seemed. All that was missing was a blindfold and a leaky tap for atmosphere.

He questioned me about Manga Boy. As I'd predicted, he'd

never called, which made rejecting him infinitely easier. Enough dud suitors and you developed a sixth sense about these things, a gift I wished I could transfer into other aspects of my life. Anyway, despite a slightly bruised ego, I was happy when they didn't call because it meant I didn't have to debate the issue with my parents. I suspected that Mum and Dad lamented having a daughter who rejected all her suitors, possibly even the less promising ones. Although to my parents' credit, they were kind enough not to burden me constantly with speeches about marriage, despite being remarkably diligent in the area of Arab Guilt—unlike Lara's mum, who would often bemoan having a daughter who was beautiful but troublesome.

"Who is going to take her?" she'd say to my mother.

Once, Lara had overheard (okay, we'd been listening at the door of my room). She'd thought it was hilarious, of course.

"Oh, for—Bloody hell! Like there isn't more to life than getting married!" she'd cried.

Dad simply felt it was his duty to remind me that I was "only getting older." "Never mind," he would say. "Still, you're only getting older, baby." Of course, "baby" would sound like "beebee," which kind of took the edge off his warning, so I would simply nod sagely in agreement.

"What was wrong with this one?" Omar said while Rabia scooped salad onto his plate.

I wasn't sure I appreciated his choice of words—as though I spent the duration of door-knock appeals looking for faults.

My brother was waiting for a response.

"He looked like a manga character." I smiled awkwardly and took a bite of my salad.

"A manga character?" The critical look again.

"You know, those Japanese cartoon characters," I said, my voice trailing off.

"I know what manga is," Omar said.

"I don't want to talk about it. Suffice it to say, he wasn't right for me."

"Enough of this, Samira," said Omar. "When are you going to realize life isn't like those romantic movies you watch and get that nonsense out of your head?"

"Leave her alone," piped up Dad. "He was no good for her."

"Thanks, Dad." I looked at him gratefully, like a humiliated contestant on a reality show, thankful for the one kind judge on the panel.

"But remember, you're only getting older, beebee."

I couldn't explain to my dad without sounding disrespectful that I hadn't been under the illusion that I was only getting younger.

"None of them have been right," persisted Omar. "That's the problem. Samira, you've rejected guys for every reason imaginable."

A slight exaggeration. I was sure, given the opportunity, I could find many more reasons to reject dud suitors.

"That's unfair. I always have good reasons."

"You rejected a guy because of the shoes he was wearing."

"Who wears tassels?" I looked around, expecting a wave of support. Surely this was something we could all agree on. Tassels belonged on curtains and military uniforms, *not* shoes.

"They're just shoes," said Omar.

"And they speak volumes about the wearer."

Omar shook his head as he picked up his fork. But Rabia winked at me in sympathy.

"I don't expect you to understand. You're a guy," I said, pulling apart a kibbeh and dipping it furiously into a bowl of yogurt.

So I was turned off by a suitor when I saw his shoes. Despite my Arab-warrior preference, I didn't really care about looks. But I had a general rule: if the suitor came in wearing shoes with tassels, a leather jacket circa 1982, and/or a moustache, the door-knock appeal would fail from the outset. A girl had to have some standards, right?

"Why don't you just get them to fill out an application form in the future before they come?" suggested my brother.

"That's actually not a bad idea, Omar. Thanks for that."

Dad laughed and shook his head. Mum fixed him with a stern look, which she then directed at Omar and me.

"If anything, I give too many guys a chance," I said casually. Even Lara would tell me it was worthwhile meeting a "mark" if he at least looked good on paper. Strictly for me, that was, because Lara completely refused door-knocks. And they often did look good on paper—especially given the tendency among some families to exaggerate their sons' achievements. Not that there was anything wrong with being a mechanic. But being a mechanic wasn't the same as being a mechanical engineer.

"You give them a chance, but it seems a bit superficial when they never make it past the first meeting," argued Omar.

"Whose side are you on? Do you think I do this for fun?"

"Not for fun, but you obviously have unrealistic standards."

"What do you want me to do? Marry just anyone?"

"Samira, don't be ridiculous. Just be realistic," said Omar.

"Nice motto. You should have some bumper stickers made up," I said a little tartly.

Omar gave me a stern look, strongly reminiscent of my mother's.

"What is bumpaar stickaar?" said Dad, looking up from his plate.

"I'm always realistic," I said. "That's why I'm still single. They're those stickers you see on cars, Dad. They advertise campaigns and things."

"You watch too many movies," said Omar, pointing his fork at me. "That's what the problem is with young women your age. You expect these heroes to come along and sweep you off your feet."

I looked around, wondering if anyone was prepared to be insulted on my behalf.

Evidently not.

"Why you say this?" said Dad. "Why would you make bumpaar stickaar?"

"Dad, it was a joke!"

"That's enough, everyone! Eat," Mum said in Arabic.

Mum's dinner table was a place for eating. Conversation was allowed, but she didn't tolerate bickering. That was only allowed outside dining room hours, when, in true Arab style, it was welcomed. Nothing like some good accusation flinging to keep things interesting.

"I kill you!" Haneen said after a few minutes, shattering the silence.

It was actually a miracle no one ran screaming from these dinners. I put it down to one essential factor: Mum's cooking was that good.

Omar began to eat his food, clearly done with me for now. Meanwhile, I felt a little like a victim of torture whose interrogator had thrown aside his tools for the time being so that he could nip out for a dinner break. What was wrong with having an ideal anyway? It worked well enough for Buttercup in *The Princess Bride*.

Okay. It was quite possible that I watched too many movies.

After dinner, as I was loading the dishwasher with Rabia, my mother asked if I wanted to see another prospect. My parents never pressured me; they simply asked. Super casual. The way a manager might place a job description in front of their employee before reclining in an oversize desk chair, fingers entwined.

My head was still spinning from my conversation with Lara that afternoon. The way Menem had left things at the engagement really had me wondering. While I was hardly an expert on social norms, was I mad to think Menem saying he owed me a coffee was because he wanted to see me again?

Mum was waiting for an answer to her question. I looked at Rabia, who shrugged but gave me the What-do-you-have-to-lose? look.

"Local or imported?" Rabia said to Mum, already on the case, like a matrimonial agent working to secure her client the best deal.

It was essential to assess early on whether the suitor was a potential visa snatcher. We had a pretty thorough screening system (seventeen proposals), but occasionally an import with no visa would slip through, and an already awkward situation would become unbearable, especially when the import would get a phone call from a friend, to whom he would smugly say, "I'll explain later. Yes, I'm *busy*." Wink, wink, nudge, nudge.

Agony.

Swift execution, please.

Amazingly enough, the ones with very little to offer were the cockiest of the lot, like some sort of twisted variation of Murphy's Law.

"He was born here," Mum said. "He works in a computer company or something like that."

"How old is he?" I asked.

"He's twenty-nine," said Mum.

"Born here, has a job, and isn't old. What's wrong with him?"

Mum looked annoyed.

"Sheesh, it was just a question," I said, frowning.

The fact was, I could have asked my mother twenty questions and it wouldn't have helped. I would only know what I was dealing with when I came face-to-face with the prospect. And he'd still be subject to Mum's test of character. Very few passed that.

"There's nothing wrong with him," she explained. "He studied late, apparently, and now he's looking to get married."

"'It is a truth universally acknowledged, that a single man in possession of a good fortune, must be in want of a wife.' How did Austen get modern life so right?"

Rabia shook her head at me, but I could tell she was amused by the exchange.

"Well, it's up to you," said Mum.

I found myself saying no. They both looked shocked. I'd even surprised myself.

I had to admit that usually I grudgingly enjoyed the pre-door-knock part: the tickle of suspense as to what the suitor would look like, his level of intelligence, his interests, and, of course, his level of religiosity—i.e., his "fundyness." And, on a side note, how he felt about the bastardization of the English language due to texting and social media.

Once, I'd decided to go out on a limb and instigated a minor "test" of sorts. I'd left a copy of Walt Whitman's poetry on the coffee table, right where he'd see it, thinking it might spark some conversation.

> Suitor: You like Whitman? [Note the familiar tone. He
>   referred to Whitman and didn't use his full name.]
> Me: Why, yes. Don't tell me you're a fan.
> Suitor: Hello? I wouldn't have made it through uni
>   without my copy of *Leaves of Grass*.

In one particular variation, I imagined him pulling out a small copy from his jacket pocket, then telling me, "I carry this with me everywhere. Here, take it."

And we'd go from there. Probably live contentedly ever after. Chuckle every time we came across a Walt Whitman book in that This-is-where-it-all-began manner that was so annoying when other couples did it.

Of course, nothing of the sort happened. What *had* happened was that my copy got in the way of his coffee, and he ended up spilling it all over the book. He might have said sorry, but it wasn't a profuse apology by any means. That had brought me back down to earth pretty swiftly.

But even though I enjoyed the guessing, reality always stopped by to ruin the party. "You know he'll be a dud," the gate-crasher nerve would say cruelly to the tiny sliver of hope.

For the first time in however long, I felt icky about the door-knock process. I didn't see the humor in it, and what had once seemed an innocuous and safe way to meet boys now felt demeaning. It occurred to me that I was on show, like a prize pony, and I hated it.

And honestly, the meeting with Menem had triggered a vaguely familiar but mysterious feeling I wanted to explore. There'd been an energy that excited me, like my electrical circuits had been fired up with just a look and a few words.

So I said no, and despite the strange looks coming my way, and the mild line of questioning from my mum, I remained firm in my decision. I'd made a simple choice, but it was as though I'd just taken a huge leap into the unknown. It felt good and a little scary all at once.

Chapter 10

On Monday morning, there was an email from Hakeem waiting for me in my inbox. I had meant to fix things with him after our "fight," but I hadn't had a chance to on Sunday after dinner.

Even though Lara was one for drama and embellishment, I had to admit that my conversation with her had thrown me a little. I generally tried not to pay much attention to what she said when it came to these types of things. Of course, Lara always thought she was right, and was never shy about saying so.

Not surprisingly, she wasn't always right. Far from it, in fact. Think abysmal miscalculation-of-weapons-of-mass-destruction-in-Iraq levels of wrongness.

I'd arrived at work a little earlier than usual, so no one was in yet. I liked it this way. It was quiet and nobody was demanding an instant-coffee fix.

As I sipped my cappuccino, I opened Hakeem's email.

Subject: ?
Dear Mary,
    I yearn for you tragically.
    R. O. Shipman, Chaplain, US Army

I knew this one. *Catch-22.*

I sensed a moment of forced introspection coming on. Hakeem had managed to not only ask humbly for forgiveness but simultaneously make me feel horrible and remorseful that it wasn't me asking for it, all by quoting one of my favorite books.

Such a gift. What a talent. But he was well within his rights to do so, since he hadn't done anything wrong. I should have been the one asking for forgiveness—I could see that now. Hakeem was just concerned. He saw a stranger showing interest, and knowing our ways, he felt obligated to tell me to be careful.

More important, this confirmed that Lara was wrong. Hakeem wasn't jealous. In fact, he always made sure I knew I was Like a Sister to him by the way he treated me. Also, by getting engaged two times, on neither occasion to me. To be fair, they'd both been quick I-want-to-get-to-know-you-the-proper-way engagements because he was straight as an arrow about that sort of thing.

Well. I wasn't too proud to apologize. This was Hakeem, after all: the person who'd hidden my indiscretions when we'd been kids so that I wouldn't get into trouble.

I drafted a reply.

Subject: Re: ?
I know this one. *The Catcher in the Rye?*
    Samira
    P.S. The chocolates you gave me from that British lolly shop were delicious. Thank you.

After I sent the email, I let out a sigh of contentment. I'd taken the high road, the path of humility, and I was feeling chuffed about it.

I began sorting out some memos on my desk, mainly an assortment of one- or two-word commands from Jeff that made no sense. That would keep me sufficiently busy for about an hour at least.

A few minutes later, as I was trying to make out a smudged Post-it, an email alert sounded. *That was quick,* I thought beatifically. Then a nudge of alarm forced its way in. Although Hakeem had initiated the forgiveness ritual, I was slightly nervous. What if he really was annoyed? I didn't want him to feel even a tiny bit of annoyance with me.

I blamed the last three days. I'd had a weird weekend and I wanted my life back! It wouldn't do at all for things to be awkward between Hakeem and me. Hesitantly, I looked up at the screen and exhaled when I realized the email wasn't from Hakeem.

Menem Chami. Menem Chami? Oh! *Menem.*

I was baffled because we hadn't exchanged any contact details. Curiously, and a little apprehensively, though with a smidgeon of excitement too, I opened the email.

Subject: Hi
Samira,
I hope you don't mind me emailing you. I just wanted to say that it was really nice to meet you (twice!). It's unfortunate we didn't get a chance to speak more at the engagement party.

Also, I heard you studied communications. One of my cousins is interested in studying it as well so I was wondering if perhaps I could ask you some questions on her behalf.

Hope to hear from you soon.
Menem
P.S. I still owe you a coffee!

Okay, no need to get flustered.

But my face was already warming up and my stomach was doing strange flip-floppy things I wasn't used to. I felt a bit sick.

Okay, calm down. No need to act like a silly adolescent over an email. I was a socially adept adult, I reminded myself.

But his email was unexpected. It wouldn't have surprised me if I'd run into him in the city given that we worked within the same vicinity. That might have gotten us talking. And that could have then cascaded into texting.

But a direct email was different. Email had its own set of rules—unwritten ones, which made them harder to follow.

Before I could properly digest this, another two emails popped into my inbox: one from Lara, the other from Hakeem. I hadn't even done a minute of work yet.

I opened Hakeem's email first because Lara's were frequently treatises and required a different level of concentration (as well as access to Urban Dictionary).

> Subject: Re: ?
> Anytime.
> And it's *Catch-22*, as you well know, Mary.
> Hakeem

He didn't seem upset. Bordering on normal actually. I moved on to Lara's email, which was shorter than expected.

> Subject: Boys suck
> How's Hakeem? You two should really discuss this. Or if you want, I can speak to him.

Has the wimpy brother contacted you? What kind of a
name is Menem anyway? It sounds like a type of curry.

Love you, babe xx

The email might have been shorter than I'd expected, but
it was authentic Lara. No need for pleasantries and airy demands to catch up soon.

Subject: Re: Boys suck
This is why I don't like telling you things. Everything is sorted
with Hakeem. I'm sorry to disappoint you, but there was
no drama and no secret confession of longing (from either
party). I'm sure you'll deal with the disappointment.

Samira xo

I decided not to tell her about Menem's email just yet.
And I hadn't lied so much as omitted, which wasn't the same
thing. I wasn't quite sure I wanted Lara's opinion on him
right now, especially as I had yet to form my own.

I returned to Menem's email and stared at it for a few moments. I reread it, then once again for good measure.

"Samira! You're here early," said Cate. She stood in front of
my cubicle, coffee in gloved hand, a beanie perched on her head.

"I had a few things I needed to get done before Jeff gets in,"
I said.

"Samina! Coffee!" came Jeff's shout a moment later.

Well, there went that idea. Cate winked at me, then walked
off to her desk, and I abandoned the email to go and make Jeff
his coffee.

Should I reply straightaway? I wondered as I opened the jar.
Was it better to leave it for a bit so as not to look desperate and

unimportant? Or would leaving it too long look *too* nonchalant? And rude?

I'd never been good at delaying correspondence. I was always concerned the person on the other end would think I was ignoring them. Never mind that people took their time getting back to me.

Menem was a stranger to me but for two brief meetings, in both of which he'd managed to step on convention in more than one way, and I hadn't minded. But I hadn't been completely at ease with it either. This was where the Arab-Muslim Guilt would creep in with alarming ease and morph into a collective. A much mightier strength of the guilt strain it was, and a good deal harder to treat. Completely blew Catholic and Jewish strains of guilt out of the water.

I could at least draft a response, I decided as I sat back at my desk after giving Jeff his coffee. Yes, a brief, polite, respectful response.

> Salam Menem,
> This is a pleasant surprise.

No, wait. Too keen? I mean, why was it a *pleasant* surprise? Maybe I should just say, "This is a surprise." But that would make it sound like an unwelcome surprise, and I couldn't say in all honesty that it was.

Oh Lord. The thing was, the email seemed a bit like an excuse to contact me. It wasn't that I had the highest opinion of myself, but I didn't really expect Menem to pass on any questions about my degree to his cousin. Of course, I'd answer them all if he did. But he wouldn't. Then again, I could be completely off the mark. It had been known to happen.

I really wasn't sure how to reply. I couldn't think clearly. I needed more caffeine. Caffeine would help; it always did. I emailed Cate and asked if she wanted to grab something in ten minutes.

"Yep!" she yelled almost immediately from a few desks away.

Before I could get back to Menem's email, another message appeared in my inbox. This one was from Zahra. Ah, the whole gang was here.

Subject: Email
Samira, I gave your email address to Malek's brother, Menem. He wants to ask you about your degree or something. Anyway, it's not a big deal, so don't get all precious about it. He's family now.
Zahra
P.S. Mum says thanks for your help on Saturday.

Oh bloody hell. Her mum said thanks? I rolled my eyes (totally involuntary reaction).

"When you pray, do you stand the whole time?"

I looked up, refocusing on my surroundings. "Oh, hi, Marcus," I said. On the one day my inbox decided to hemorrhage, of course Marcus would come by for a scripture lesson. But then Cate called out and waved me over, so I made an escape.

Outside, the weather was divine, with clear blue skies and a freshness that made returning to the office even less attractive than usual. When we could spare a moment, Cate and I would find a shady spot in the adjacent park to have our coffees. This was our catch-up time, during which many a dud door-knock and many a dud date had been dissected.

We went to our favorite coffee place, a small coffee bar in MetCentre, the shopping center near our building. We ordered, then continued our conversation while we waited.

"So did your cousin look good?" asked Cate.

"Yeah, she did. Her dress was pretty, and she had her hair and makeup done nicely."

"Was the dress off-the-rack?"

"Nope. She had it made specially for the engagement."

"Ah, she's one of those," said Cate.

"One of those what?"

"A bridezilla. Trust me. Bridezilla before you can say a hundred fifty a head. You think you had it tough with the engagement, just wait for her wedding," she said, taking out her coffee card.

"I'm not too worried. It shouldn't have any impact on me." I shrugged.

If Zahra wanted to have a big fancy wedding, she could be my guest. Or rather, I'd be her guest.

"Here you go, bella," said the barista, Frank, an old Italian man who often complimented me on my scarves.

He stamped our coffee cards and returned them to us with a flourish.

Just as we were walking away, I heard someone say my name. I turned around, curious.

Cate turned with me, and I found myself face-to-face with Menem.

"Hi," he said. Then he smiled, a little shyly I would have thought.

Cate hooked an eyebrow and looked at me. I was busy turning red, but I managed a feeble hello back.

"Your building *is* close by," he said.

Cate kicked me in the shin and I winced.

"Oh, um, Cate, this is my cousin's future brother-in-law, Menem," I said, looking between them. "Cate is a colleague. You might remember her from team building."

Cate smiled and greeted him.

"Hi," he said with a small wave. "I was just going to buy a coffee." He looked down at our hands cradling coffee cups. "But I see I'm too late to make good on my promise."

I smiled at the sweetness of his gesture. "It's okay. We just needed a quick fix."

"I emailed you, by the way. I hope that's all right," said Menem.

I looked briefly at Cate, who hooked the other eyebrow, her expression growing increasingly amused.

"Yes! Um, I was planning to reply to that soon. You know how it is! Mondays!" I laughed awkwardly and looked down, wishing the floor would crack open and I could dive right in.

What utter pants. *You know how it is, Mondays?* This was too uncomfortable for words. Where was my confidence and wit from the team building?

"No, no, it's fine, no rush," said Menem. "I just hope you don't think I was too forward."

"Not at all." Maybe a little. Or maybe I just had no real compass for this sort of thing.

"Okay, well, I should leave you to your caffeine fix." He smiled and nodded once before going to Frank's coffee bar.

"You're one for secrets," whispered Cate as we made our way back to the office.

Chapter 11

Hi Menem,

Thank you for your email. It was nice to meet you too, and a surprise to run into you in the city today! Isn't it funny how these things happen? It's like when you hear a new word for the first time, then hear it numerous times over the next few days.

About the communications degree—I'm afraid what you heard is true, but please don't hold it against me. I'm not a latte drinker and I couldn't care less about Nietzsche. It's not too late for your cousin. She can be saved. Nevertheless, in order to ensure she has all facts at hand, I'd be happy to answer any questions.

Samira

This was only my thirtieth draft. What was the big deal? I'd never had to agonize over an email to Lara or Hakeem. But here there were issues of appropriateness, of what kind of message I wanted to transmit. In this case, I wished to be polite and friendly, but I didn't want to seem interested per se. I didn't even know Menem, after all. Hakeem said I was too trusting, and even Lara agreed. Well, they were just plain wrong.

Still, I was racked with doubt. Biting my lip, I deleted half the email, then a second later decided to keep it as it was. I couldn't look at it anymore. I hit reply, pasted in my message from the draft email I'd been using, then I hit send without reviewing it so that I wouldn't begin version thirty-one.

"Samina."

"Hi, Jeff."

"The ads."

"The—"

"The ads, for the cadets. What's the status?"

"Oh, um, I have the final drafts here—you just need to sign off on them." I fumbled through the stack of folders on the corner of my desk.

"Well, I would sign off on them if I had them, wouldn't I, Samina?"

The ads weren't running for a couple of months, but this was typical Jeff. Never mind that I'd emailed every single version to him.

I sighed inwardly as I located the piece of paper containing the two cadetship ads: one for three journalism positions and another for two photography spots. We always ran the cadetships, only reducing the intake during the financial crisis, and even now, they paid peanuts.

"Jeff, do you remember our conversation about me applying for a cadetship?" I said, handing him the paper.

He sighed. "Did I ever tell you what happened to me at my first job?"

"No, Jeff. I don't think so."

"I got fired, Samina. Fired." Then he gave me a look that said, "My point exactly," even though I had absolutely no idea what he was on about. Then he walked off.

I directed my attention to actual work, sifting through the

mountain of papers Jeff had left for me last week. It wasn't long before my mind drifted back to Menem's email and our unexpected meeting. It was such a coincidence—the kind of thing that happened in movies, not real life. Or, at least, not in my life.

There had to be something wrong with this equation. Did he have a secret past? Or a string of fraudulent business deals? Was he involved in Ponzi schemes?

An hour and three monthly budget sheets later, an email arrived. Nervously, I looked up at the screen, surprised to find it was another message from Hakeem.

> Subject: ?
> You sent this to the wrong person. My apologies for reading it—I didn't realize it was meant for someone else.
>   Hakeem

Confused, I scrolled down, and my heart stopped. There was my email to Menem. I stared dumbly at the words. *This can't be right*, I thought frantically. I went to my sent messages and clicked on the email. Sure enough, it was addressed to Hakeem. I clicked back to my inbox. Menem's email, which I hadn't replied to, sat beside Hakeem's last response.

Crap. Things were already weird between me and Hakeem, and now he'd read my email to Menem and probably gotten the completely wrong idea.

My face flamed hot. Pure panic settled in and put its legs up on the coffee table beside humiliation. "Make yourself comfortable, boys," said humiliation. "You might be working overtime on this one."

I took a deep breath and did my best to suppress the nerves. I reread Hakeem's response, with almost one eye closed.

I didn't know why it bothered me so much, but it did. It really did. *It wasn't* meant *for him,* I thought with a mental whimper. Something deliciously private had been revealed before I'd wanted it to be.

After I'd waited a few minutes for the traces of embarrassment to subside, I realized how silly I was being. What was I thinking? So what if Hakeem saw the email? I had nothing to hide.

I hit reply, this time checking I'd typed in the right email address.

> Subject: Re: ?
> Sorry about that. Menem—Malek's brother (Zahra's fiancé)—emailed me, as he wants to ask me about my degree for his cousin. Thanks for your reply, though.
>   Samira
>   P.S. I didn't give him my email address, just so you know.
>   P.P.S. Zahra did.

I bit my lip, then put the lower part of my face in my hands. I felt like I was in some bizarre alternate universe. Too many things were happening at once.

Hakeem replied quickly.

> Subject: Re: ?
> No problem.

Before I had time to overthink things again, I copied my email to Menem and sent it, triple-checking the address.

It didn't feel as good sending the email now. I almost didn't care if Menem responded or not. It was all tainted by my stupidity.

Even though Hakeem had said it wasn't a problem, I was sure he disapproved. He was probably disgusted and annoyed and wishing he hadn't given me a book that required me to use my intellect.

I'd expected Menem to take his time replying, but apparently not. Ten minutes later, his name appeared in my inbox, and I involuntarily found myself smiling, my stomach burning, my curiosity piqued.

An email chain followed. Each time I replied, I wondered if it would be the message that put him off. So far, nothing he'd said had put *me* off. But I was amiable and easygoing.

It was hard to tell what he was thinking over email, but I slowly gathered more information about him. It turned out he'd only recently started working nearby. He was on secondment from another branch of whatever company it was he worked for.

We weren't likely to cross paths every day, but momentarily I felt like a Jane Austen character who lived in a quiet little village: a young, single woman from a middle-class family with humble connections and suddenly a young, dashing businessman had come to the village and rented an extravagant mansion.

I pictured Menem in one of those period costumes. He'd look the part, considering he was fair skinned and dark blond. I could imagine him bowing as he entered our estate and inquiring after me in a posh accent.

"Is the lady well today?"

And I would nod politely and smile before replying with, "Why, yes, sir. Indeed I am."

But that's where my daydream sort of fell apart because my hijab didn't really go with the types of dresses women had worn back then.

Nevertheless, when I looked at the situation in Austen terms, it didn't seem so odd that Menem worked a few buildings down from me. Meeting him at team building was like meeting him at a picnic. And seeing him at the engagement was like stumbling across him at a ball. In fact, when I thought of it that way, it was almost logical.

So when we ran into each other again while getting coffee a couple of days later, it seemed completely normal.

I realized that I felt more at ease about running into him too. I was able to smile, normally, and while there were somersaults in my tummy, they were the nice kind. And when Menem asked if I had time to sit for a bit, I didn't hesitate to say yes despite having a mountain of work to get through.

"You're a big coffee drinker," he said.

"I think I'm medium-size actually."

He grinned. "Nice one." Then he insisted on paying for the coffee, and asked me to choose a couple of pastries to go with it. "Not very impressive on its own," he said lightly, causing me to smile, because I liked the idea that he was trying to impress me.

I suggested a doughnut—a pink *Simpsons*-inspired one I'd had before.

"Sure, but we can do better than that." He bought the doughnut and two cupcakes as well.

"You are such an Arab," I told him and he laughed. "Force-feeder."

"I've got nothing on my mum."

With coffee and sweets in hand, we found a table nearby

and sat down. Menem invited me to dive in first, and I used a plastic knife to cut the doughnut in half.

While we ate, we swapped war stories and laughed over the force-feeding that occurred in our respective households.

"The worst thing is, I've caught myself doing it to other people," Menem said.

"Teasing aside, I doubt your version of force-feeding is quite the same as an Arab mum's."

Menem paused, played with the lid of his coffee cup. "This is nice," he said. "No loud Arabic music to compete with. No annoying brothers and cousins needing us at their beck and call."

"You understand the pain," I said, grinning like an idiot.

"More than you know."

Menem glanced at his watch. I had to get going too. We'd been there half an hour, and I actually did have lots of work to do. But it seemed neither of us was ready to leave.

"Do you enjoy your work?" I asked.

"Yeah, I do. I love it, in fact. It's the one thing I can make sense of," he said.

"Just the one?"

"Well, it's not as complicated as other life . . . matters."

"Right."

Dangerous, choppy waters. Could get flirty and/or suggestive. For example, I could say, "Such as?" Then Menem would say, "Well, love." Then I would blush and feign innocence, pretending that I hadn't seen that response coming from five football fields away.

"What about you?" said Menem.

"What?"

"Work. You like your job?"

"No."

"Really?"

"Pardon?"

"You said, 'No,' as in you don't like what you do?"

"No."

"No, you do?" Menem asked, puzzled.

"Um, okay. Sorry, can you please repeat the question?" I said, flustered.

"Do you enjoy what you do?" he repeated.

"Sometimes," I replied.

"Okay, well, that's not good enough. Find something you enjoy at least most of the time," he advised.

"Yes," I responded weakly. Hopeless.

"Do you think we could do this again sometime?"

"Like, accidentally run into each other?"

Menem nodded, his eyes meeting mine. "Yes, that."

"That would be nice."

Menem smiled, but he seemed nervous. "So . . . can I have your number? Texting is easier."

My face blazed red, but before I could worry about appropriateness, I acknowledged the multitude of emails and growing number of interactions. It would be hypocritical to refuse.

"Of course."

Menem gave a relieved smile, and I recited my number.

"I'll prank call you now."

I watched as he walked away, his head lowered to his phone. Then, a few seconds later, my screen lit up with his number, and my stomach continued with the somersaults.

Chapter 12

Lara, Cate, and I were sitting in Sahar's kitchen, devouring a mud cake with layers, as Cate and I retold the story of my harrowing experience on the flying fox. Cate and I had been stuck at work late, so I'd invited her to come along, and, well, she wasn't going to say no to cake.

The topic of conversation then segued (unintentionally, of course) toward the Arab-warrior types one might find in the Arab world. Or, as Lara reminded us, in a number of convenience stores throughout the Sydney metropolitan area.

Lara was extra pleased about that, because any time she went into one of those stores, the guy behind the counter would take one look at her and practically give up his shop for her. They nearly lost their minds when they realized she was also Arab (her favorite gold necklace, which had her name written in Arabic, was the giveaway).

Lara would go in, unperturbed if it turned out to be a Pakistani or an Indian behind the counter because they tended to gravitate toward her too. There'd be a conversation, during which the convenience-store assistant would ask Lara where she was from. Following that, they'd laugh over the fact that they were both Muslim, or in a couple of cases, Palestinian, which would then lead them to try to figure out how close their villages in the homeland were to each other.

Of course, he'd have no idea that Lara barely remembered the name of her dad's village.

Then Lara would leave with a handful of free chocolates or a bottle of Coke at half price, which, admittedly, worked out well if we were on our way to a movie.

"The fact is, you're going to have to go overseas if you want an Arab-warrior type," Sahar told me.

I almost choked on my cake. "Overseas? I can't find someone here and I have things in common with these guys. Imagine how incompatible I'd be with a guy from there."

"What about a Westley type?" said Lara, invoking the name of the hero from *The Princess Bride*. "Surely they've got those?"

"Very funny. You know, here I am thinking my friends want the best for me, but instead I'm getting lectured about marriage." Seriously, what was it with loved-up friends who suddenly felt this overwhelming need to get everyone else paired up too?

"Sahar, can I strip?" I said.

"Nobody's here, as usual," she replied, arranging her own hair into a ponytail.

Sahar's parents were out most of the time. Her mother ran a local Muslim organization and spent most of her time at the office. Her father owned a mixed business—one of the few left in our area. He was still the go-to person for Arabic delicacies, like olive oil from the West Bank, cheeses, labneh, and za'atar spice mix. Even now, he would give me free lollies whenever I went into the shop.

I removed the pins from my headscarf—two on top, one safety pin at my throat. With a flutter, the scarf and the cap I wore under it fell onto my handbag. Then I removed the elastic holding my bun and shook my hair out.

I exhaled. "That's better."

"Oh my God," exclaimed Cate.

"What?"

"You look so different!"

Lara glanced up from her cake. "You've never seen Samira's hair?"

Cate shook her head in awe. "You're beautiful, Samira," she said. "I honestly wouldn't have recognized you if I'd passed you on the street looking like that."

I blushed to the roots of my hair. "Thanks, Cate. You're exaggerating, though."

She shook her head. "Seriously, I can't believe what a difference a headscarf makes. I mean, you're beautiful either way, but . . ." She stared at my hair, which fell just below my shoulder blades, as though it was lost treasure. "Is this your natural color?"

I caught Lara's expression and inwardly cringed. I knew Cate meant well, but I was starting to feel uncomfortable. "Yep."

"I didn't expect it to be so light. I knew it was brown, but it's almost golden." She looked at me with a mournful smile.

"You're just not used to seeing me this way," I told her.

"Maybe. Sorry, I'm being a jerk. It's just . . . this is all hidden."

There was an awkward silence. Sahar was at the sink, pulling on gloves to wash the dishes. She'd been watching the exchange, but I wasn't sure how she felt about it.

"I don't know how you do it," Cate said.

Sahar began a spiel on sacrifice, but Lara broke the tension. "Yes, fabulous, Sahar, but can we talk about boys again?"

I gave my less-than-subtle cousin a look of gratitude.

Cate raised her hand with a laugh. "Okay, but you're going to have to bring me up to speed here," she said, turning to me. "Define Arab-warrior type."

"Oh, right," I began. "Beard, dark skin. Tallish, broad shouldered. You can imagine him riding a magnificent horse in the desert, a white cloth wrapped tightly around his face."

Not that I'd thought about it much.

"A cloth like Yasser Arafat's scarf?" inquired Lara. I wasn't sure what was more shocking—that Lara would suggest the Arafat look in the Arab-warrior context (completely off the mark) or that she knew who Yasser Arafat was.

"Like Hakeem," said Sahar unexpectedly, abandoning the dishes. There was a moment of silence before I realized they were all looking at me—Sahar with a look of revelation, Lara looking a bit smug, Cate with a raised eyebrow.

"I guess," I said. I had been going for airy, but it came out a little dismayed. "I mean, I've never thought about it. Here, let me help you, Sahar."

Maybe a tiny, baby white lie there. Hakeem did have the Arab-warrior look. He fit the description. Or at least *my* description, which by no means was the definitive one. But I didn't regard Hakeem that way. Not even a bit. I might have had a crush on him once, but it was so long ago, I could barely remember it. I'd been in the throes of puberty, realizing I could experience strange flip-flop movements in my stomach when a certain guy was around.

But the mention of his name ruffled me. I was still feeling

a bit annoyed at myself about the email mishap on Monday. I hadn't heard from him since his last reply. If he didn't initiate conversation, it would be strange.

"Why don't you just marry Hakeem?" said Lara, snapping me out of my reverie.

Standing beside Sahar, helping her wash up, I dropped the bowl I was holding into the sink with a thud, feeling my face warm up. I really needed to see a doctor about that. I'd heard about a condition where you blush frequently and easily. Perhaps I had that. Assuming you could develop the condition in your late twenties.

"Okay, how about no way?" I replied a little too shrilly, twisting around to give Lara a death stare. "He's like a brother to me. And I'm not his type!"

"But he's *your* type," persisted Lara, totally aware of my discomfort but not caring.

I opened my mouth to speak but had no idea what to say. What could I say that would make an ounce of sense? Hakeem and I didn't match. He'd want a quiet, shy type who could vacuum while making a rice pudding or something.

I could feel Sahar's thoughtful gaze on me. "Maybe he's not her type," she said finally, her face a little pink.

"Can we change the subject?" I said.

"Must we?" said Cate, looking captivated. "I've worked with you for over a year and you have never once told me about this guy!"

Lara shrugged. "He's only completely in love with her."

"Lara!"

She ignored me.

"What happened with that guy from Zahra's engagement?" said Sahar.

Lara straightened up. "You mean Malek's wimpy brother? Has something happened with him?"

"What, and miss out on your Muslim matchmaking skills?" I smiled, but my back was to her.

"Is he that cute guy we ran into the other day?" chimed in Cate, her mouth jammed full of chocolate cake.

I looked over at Sahar and remembered her disapproval at the party. She didn't say anything, and if she was surprised, she hid it by busying herself with drying the dishes. I knew she would not approve, and I hated to disappoint her, so I had to be careful here lest I reveal too much. And use words like "lest."

"We're in contact," I confessed. "But nothing's happening, really."

Apart from daily messages, emails (because they're easier to reply to when you're at work), and "accidental" meetings at MetCentre. I didn't feel like we were in deep. But the contact was regular and playful, and I felt a bit of a boost whenever I saw Menem's name appear.

"Are you attracted to him?" demanded Lara.

"There's nothing to report," I said, feeling oddly protective of this connection.

"He's really cute," said Cate, helpfully.

I felt my face warm up. I was deeply attracted to Menem, but I wasn't ready to show it.

After dinner, I left Sahar's place with Lara. I was driving her home, and we were barely a hundred meters down the road before she turned to me.

"So out with it," Lara ordered.

"What?"

"Samira, I have known you all your life, and you're a terrible liar. Don't play innocent with me." She connected my phone to the speakers and selected a track.

"What are you on about?" We stopped at a red light and I turned to my cousin. She narrowed her eyes at me.

"I want every detail. I love it when I'm right," said Lara, laughing evilly.

"Right about what?"

"Hakeem and the wimpy brother."

"Lara, you don't even know him! And his name is Menem," I said. The light turned green, so I accelerated and waved her away. I wasn't in the mood for more wild theories and recrimination.

"I don't have to know him," she said. "He's a flirt, so I don't like him. And I'm sticking with 'wimpy brother.'"

"Since when do you hold flirting against a complete stranger?"

"So he *is* a flirt!"

"No! He is not!"

"Samira," she said, sounding ominously like my mother.

"I told you: he emailed me."

"And how'd he get your email address?"

"Zahra gave it to him." I told her about Zahra's email and Lara burst out laughing.

"The plot thickens. Okay, any word from Hakeem? Ooh, tell him wimpy brother emailed you!" Lara squealed.

I was silent. I still felt a flush of embarrassment whenever I remembered. I studied the roads, wondering if perhaps there was a shortcut I could take.

"Samira?"

"Hakeem already knows about the email."

"Get out of here! The student becomes the master!" Lara put one hand to her mouth, her voice projecting pride.

"No, I didn't do it on purpose! I'm not you!" I braked a little too suddenly at another set of lights and we both tumbled forward, then back again.

Lara didn't skip a beat. "Ouch, that hurts. But it's true. So how does he know about it?"

"I kind of accidentally sent my reply to Hakeem," I said, biting my lip.

Lara guffawed. "Oh my God, this is precious." She looked out her window and shook her head. We didn't celebrate Christmas, but it had come early for her this year.

"Lara, it's not funny! If you want drama, watch *Days of Our Lives*."

"And miss this? I'm sorry, sweet, but please don't tell me you can't see the humor in this. You're not letting it bother you, are you?"

"No, I was embarrassed, but I got over it."

"Good. What did Hakeem do?"

"He just said, 'No problem.'"

Lara was quiet for a moment. "Okay, look. I know I tease you, but can't you see that I'm right about Hakeem? He's jealous. He's totally into you."

"No, I cannot see that. Lara, look—"

"How many thirty-four-year-olds do you know who go to family dinners?" she interrupted.

"What?"

"Answer the question," she commanded.

"First of all, he's thirty-one in a couple of weeks, not thirty-four," I said.

"Minor detail. Point is, Hakeem's hardly a social butterfly, and he's not the wimpy kind who goes to every family function. So how many thirty-year-olds do you know who'd do that?" continued Lara.

"His father is all alone here, so it's natural Hakeem would go with him." Hakeem's mother had died three years ago, and I instantly sent up a prayer for her. Hakeem had an older brother, but he lived in the Gulf with his wife and kids.

Lara shook her head. "He comes to those family dinners because you'll be there and it's the only way he can see you without doing something wrong," she said, stopping short of rolling her eyes. "I mean, no offense, but no guy who's single and free like Hakeem would voluntarily come to those dinners. You're not even family."

I wasn't offended because I knew exactly what she meant. Family dinners did get rather chaotic, especially on the occasions when we pulled out the Scrabble board (usually when my cousin Jamal was over). Scrabble would mutate into another subspecies of game entirely if Dad insisted on playing. No matter how many times I explained the rules to him, he'd still get confused. One time he found a deck of UNO cards, and it ended in disaster. Dad kept forgetting to say, "Uno," which led to turmoil. There had been actual tears.

Mercifully we arrived at Lara's place, and despite her urging me to come in for a while, I insisted that I couldn't stay.

"Life would be so much easier for us all if you'd just accept that I'm always right," said Lara, her hand poised over the door handle.

"Yes, and modest too."

"Who taught you that boys suck?"

"You did."

"Exactly. Now, will you just admit that Hakeem likes you?"

I still didn't believe even for a moment that Lara was right about this. "If that was true, why hasn't he asked for me? There's nothing to stop him from asking to marry me," I pointed out. Hakeem's father was my dad's first friend in Sydney, according to the Abdel-Aziz folklore. Our families were tight. It would be the simplest thing in the world for Hakeem to make the move.

"Lesson one: boys suck. Lesson two: they're complicated and don't always know what's good for them," said Lara. "Particularly ones like Hakeem. He's probably torn with guilt just for liking you. It's probably against his rules." Lara crossed her arms and looked ahead thoughtfully, as though trying to unlock a great secret of the universe.

"If he liked me, he'd like me. Simple," I countered.

"We're talking about a man who's been engaged twice."

"He didn't find what he wanted. So what?"

"That's just it. He wants more, but he's too afraid to go for it. It's probably destroying him."

"You've been watching trashy romances again, haven't you?"

"Don't you get it?" Lara said, her eyes getting progressively wider. "Hakeem will never do anything about it unless he's forced to. The problem is, he has low emotional intelligence. We all do. It's because of the way we were brought up. I read a book about it."

"Okay, Lara." I rubbed my forehead, preparing myself for the headache with which my cousin would leave me.

"Or maybe it was in *Cosmo*. Anyway. Hakeem's a pigtail puller," said Lara. "The new guy probably is too. They all are."

"Pigtail puller" was Lara's term for the emotionally stunted men who came our way, the ones who, much like their kindergarten-age counterparts, would make life difficult for the girls they fancied.

"What are your plans for Saturday night?" Lara said, finally dropping the subject. "I want to go to the movies. Let's watch something pretentious."

I nodded, happy to change the subject, and relieved that I had kept my meetings and messages with Menem to myself.

Chapter 13

The next day was the first in a few that I didn't open my inbox to a new message from Menem. Nor did I run into him when getting my midmorning coffee. It oddly affected me. I felt disappointed but also tried to stem the influx of negative thoughts that seemed eternally on standby.

But then, in the afternoon, while I was having a late lunch in the MetCentre food court, he found me alone, doodling, of all things.

"You know, they say doodling can tell you something about a person."

I jumped in fright, then looked up to find him standing beside me with an expression of amusement on his face. He wasn't wearing a jacket or tie. His top button was undone, and he had his hands in his trouser pockets. The look suited him, and my stomach made some odd jumbly movements.

I found him very attractive. But also there was something awfully comforting about his presence. I almost felt . . . safe when I was with him. I was surprised at the wave of relief that rushed through me. He hadn't been avoiding me.

I stared at the page of doodles and felt slightly foolish. They were hopeless drawings. If I had a shot at anything creative career-wise, it certainly wasn't drawing.

"Right," I said, a little embarrassed.

Menem sat down opposite me. "May I?"

I nodded, and he turned the notebook toward him. "So you're an expert on scribbling, are you?" I said as he studied the page.

"Yes, I'm a doodler myself," said Menem mock-proudly. "Now, see this right here?"

"That's a flower," I said quickly. At least it was meant to be a flower. It actually looked more like a mutant raindrop.

"Yes, I can see that," he replied. "Notice the way you've drawn the petals? That symbolizes burdens."

"You're making this up," I said.

"I am not!" he said, affronted, but he laughed.

I regarded him skeptically.

"See this star?" He pointed again at the page.

"Uh-huh." I couldn't help smiling. Pathetic. I wondered if I was becoming one of those silly girls who bat their eyelids at the boy they fancy.

"That star suggests aspirations," continued Menem. "Dreams unfulfilled. Does that sound about right?"

I nodded in amusement. "Well, I guess you have me figured out then."

"Not quite," he said with a smile. "But I'm getting there."

Chapter 14

It was a Monday evening, and I was to undertake the weekly shopping for Mum after work. There was something therapeutic about supermarkets. I liked the way everything was so colorfully and methodically set out. I appreciated the order and the vastness, but I only liked shopping in them at night, when it was quiet and little more than the sound of beeping registers and really bad '90s music could be heard.

So I happily set off after dinner, shopping list in hand. Admittedly, I was in high spirits because (a) Menem was playing on my mind, and (b) there'd been a brief period of respite from Zahra's wedding inquiries. Meaning, I had enjoyed two days of silence following a barrage of requests to do with shoe retailers, Sydney's best bridal stores, venue breakdowns, and back issues of *Bridal Bazaar*, to name just a few.

But as I was inspecting my ice-cream options in the frozen-food aisle—cookies and cream or strawberry—Zahra appeared, doing her little tilted-head walk toward me.

"Samira!" she gasped.

I gave her a pained smile. "Hi, Zahra."

We made small talk, Zahra flashing her engagement ring every five seconds by straightening the strap on her Miu Miu handbag or scratching a nonexistent itch on her face.

Then she studied me, an amused expression on her face. "Malek's brother seems to have noticed you. Don't worry, I warned him that you're a total innocent and spend all your time watching romantic comedies."

I felt my cheeks burning, but I wasn't going to let Zahra pull me into her tornado of digs. Before I could start calculating the potential damage she had done with her review of my personality, I opened the freezer door to make my selection: cookies and cream.

It was clear Zahra wasn't going to leave, so as I placed the tub in my cart, I turned to face her.

"My mum said your wedding is in a couple of months. That's kind of quick, isn't it?"

Zahra rolled her eyes and sighed. "When you know, you just know. It's hard for you to understand."

Another obligatory put-down.

Then Zahra did a head-tilt smile that I'd always found annoying and had always led to some rather unsavory mental images that involved the yellow *Kill Bill* jumpsuit.

"Anyway, I may as well let you know now that you're going to be a bridesmaid," she said.

I was gobsmacked. "Um, I don't think so," I replied with a laugh.

My cousin didn't move, standing beside my cart with her feet positioned like a ballerina's, her arms crossed.

I'd no doubt the decision to include me in her bridal party was less than an affectionate gesture and I wanted no part of it. There was also no way on God's green earth I was going to be a bridesmaid if it was a big fat Arab wedding. Seeing as Mum was fairly conservative, I knew I'd have her backing on that, and she wouldn't bury me in guilt for refusing.

"I'll adjust your outfit for your headscarf," Zahra said. "And it's not going to be a massive wog wedding, so don't worry."

I found this hard to believe, given the size of the engagement party.

"Zahra, look, no offense, but I don't want to be your bridesmaid. I don't want to be anyone's bridesmaid."

I was bloody sick of weddings, in fact.

"Lara's going to be one too," she said, mildly put out.

"And does she know about that?"

Zahra's face was fixed in a tight frown, and she shook her head imperceptibly.

"Why aren't your friends your bridesmaids? Najwa isn't all over the wedding?" I tried to remember the names of Zahra's other friends, but Najwa was the only one I'd ever had a conversation with, and she was as fond of me as Zahra was.

My cousin momentarily stiffened, then adjusted her handbag, offering one more flash of the rock on her finger. "It's going to be family only in the bridal party. We're all on the same table."

"But—"

"I'll call you about the dress fittings next week."

I felt like she was withholding crucial information, but I also suspected that it had already been agreed upon between our parents and I had no choice. As my mood deflated, I wondered if I should get the strawberry flavor too.

With a glance at the tub of ice cream in my cart, Zahra touched her stomach and smiled before saying, "Salams."

By Thursday I was in the foulest of moods, unable to shake the feeling that I'd been set up by those I should have been able to trust the most. Not even a cheeky meme from Menem could cheer me up.

Cate didn't so much sense that something was wrong as notice it when my stapling was louder than the hum of the printer.

"Are you okay?" she asked, resting her arms on my cubicle wall.

"Just dandy!"

"Another dud?"

"No. My cousin told me I have to be a bridesmaid at her wedding." I began beating a set of reports with the blasted stapler because it kept getting stuck.

"Okay, so I'm going to take the stapler off you," said Cate, coming over to disarm me. Gingerly, she removed the stapler from my hands and sat down on my desk. "Now, let's back up a moment. You don't want to be a bridesmaid because . . . ?"

"Well, because I don't want to," I complained. Realizing that wasn't an adequate explanation, I continued. "It's just amazing that someone who didn't even tell me she was getting to know a guy before she got engaged is expecting me to spend a weekend driving around Sydney to find the right shoes for her 'specially made dress with Italian fabric,'" I said, mimicking Zahra, who'd put in the "request" on Tuesday.

"Poor you. That sucks."

"Well, it serves me right for having a car."

I was slowly but surely going to be swept into an alternate universe where everything was about Zahra, but worse, because it also involved weddings—two of my least favorite things.

It should have stopped at Zahra's request for back issues of *Bridal Bazaar* and retailers. Instead, there was the supermarket meeting and Zahra's subsequent "fabric" request. Then my mother called me at work this morning to tell me we were going to Zahra's place tomorrow night to help with something wedding related.

I felt the need to resist somehow. To fight the inevitable.

My schedule was slowly but surely being taken over by Zahra's wedding. The idea of being at my cousin's beck and call, when she always went out of her way to make me feel insignificant, was overwhelming.

Before Cate could offer me counsel, Marcus swung into my cubicle and plopped down on the floor beside us.

"Hello, ladies," he said. "Samira, I have a conundrum for you."

"I'm no good at conundrums," I deadpanned.

"Well, it's more a 'What would you do?' situation," he said.

"Okay," I said.

"You're stuck on a deserted island with a man. There's only the two of you. Can you get married? I mean, let's say you had no idea if you'd be rescued. What would you do?" he asked, sounding genuinely interested.

Cate leaned down and slapped Marcus on the arm.

"Ow!" he cried.

"Be gone!" ordered Cate.

"You know, that can constitute workplace harassment," he said, rubbing the sore spot. "I watched the OH&S video."

We all had. And even though the topic was a serious one, eventually the hammy acting and the cheesy soundtrack had led to a few sniggers. Then Jeff, with his arms crossed, had yelled, "Shut the bloody hell up! You have to answer a bloody quiz about this! It's my neck on the line!"

Marcus gave Cate a look like an injured puppy dog. There

was definitely more to his hurt expression than usual, and if I were in any other mood, I'd have felt sorry for him.

"I like your headscarf today, by the way, Samira," he said, glancing my way.

"Thanks, Marcus. And to answer your question, I really don't know. I can ask someone, perhaps." Like, never. I wasn't about to pull aside a sheikh or an Islamic teacher to ask them about it. They'd look at me like I was mad. Following that, they'd most likely remind me that men and women shouldn't be alone together unless there is a reasonable purpose—a rule that no one I knew managed to follow.

Marcus erupted into his hyena laugh.

"Like a sensei?" he guffawed. "Ow!"

"Go!" commanded Cate. And go he did, but not without another hurt look.

"Sorry, Cate, I have to go too. Photo shoot." I got out of my chair and began to pack up.

"Gabriel?"

"Yep."

Cate sighed. "I love him."

"How are things with Marcus?" I asked.

Cate blushed. "Fine."

"Fine?"

"That is all I have to say."

She still hadn't told me about their first date, nor what I presumed were the second and third and fourth ones. Her secrecy was a little alarming; post-date discussion was par for the course, so I didn't understand why this was such a big deal.

"You know you'll tell me more eventually," I said as I swung my handbag over my shoulder and hugged a plastic envelope to my chest.

Cate twisted her mouth every which way, assessing the validity of my statement. "Well," she said, "there isn't really anything to say just now." Then she shook her head at me. "I can't talk about it yet," she said in a near whisper. "I'm not sure how to deal with the situation."

"Wow, this must be serious."

Cate blushed a deeper red. "Maybe," she said with a shrug. "I'm not sure yet."

Chapter 15

I had allowed myself enough time to walk at a leisurely pace to the shoot location, taking advantage of the winter sunshine bathing the city. Ordinarily it took about fifteen minutes to get from the office to The Rocks, the setting for so many of our magazine spreads and just about every Sydney wedding. Today I sucked up half an hour, realizing as I walked along Hickson Road that I should do this more often.

I stopped by a bakery and bought a caramel slice, which I balanced out with a Diet Coke. I continued my walk, trying my best to block out annoying thoughts, to find some calm. Knowing I'd be on a photo shoot helped me to achieve this. I much preferred watching Gabriel at work than office drudgery. Not even the occasional writing opportunity seemed as interesting as capturing the right image.

I spotted Gabriel dragging equipment from his car as I neared the Nurses Walk.

He smiled and waved when he saw me approaching. I rushed up to join him and grabbed one of the bags.

"Hey, girl!"

"Hey. How's it going?" I took a couple more bags off him, repositioning the things I was already carrying.

"I've got my health and I love my job. What's there to complain about?" he said.

"Fair enough." I laughed.

We took the pathway down to the Nurses Walk, a full load between us.

"You're just in time to help me set up," Gabriel said.

"The model isn't here yet?"

"Relax—she's in makeup."

"Oh, good. What can I do?"

"The usual."

"Really?"

"You've been doing a pretty good job so far. Why stop now?"

"Thank you!" I felt a bubble of excitement as we placed the bags and cases in a suitable spot by the makeshift dressing room.

I unlatched the tripod case and carefully removed each component. Once I'd set it up, I scanned the rest of the bags. The camera came out next—a swish Nikon. It was one of the best in the range, strictly for the pros.

Gabriel crouched down to my level, and after a cursory glance at his bags, he looked at me expectantly. "Are you going to get that thing set up properly or what?"

"Come on, you know I get nervous with this stuff. It's so expensive," I told him.

He shook his head. "You're fine. Just get it up on the tripod."

I understood Cate's crush on him. Gabriel had beautiful blue eyes, which canceled out the somewhat grungy look he seemed to favor. His hair was a dirty blond, he had one ear pierced, and today, like most days, he wore tight jeans, a white muscle tee, a studded belt, and a checkered shirt. I wouldn't have placed him as older than early thirties, but he dressed like a teenager.

Gabriel made location shoots more tolerable for me. I'd started to ask him photography-related questions early on, not realizing I was doing it so often. Then, out of the blue, he shoved one of the smaller cameras into my hands after a session one afternoon and told me to point and shoot. I had been intimidated and thrilled by the prospect.

After that, whenever we waited for models to get changed or have their makeup done, Gabriel would instruct me on the functions of a digital SLR. Sometimes, if I was very lucky and the shoot was in the afternoon, he would stay longer and give me a proper lesson.

He taught me about aperture, metering, shutter speed, and composition. I liked the theory behind photography. I loved that you could never be sure what you'd end up with, but like most things, there was still a formula to help you get there. And Gabriel made it seem so simple.

He encouraged me to take photos, anytime, anywhere. "Just buy a small camera to start with, and keep it in your handbag," he suggested. I did, but I wasn't sure the photos were any good. I tended to photograph landscapes and objects. They were less complicated than people, who demanded a more tailored approach.

Not that I dedicated a whole lot of time to it. It was fun on location shoots, and I preferred being under Gabriel's instruction. I seemed to forget everything he'd taught me when I was alone.

We stood up, my hands framing the very expensive Nikon. I secured the camera to the tripod, then positioned it on the paved walkway.

Gabriel scooted over and made further adjustments. "Based on how the light is filtering through," he said as he repositioned the tripod. I watched as he fiddled with the complex menu on the camera, searching through the various functions, pressing buttons efficiently and quickly.

"I'm going to need you to hold a reflector," he said, leaning down to take a test shot.

"Too much sun?" I ventured.

"Good girl. Even with the best equipment, sometimes the light just sucks." He changed the settings again and took another shot. "Remember what I told you about direct sunlight?"

"You want to avoid it and work with reflected light only," I recited, verbatim.

"And why do we do that?" he prompted, turning back to his bags. He searched through a couple until he found what he was looking for: a shorter lens.

"This not only avoids stark contrast but also eliminates squinting due to harsh light," I said.

Gabriel nodded, impressed. "And we use a fill flash to minimize shadows under the eyes, then hope like hell the subject can avoid squinting," he reminded me. He located a reflector: the large, white, floppy thing that's held to the side of the person being photographed. "And this does what?" he said, flapping a shade.

"It balances light and shadow," I said, chuffed that I remembered it all, and, even better, that I understood it.

He had another, larger reflector, which he set up on a stand on the other side. The model, Josephine, now stood in place, in a dress that was Cinderella-stunning. Snow White and Rapunzel blow-me-out-of-the-water exquisite, and somehow not ostentatious in the least.

She motioned to me, and I rushed over to assist her. With

a smile, she gestured to the back of her voluminous skirt. I leaned the reflector against a pillar, then stepped behind her to straighten out the fabric, which was laced with pearls. Next, I smoothed out the short, lacy sleeves and adjusted the boatneck bodice, leaning over so as not to step on the hem of the dress.

She thanked me with another luminous smile, then I stepped back and retrieved the shade.

"Okay, let's go," said Gabriel.

I stood to the left of Josephine, holding up the reflector. My visibility was limited, but I could still see her if I leaned my head to the side just a little.

I felt a twinge as I watched her confidently pose in the dress, her hand resting lightly on her hip, her hair elegantly styled in a French knot. She radiated happiness, as though it really was her special day. I found my reaction odd, given I'd never thought much about wedding gowns for myself. I didn't think I'd ever contemplated an actual wedding.

I suddenly felt more than a little frumpy in my hijab, black trousers, and blouse vest ensemble. *I'd never be able to wear something like that dress,* I thought. Or if I did, it would only be in the company of other women. The men in my family didn't count, and while my future husband could see me in it, of course, he wouldn't be beside me the whole night because I could only wear it if it was an all-girls party.

My hijab and its requirements had never bothered me much, so I was surprised at the feeling of regret that washed over me.

I returned to the office at 4:30, feeling a little exhausted after a day in the sun. Marcus was hovering around my desk and seemed poised to begin another session of Twenty Questions. Honestly, he should've had his own TV show.

I smiled politely at him, then switched on some music, navigating earphones under my headscarf. I checked my emails and responded to a couple from Jeff. There was also a message from Lara—a meme of a cute cat thinking psychotic thoughts. Maybe I was just tired, but I found it disturbing.

"Tiaras."

I looked up from my computer. "Pardon me?"

"I need five hundred words on tiaras. We have an empty column," explained Jeff.

"Okay, and—"

"Samina." He sighed. "I'm telling you because you're to write it. Yeah?"

"What exactly am I writing?" I asked, bewildered.

"Five hundred words on the wonder that is the tiara. Be creative. And get me the survey results from marketing. Now."

I was trying to figure out exactly what was so wonderful about tiaras when my inbox pinged. It was Lara again.

> Subject: Hmmm
> I was talking to Hakeem the other night. Interesting.
> You can thank me later. Has wimpy brother popped the
> question yet?
> Miss you
> Lara xx

Oh bloody hell. Lara needed adult supervision sometimes. This is what happened when she was bored.

Subject: Re: Hmmm
Lara! What have you done? You can't be left alone on
the internet!

Remembering Jeff's request for the survey results, I quickly
printed off the report that marketing had sent through earlier.
As soon as the pages were ready, I rushed them over to Jeff and
placed them on his desk.

"Here you go," I said.

"Samina. Five hund—"

"Yes, Jeff. Five hundred words on tiaras."

"By ten a.m. tomorrow, *please*. That's morning, *a.m.*"

All I could think about was whether Lara had responded yet.
Of course, I knew I should've been more enthusiastic about being
asked to actually write, not just tweak or copyedit, a whole five-
hundred-word piece. But priorities! I hurried back to my desk.

Subject: Re: Hmmm
Are these the words of someone who trusts someone? I think
not. By the way, quick question: Team Aniston or Team Jolie?
After all these years, it still bugs me. You can go either way
here and no one will think less of you.
    Lara xx
    P.S. I'm waiting for an update re wimpy brother! Don't you
be holding out on me!
    P.P.S. DON'T ELOPE.

I had no idea where eloping came into this, particularly as
I was hardly the type to do something that outrageous. And I
couldn't imagine it without horses and Austen-era capes.

Subject: Re: Hmmm
It's not about trust. Don't try to change the subject. What
have you done?

P.S. Team Aniston (still).

By now, I'd given up pretending to work. A horrible knot of
anxiety was threading its way through me as I awaited Lara's
response, which finally arrived ten minutes later.

Subject: Re: Hmmm
Why is it that if you need something done you have to
do it yourself? Please find attached an excerpt from my
conversation with Hakeem. I was hoping to show it to you
in person so you could get my accompanying commentary.
But I would like to prove that I am, once again, right. Feel
free to forward this on to wimpy brother. That ought to kick
him into gear!

So you're still Team Aniston, huh? Go figure. You always
gun for the underdog.

Lara xx

P.S. I think Hakeem blocks me on Facebook sometimes.
I've no idea why. Who wouldn't want to talk to me?

EXCERPT FROM LARA'S CHAT WITH HAKEEM
(which proves she's right):

Lara: This bloke kept driving even though the lady was
    crossing the street. And there was a crossing.
Hakeem: Maybe he didn't see her.
Lara: Oh, he saw her.

Hakeem: Why assume the worst of people? It's not good to
think that way.

Lara: Uh-huh, whatever!

Hakeem: You have a lot of sugar in your diet, don't you?

Lara: Samira says the same thing, you know. I miss her. I
hardly get to see her these days.

Hakeem: Inshallah, you can make time then.

Lara: She hasn't been in touch much. There's obviously
a guy in the picture.

Samira, he totally paused here!!!!

Hakeem: Well, she needs to be careful.

Lara: Totally. But she's smart enough to handle herself.

He paused here too! (Not just a short one—a long pause.)

Hakeem: I've told her to be cautious. She can be too
trusting.

Lara: True. Still . . . Imagine if she gets engaged. ;) Wouldn't
that be fun?

And here!!! (HE MUST'VE FAINTED!!!)

Hakeem: Zahra's fiancé's brother appeared interested. I
upset her. I told her to be careful about him. Anyway,
she's a grown woman. She can handle herself.

Lara: Totally. Besides, he can just ask to see her at her place,
and all's good.

Hakeem: It's a bit strange he hasn't yet, isn't it?

Lara: How so?

Hakeem: He should go directly to her parents. He's a
stranger to her.

Lara: I suppose. But you know how it is with Arabs. You meet
one person, you know their whole family. He figures she's
Zahra's cousin.

Hakeem: So he's interested officially?

Lara: Well, he hasn't asked for a visit yet. But he's definitely
making it obvious that he's interested.

Hakeem: And is she interested?

Lara: Well, you'd have to ask her. Not sure. But like I said,
she's never around! Oh Lord, I have to go now.

I reread Lara's email three times before drafting a response.
I wasn't sure what to make of it. Hakeem seemed curious, but
so what? No alarm bells going off.

Subject: Re: Hmmm

Lara, what were you hoping for him to say exactly? You've
got nothing!

I went back to work, and I tried so hard to concentrate on tiaras. But my mind kept flitting back to Lara's conversation with
Hakeem. I didn't find the pauses from his end (so thoughtfully
indicated by Lara) that strange. He'd always been the protective
type: stern, commanding, and disapproving. But then maybe it
was hard for me to tell because I knew him so well. I really had
no idea.

Chapter 16

Morning coffee the next day and it was just Menem and me in the near-empty food court.

"So when you're not working the bridal scene, what do you like to do?" said Menem, while we waited for our order.

"The usual. Reading, movies. I'm thinking about taking a photography course," I said, surprising myself. I didn't even own a digital SLR camera yet.

"That's great," he replied.

"Actually, I'm a bit of a hermit sometimes," I confessed.

"Why's that?"

"Because I'm bored?"

"Maybe you're bored because you're a hermit."

"No, that can't be right," I said, pondering this and then shaking my head. "What about you?"

"Well, when I'm not working on computers, I'm either working on computers or fishing."

"Fishing?"

"Yeah," he said, a little embarrassed. "A bit of an oldies thing, I know."

"Not really. It's just an interesting hobby. Do you set the fish free after you catch them?"

"It depends. Generally, no."

Frank handed us our coffees, and Menem pointed to the exit. "Want to walk for a bit?"

We strolled toward a small park behind my company's building.

"Do you like reading?" I said.

"Not so much. I don't have the patience for it, to be honest."

Then he asked me what my favorite book was.

Too many to pinpoint one, I apologized.

He tried to help me to break down my list of favorites by playing the desert island game. "If you could take only one book with you—aside from one on religion—what would it be?"

I still couldn't answer. But we talked about the desert island game and how logistically, and in all other ways, it made very little sense.

We continued with some small talk. The weather. The annoying elevators in our respective buildings that never seemed to operate well. Whether or not there was a significant difference between lattes and flat whites. As I was a cappuccino drinker, I had no idea. Then we compared coffee bars, which was something I did have some idea about.

"So do you do any sports?" he asked after we realized there was little disagreement on the subject.

We'd found a bench, and Menem positioned himself so that he was facing me, one arm relaxed along the back.

"I used to. I was a pretty good runner," I said, meeting his gaze. That had been a long time ago, so I wasn't even sure it deserved mention.

He seemed impressed. "Short or distance?"

I nodded once. "Distance. But it was ages ago. Like, during adolescence." I focused on my coffee cup so he wouldn't see the way my face had flushed.

"Why'd you stop?"

"I just got older, I guess."

"Okay. But what does that have to do with anything?"

If I hadn't known better, I'd have found it impossible to believe he came from an Arab Muslim family. Granted, they didn't seem like the stuffy type, but Menem seemed completely and sincerely confused by my response.

"It's a little bit hard when you wear a headscarf," I explained.

"But you can wear long pants and those scarves that don't fly off," he said with an easy shrug.

"I guess I wouldn't feel comfortable," I said.

Menem was about to say something but instead our eyes met and he studied me.

I was the first to break. "I should get back. Once I've filed a potentially award-worthy piece on tiaras, I have to start researching how people are making white weddings green." True story. A new assignment from Jeff, and to be written up in more than 400 words.

"It was nice running into you," he said, and I offered my agreement.

He gave me another serious look and I felt an agonizing jet of nerves—the same feeling I got the one (and only) time I rode on a roller coaster.

Chapter 17

The next week passed uneventfully and, in a rare occurrence, was lighter in terms of workload. Nevertheless, there were more requests from Zahra to fill the gaps—bonbonnière "prototypes," hen party "suggestions," and a cake-tasting session that, admittedly, almost made the life of wedding servitude worthwhile. I'd never realized just how much one could do with flour and eggs. Nor had I ever considered marzipan to be edible before Zahra dragged me to that fancy cake shop.

We went to Paddington after work on Wednesday. I had no idea why she'd requested my assistance, given she didn't need my car, and I doubted that anyone had forced her to bring me. I'd have almost ventured that she actually *wanted* my opinion.

Despite my surprise and slight discomfort at my beefed-up role as wedding assistant, I didn't mind tagging along. There was no getting out of any of it now anyway. It was like quicksand: the more I struggled, the deeper I sank into Zahra's Wedding Extravaganza.

With minimum fuss, Zahra settled on a design and cake—fruit cake, but no lie, it was scrumptious. Nothing like those soggy Christmas puddings you'd get as an end-of-year gift from your boss. It was a beautiful three-tiered cake with white marzipan icing. Each tier was square shaped and marked with a different pattern, like quilted boxes.

I didn't run into Menem every day (he was on a deadline), but he had emailed me on Tuesday.

Subject: Books
How can you not know what book you'd take with you?
What if we categorize them?
Menem

By Friday, Menem had conceded that I, in fact, did not have a favorite book. He further acknowledged that I wasn't simply being difficult, although I could understand how he might have thought I was being playful or flirty or something.

On Sunday evening, Mum announced that we were having a family dinner plus guests.

By 6:30, it was Grand Central at our house. I wondered if perhaps some neighbors had wandered in when they'd seen the guests converge, hoping to blend in and have a free feed. A party *was* a party.

I was with Mum in the kitchen, sorting out the food she and Dad had bought for dinner. Mum wasn't cooking tonight, but the menu was still very appetizing: four stuffed chickens; three boxes of spinach pies; two trays of meat and za'atar pizzas; two tubs of creamy baked potatoes; one jug of something liquidy. And a partridge in a pear tree.

Mum gave me instructions: I was put in charge of salads. Well, salad (singular). After a few minutes, she came over to examine my cutting and used her knife to turn over the tomatoes.

"Make them even, Samira," she said.

So much for taking a creative approach to the salad. *Artistic vision was crushed in this family*, I thought bitterly. I began to cut them evenly, but I wasn't happy about it.

"Who's coming tonight?" I asked.

"Abu Ibrahim and Hakeem," said Mum. "And your aunt Kareema's family."

"Why didn't anyone tell me we were having a big dinner?"

"We did tell you," said Mum.

"No, you didn't."

"Well, now you know."

"So evi—Zahra isn't coming?" I said hopefully.

I'd had fun cake tasting. There was no denying it. But yesterday I'd had to drive out to a factory in a suburb I'd never heard of to collect the materials for Zahra's bonbonnières.

"Buying in bulk, Samira," Zahra had explained. "Don't you understand that it saves me a fortune if we assemble them ourselves? So what if I have to drive an hour out of Sydney to get them?"

Not a problem at all, except that *I* was the one driving an hour out of Sydney.

"They're not coming tonight," confirmed Mum.

Admittedly, I was feeling edgy about seeing Hakeem. I still hadn't spoken to him properly since the email incident, which was unsettling and weird and completely unlike us.

I had a birthday gift for him, but I was feeling rather nervy about it. And then, of course, I was annoyed that I was so nervous. It was a horrible, vicious spiral. To top it off, I knew *he'd* be annoyed at me for buying him a birthday gift because he didn't like celebrating that kind of thing.

Every year I'd buy him something, and every year he'd lecture me on why I shouldn't have. But he'd still accept the gift. Then we'd argue again. He'd always buy me one too, but usually *around* the time of my birthday. Then we'd argue, but generally not in relation to the present.

Just as I'd finished with the evenly cut tomatoes, the doorbell rang. The feeling of dread in my stomach deepened. There was nothing to be worried about, but the nerves were on standby. "We're not going anywhere," they declared.

Dad answered the door, and I heard him welcoming Abu Ibrahim and Hakeem in his typically hospitable manner, beckoning them into our lounge room. My mother swooped into the kitchen a moment later and examined the trays.

"Yallah, Samira."

"Okay, Mum, I'm doing it."

"Go and get changed," she ordered.

I left the kitchen and went to my room to get dressed in something more appropriate than my PJ bottoms and shirt. When I reemerged, I could hear laughter coming from the sitting room. I grabbed the plates and cutlery, then made my way to the dining room.

As the dining and sitting rooms had no wall between them, I couldn't avoid our guests. I put down the plates and sent my greetings from the dinner table. Abu Ibrahim acknowledged me back. Hakeem nodded, but his smile was tight. *At least he came,* I thought.

We'd brought out the extra table for the evening. I didn't know any other family who had to buy two identical dining tables from IKEA and push them together whenever they had family dinners.

As usual, Omar sat opposite me at dinner and threw questions at me, each one followed by his customary look of assessment. The fun part was having the extended family around to witness it all. Tonight's topic wasn't marriage, though, thank the Lord.

"Have you spoken to your boss about career progression?"

Before Omar could pounce on my lack of aspiration, I bailed to the kitchen. I was getting tired of McCarthyesque trials at every dinner.

I decided I'd be useful without being asked, by preparing dessert, which primarily involved unwrapping the trays of kanafeh and baklawa that Abu Ibrahim and Hakeem had brought with them.

"Did you put on the kettle?" said Mum as she walked into the kitchen.

"Not yet."

"Then put on the kettle."

"Yes, Mum." I put on the kettle.

Aunt Kareema walked in next. She was the one who'd sent me Manga Boy. I should've been affronted by the setup, but the sensible side of me knew that she meant well. She merely wanted to free me from the shackles of singledom censure. An honorable mission, even if it was one doomed to failure.

"Now, why didn't this young man work out, Samira?" she said in Arabic. Easing me into the conversation, you understand.

Mum smiled knowingly as she brought out some teacups from the cupboard.

What was I to say? He had better hair than me? He probably attended comic book conventions? He most likely owned a bottle of black nail polish?

"Um, he wasn't interested, Khaltee," I said, smiling humbly.

It was a smile that said I could handle rejection, that despite the trauma of the rebuff, I'd be okay.

"And your mother told me another nice man asked to see you and you said no," said Aunt Kareema, waving a hand, gold bangles jangling all over the place.

Damn it. Was nothing private in this family?

"I don't understand what you young people want these days," Aunt Kareema said with a sigh as she went over to Mum, who was putting tea bags into a pot. Mum nodded, still smiling.

Betrayed!

"When I was younger, we met someone at our house and made a decision straightaway," my aunt continued in a poignant Those-were-the-days-of-war-and-hardship-but-at-least-the-men-were-all-gentlemen tone.

I bit my tongue and smiled politely. *Please don't start talking about how you met and fell for your husband,* I thought frantically. I always hated those conversations. I didn't like thinking about my older relatives as once being young and carefree.

"These young men nowadays have much more to offer too," she said.

"Yes, Khaltee, but I think he was a bit different from what I need." *He had a bigger hair-product collection than me for starters,* I thought.

I was still waiting for my mother to jump to my defense. After all, she hadn't been thrilled with the family either.

"All these new ways of communicating," said Mum. "We never had computers. Phones. Chatting."

Any minute now.

"Yes," my aunt agreed. "I can't get Jamal off the computer half the time. I checked his history once, but it was all cars and Islamic pages."

Our parents needed our help setting up outdoor tables, but checking internet histories they could do.

Aunt Kareema had six children (praise Allah): Salah, Salha, Hassan, Hussein, Jamal, and Jameeleh. Two lived overseas, three were still here and married, and Jamal was the remaining singleton. He was an IT nerd and mechanic to boot, and was the only one we ever really saw these days.

Their matching names had been given in accordance with the grand tradition of Arab naming conventions. For example, my mother's name was Salmah, and one of her brothers was Salim. Thankfully, our parents spared us this particular convention within the extended family, diversifying so far as Samira, Zahra, Lara. We coped admirably well with it. Aunt Kareema's husband was named Kareem, but the name similarity there was purely coincidental.

"To be honest, the family weren't really our type," acknowledged Mum finally. I knew she wouldn't let me down.

"I don't know them that well," said Aunt Kareema. "But they came highly recommended, and the son seemed nice."

"Oh well, these things happen," said Mum diplomatically, as though she was talking about a faulty toaster. "The boy was a bit strange," she added more softly as she dropped some sage into the teapot. She wasn't a gossip by any means, so to hear her disparage someone besides me was a bit delicious.

"That's a pity," said Aunt Kareema. "When I saw him, I thought he was very nicely dressed and presentable. Don't you agree, Samira?"

"Yes, Khaltee. In fact, I think he was a better dresser than me."

Chapter 18

I was in the kitchen cleaning up after a game of Scrabble, which had featured a lot of air punching from Jamal after every play, and me saying, "Oh my God, Dad, oh my God," each time he changed the rules. In the end, Dad had won, even if his conduct had been questionable.

Our parents had gone out to visit someone for something or other, but Omar and his family lingered. Rabia was resting on my bed while my nieces watched a Disney movie. Hakeem also remained, as did Jamal.

I loaded the dishwasher, then moved on to the glasses and crockery. I hadn't forgotten about Hakeem's birthday gift. I was busy cleaning up, as I was meant to, and at the same time successfully procrastinating. Two birds with one stone.

A few minutes later, I heard someone enter, and without looking up from the sink I knew it was Hakeem.

"Sorry, where should I put this?" he said, holding a tray of teacups.

"Just on the table is fine," I responded, wiping some soap from my face. Before he could leave, I said, "So how are you?"

"Fine. You?"

"Yeah, good. You know how it is," I said. "I have something

for you." There, that wasn't so hard. Except my face was already warm. And my nerves were nibbling away at my internal organs.

Hakeem looked surprised. "Why? What is it?"

"Um, it's a birthday present," I said awkwardly. I dried my hands so that I could go and get it from my room.

"That wasn't necessary."

"I know."

I was out the door before he could protest further.

In my room, I located the small package in my bedside table drawer, neatly wrapped, even if I did say so myself, in silver paper and a sheer ribbon, a small card tucked under the bow. I didn't usually include a card because Hakeem was funny about things like that. Looked fabbo. I could totally wrap presents for a living should communications continue to prove unfulfilling.

Back in the kitchen, I handed him the gift. Brief smile. No eye contact.

Nonchalant. Unflappable. Insouciant. I went back to the sink and turned on the tap when I heard Hakeem sigh. A wail of despair could have easily followed given the depth of it.

"Samira, how many times do I have to tell you that you shouldn't be buying me gifts?"

"I know, I know. It's just something small for your birthday. Something I thought you might like!" I wasn't concentrating and dropped in the sink the soapy glass that had been in my hand. It cracked neatly down one side. *Lovely.*

"Are you okay?" he said.

"Fine!" I said, a little too brightly.

I think I'd actually cut myself when I tried to keep a grip on the glass, but never mind. I was being silly. But it was the snowball effect: the more I tried to act normal, the weirder it all got.

"What's wrong with you tonight?" Hakeem said.

"Nothing."

"You seem distracted."

"I'm just preoccupied."

"With?"

"You know. Work and stuff."

Which reminded me: that was my new rule. In any awkward situation, blame work. I'd read somewhere that projection was healthy.

"Oh, right," said Hakeem. He shrugged and looked like he was about to leave. Then he stopped and said, "Did you sort out your email mistake?"

I examined the sink. "Uh-huh." A normal, self-assured person would have left it there, but naturally I kept going. "Funny thing, really." I laughed, but it came out sounding a bit strange. Why could I never master merry laughter? What even *was* merry laughter?

"Well, he's certainly not shy. Has he asked for you yet?"

I dropped another glass and heard it crack. *Damn it.* My mother was going to *kill me.*

"Samira, seriously, are you okay? You're very clumsy tonight."

"I'm fine!" Bordering on farcical now, actually. "Okay, look, why would you ask that?" I said, turning to face Hakeem. "I've only just met him."

Seriously. It had only been a month since Zahra's engagement.

"That's how it's done, isn't it? If he's interested, his family will approach yours."

"Yes, well, I guess he's not interested then, because no, he hasn't asked for my hand."

He certainly seemed interested, though, if his emails and general behavior were anything to go by. I'd been seeing him more and more lately. And, well, we'd pretty quickly graduated from awkward emails to awkward encounters to cautious messages.

"It was just a question," Hakeem said, an oh-so-subtle hint of amusement marking his face.

"Yes, well, it was a silly question."

"That's good. We don't know them well, so you can't be sure he's trustworthy." Hakeem had now adopted his paternal voice.

I sighed and washed the soap off my hands so that I could clean up the broken glass. A couple of my fingers were sporting impressive cuts.

"Samira, you need to get away from the comfort zone you're in. You should find out what real people are like. Life isn't what you see in *The Princess Bride*," he lectured.

"Oh God, Hakeem, give it a rest, please. Is it that bad I like the movie?"

"Not at all, but for such an intelligent woman, I'm surprised at how innocent you are at times," he said.

"You think I'm intelligent?" I said.

Yes, that was the best response, I thought the moment it passed my lips. Never mind defending how I spent my time.

"Samira." Hakeem looked at me with disapproval.

"Why are you so hard on me?" I asked a little desperately.

"Because I want more for you," he said.

It took me a moment to realize my mouth was open. Hakeem looked away, as though he had been caught out on something.

I wasn't quite sure where to look.

"Thanks for the present," he said. He left the kitchen, tucking the package into his bomber jacket.

"My pleasure," I said to the empty kitchen. I remained at the sink, still feeling a bit stunned by what Hakeem had said. And how he'd said it.

Jamal walked in. "Cuz. What happened to your hands?"

"Nothing." Just a few rivulets of blood—nothing to be alarmed about.

As I lay in bed that night with bandaged fingers, I thought about Hakeem's behavior. He was certainly protective of me. But he didn't seem jealous, as Lara had suggested. Granted, I didn't have much experience in the jealousy department. If anything, he was probably disgusted with the whole situation.

I wondered if he'd read my card yet. I'd already realized the gift was a mistake. It was a movie. And not just any movie—the one movie he thought I based my existence on, which obviously was an irrational accusation. Liking a movie didn't mean you expected the same to happen to you. There was a giant in *The Princess Bride*, and there were definitely no giants in my life. And Buttercup was totally a princess and a size 8, neither of which applied to me.

Anyway, the movie had seemed appropriate at the time I bought it. I'd thought it was a bit symbolic or something. And then I wrote him the card, putting only a single quote with a question mark below it: "My words fly up, my thoughts remain below: Words without thoughts never to heaven go," which I'd chosen because it was about guilt and repentance.

My phone rested on the bedside table and I toyed with the idea of messaging him. Before I could decide, however, he messaged me.

Hamlet, William Shakespeare.

P.S. Thank you for the gift. I'm curious about *The Princess Bride* now. I'll let you know what I think.

I felt something release in me, and suddenly I was very sleepy. But just as I was about to shut my eyes, I got a friend request from Menem on Facebook. It was something I'd been hoping for a while ago, then forgot about because seeing him felt more significant. Still, I felt a tiny thrill of excitement.

I'd accept right now, but if I did, I just knew I wouldn't be able to resist stalking him.

So I went straight to sleep, trying my best not to think about a single thing.

Chapter 19

Aside from my significant coffee-making duties, I did actually have a ton of other tasks to undertake in my daily work routine, and managing the comments on our social media accounts fell under my expansive job description. I felt a bit of a rush invoking the ability to ban offensive commenters, but the real negative was bridezillas en masse.

"Nobody understands the pressure of being a bride! [Insert various My-life-is-over-but-in-a-self-indulgent-way crying emojis.]" Which would generally be followed by an onslaught of fellow bridezillas who apparently *did* understand the pressure of being a bride. [Insert various We-shall-indulge-you sympathetic emojis.] Then there were your standard flamers and trolls: "You're making a big mistake! Marriage is a form of slavery!"

I spent ten minutes making sure everything was in order, methodically scrolling through each post and deleting the trolls.

Afterward, I went to my own Facebook. I had accepted Menem's friend request a couple of days ago but hadn't yet had a chance to explore his profile, so I went straight to it.

I hardly used Facebook except for Messenger and the occasional update, and to keep up with Lara, for whom it might as well have been invented. In her current profile picture she was sitting in the lap of a Ronald McDonald statue, kissing his cheek.

After a good hour trawling through Menem's page, it became apparent that he was an incredibly active and social guy. He had photo albums for fishing expeditions, bushwalks, and trips to the Gold Coast, Melbourne, New Zealand, and even Lebanon. Had I not known how lovely and down-to-earth he was, I'd have felt completely intimidated by his liveliness. I marveled at it, before feeling a pang in my stomach that lingered. I wasn't sure if I was a little jealous because I had so little to show for myself in comparison, or if it was that everything I saw of him made me like him even more.

Following the Facebook investigation, I opened Messenger. I could see that Menem was active, and I waited for a few minutes, but he didn't message me. I felt a mixture of relief and disappointment. I stared at the screen for a moment, then resolved to get back to work. But just as I was about to, a new message notification appeared.

Menem. Stomach muscles released. Breathing returned to normal.

Pathetic.

Still, I smiled, a feeling of anxious excitement working its way up my throat.

> Menem: Who is Lara and why is half your page taken up with posts from her?
> Samira: My cousin. Zahra's cousin too. She has a lot of sugar in her diet.
> Menem: Haha. She's pretty funny.
> Samira: She certainly thinks so.

Menem: You're very close?

Samira: Yes, very. She's like a sister to me.

Menem: And Zahra? Are you close to her as well?

Samira: Well . . . Not exactly.

Menem: It's OK. I'm picking up on the "don't go there" vibe.

Samira: Yes, maybe change the subject.

Menem: Consider it done.

Samira: OK.

Menem: So why don't you get along?

Samira: Stop it! :P

Menem: OK, OK. I'm just teasing. For what it's worth, even though she's my sister-in-law-to-be, I'm on your side.

Samira: That's good to know.

Menem: No need to thank me.

Samira: OK.

Menem: Unless you really want to.

Samira: How about I wait until there's a need to thank you?

Menem: That might work. I'll hold you to it.

Samira: No problem. Done any fishing lately?

Menem: Are you making fun of me and my fishing hobby?

Samira: I'm hurt you'd think that.

Menem: Well?

Samira: OK, I'm smiling, but I'm not making fun. I just don't know anyone who does the fishing thing.

Menem: The fishing thing? You need to try it. If you did, you would never dismiss it like that.

Samira: Erm, I'll pass. But if it's any consolation, I liked your fishing expedition photos.

Menem: I saw that. Thank you, I appreciate it. I like your photos too.

Samira: You mean photo. Singular.

Menem: It's a nice photo. Singular. Why don't you have
    anything else up?

Samira: Not sure. I guess I don't have much to show.

Menem: I'm sure that's not true. Zahra's mum mentioned
    some photos you took of your nieces. She said they were
    beautiful.

Samira: Well, aside from family, whom I don't put online,
    there was my trip to the Blue Mountains five years ago.

Menem: Haha, fair enough. Do you mind if I ask you
    something personal?

Samira: Depends on the question.

Menem: OK, well, I'll ask and you can tell me to buzz off if
    you don't want to answer.

Samira: Works for me. Shoot.

Menem: How long have you worn hijab?

Samira: About six years. And no, no one forced me. :)

Menem: I didn't think that at all. I was just curious. Do you
    ever think about taking it off?

That question threw me. What on earth could he mean by
asking me that? Did he not like hijab?

Oh God. I'd assumed he was observant if not very strict.
Totally non-religious boys tended not to gravitate toward girls
who wore a headscarf. Not that the boys would never end up
with a hijabi; it was just less likely to happen.

A few door-knocks had failed from the moment I'd entered
the room, essentially because the suitors struggled to hide their
disillusionment when they saw me walk in with hijab. Those
guys were easy to detect; I knew how to recognize the signs.
There was the wide-eyed look first—the sort that swiftly turned

from dismay to *How can I make it look like I didn't just look dismayed?* This was followed directly by a bright smile, no eye contact. Then the mental countdown: *How long do I have to stay so that it doesn't look like I'm put off by the hijab?* Finally, there'd be some uncomfortable shifting on the couch.

Those were forever after deemed the Sellout Suitors. They were lower on the scale than the FOBs, the Metrosexuals, the overly anxious Fundies, and, of course, the Mangas. They barely edged out the Delusionals, who comprised would-be suitors denied the actual visit, usually due to unreasonable and/or perverse pre-door-knock demands. These demands ranged. Their mothers called ahead with the rider list, but instead of requesting five cases of sparkling mineral water, a bowl of yellow peanut M&M's, and scented candles, they had particular needs that had to be met. Their sons' very well-being depended on it.

There was the one who'd insisted he see me without my headscarf at our first little meeting in case, I presumed, I had frightening bangs or something equally traumatizing. Mum said it wouldn't be a big deal if the suitor's mother saw my hair. I begged to differ. Mum regaled me with tales of how things were done in the village once upon a time. I was unmoved.

Mum issued a polite refusal, adding something about how it was all destiny, which no one could ever argue with. Ma'fish naseeb. Next. And it worked for unlikely couplings too: subhanallah, keef il naseeb—which basically meant those two would never have gotten together without divine intervention.

Now here was Menem asking me if I'd ever considered taking off hijab. What if he liked me but was hoping I'd eventually go au naturel? He probably thought I'd be totally glam without it, all luscious locks spilling over my shoulders!

Menem: Sorry, I hope you don't mind me asking that.

Samira: No, no, it's OK. To answer your question, not really.
I have my moments, I guess. I miss the anonymity, just
blending in. I miss little things, you know?

Menem: I can imagine.

We continued talking for about an hour. We would have kept going too, except I had work to finish.

I couldn't deny the effect he was having on me—curiosity, a rumbling of an excitement that felt familiar but also new. I wanted to know what he thought about things and why.

I liked him. And I wanted him to like me in return.

Chapter 20

The next morning, I undertook a coffee run at work. I was alone this time, as Cate was busy. While I waited for my order, I assessed whether a small danish pastry would be a wise move a couple of days before my first bridesmaid dress fitting.

Just as I was about to head back to the office, Menem came by. I had coffee orders to fulfill, so I couldn't linger. Not that I intended to linger or anything. Besides, I had a bunch of meeting minutes to type up and send out. Uni education repayments well spent.

"How's your day going so far?" he said.

"I can't complain," I said politely. A complete and utter falsehood, as I could have complained until the cows came home three times over. "And you?"

"Deadline after deadline," said Menem. He looked a bit stressed. "I'll be working late."

"Do you work late often?"

"Yes. Too often. Anyway, what's new?"

"Since yesterday?" I said with a smile. "The usual." Annoying texts from Zahra with wedding reminders.

"Zahra driving you mad?"

"Get out of my head."

Menem laughed. He had a nice one: soft, but the way it made him smile was rather lovely.

"Bella! Your coffees!"

"That would be me. I'm Bella," I told Menem with exaggerated modesty.

"That you most certainly are," said Menem.

I took the coffee tray, my heart beating fast, the blush remaining all the way back to the office.

Saturday was the day of our first dress fittings. Zahra had already picked out the dresses, hers included, and she'd done all the measurements and begun the major adjustments a while ago. Now we needed to check that my and Lara's sizes were right and take care of any alterations.

Lara was, not surprisingly, unenthusiastic about it. "Why should we have to give up valuable time for snot face?" she whinged to me the night before.

I did my best to placate her, noting with unease that I was now unofficially a counselor to those affected by Operation Zahra's Wedding. But Lara just wanted to complain. We both knew she'd be going, mainly because, as much as she rebelled against The Establishment (*any* establishment, for that matter), Lara was still a good Arab-Muslim girl who did her duties. Even if she did them in her own unique way. That and she wanted a free evening dress.

In the morning, I picked up Zahra first. We didn't say much as we drove to collect Lara, who naturally kept us waiting. When she finally got into the car, she was pouting. She actually looked rather glamorous when she did that, but it was a mood setter too. I mentally sighed, preparing myself for more counseling. Although, I'd be the one seeking it if things stayed like this much longer.

"Sorry I'm late," said Lara, still pouting. "I didn't want to look fat for the fitting," she explained.

"You're being measured, you dunce," retorted Zahra. "You can't hide the curves." She shook her head and rolled her eyes.

"True, so how will *you* manage, Zahra?" said Lara.

"Okay, ground rules: no arguing," I said. "And, well, if I think of any others, I'll add them later."

We drove in peaceful silence for several minutes.

"So what color are you making us wear?" asked Lara finally.

"Lemon yellow," replied Zahra as she wrote down something in her wedding organizer—an off-white journal specifically purchased for her wedding planning.

Lara snorted. "Oh yeah, lemon yellow will do wonders for our complexions!"

"What's wrong with yellow?" said Zahra, looking up from her organizer and turning to look at Lara.

"Hel-*lo*? Yellow? On us? Are you that insecure that you have to make us look crap?" said Lara.

Zahra was silent. Lara had clearly hit a nerve. Nevertheless, I sent Lara a reprimanding glance in the rearview mirror. Zahra wasn't due for her angel's wings anytime soon, but she hadn't provoked Lara in this instance. Although Lara did have a point. At least about the lemon yellow, if not the insecurity bit. It wasn't likely to look very nice on us.

"Can you stop whinging?" said Zahra, more herself again. "It's not like you were my first choice for the bridal party."

There it was.

"Happy to bow out anytime," said Lara.

"Fine by me," said Zahra. "And I'll happily tell everyone

it was your choice because you're afraid of looking fat in a yellow dress."

"Why, you litt—"

"Guys!" I practically yelled. We came to a stop at a red light, my mind populated by all the potentials of why Zahra's friends weren't in the bridal party.

"Why ask us?" I said, glancing Zahra's way. "Really. We're obviously not who you want beside you."

Zahra froze for a second, but then she shook her head and met my gaze. "God, you make it sound worse than it is. Look, my friends couldn't confirm they'd be in town. The wedding was arranged without much notice."

I sensed there was more to the story, but the light turned green so I directed my gaze back to the road. "Look . . . Lara is right about the color. We're both pale. Is it your final choice?"

"Well, no, Samira," Zahra whined. "If you're both going to whinge about it, we can change the color. But the design stays!" She returned to scribbling notes.

"Blue. It should be blue," said Lara a moment later. "Samira's eyes will pop."

Following the dress fitting, Lara and I dropped Zahra at her place, then went on to my parents' home. We were going to Cate's in the evening for a housewarming party. She had bought an apartment a few months ago and had finally gotten around to arranging a get-together.

Lara seemed out of sorts as we drove. "I kind of got booted out of my placement," she confessed while she scrolled through a music playlist.

"What?"

"It wasn't my fault. I had a fight with my head nurse last night. He told me off for something, so I threatened to report the harassment, and then he said I've received all the warnings I'm going to get and to leave."

"Wait, wait. Harassment? When?"

"One of the doctors kept asking me out. Tosser. Like, hello! He's married. As if!"

"Oh my gosh."

"Anyways, I am officially jobless." Lara sighed. "Again. Why do I always end up working for tossers?"

"Maybe you're going for the wrong jobs. And it's not like you love studying."

Lara half-heartedly shrugged and nodded in agreement. She had managed to get halfway through two other degrees before finding an interest in nursing. But the wheels had started to come off once she was placed on rotation in hospitals.

When we arrived, the ever-unflappable Lara greeted my father, as always calling him her "fave uncle," her future employment woes already in the rearview. As usual, Dad smiled shyly and said, "Get out!" in his thick accent.

Jamal had texted me earlier to announce that he'd been interviewed by a show on the ABC TV network about an Islamic school under construction because he was now the spokesperson for his local Muslim association. The school was causing a bit of a ruckus (of the white supremacist kind).

While Lara and I sat in my room, waiting for the news to begin, I divided her hair into two braids and she downloaded about being let go at work, wishing aloud that she had quit before they could fire her.

A few moments later, Jamal, looking very sweet and handsome in tailored trousers and an ironed shirt, appeared on the screen.

"*That's* your cousin Jamal?" Lara said in amazement.

"Uh-huh. Why?" I asked, finishing off the braiding.

"He's gorgeous!" she said, transfixed.

"Lara, it's Jamal. You've known him all your life."

"I haven't seen him in ages."

"He's younger than you," I said.

"How much?"

"He's twenty-six."

"I'm only twenty-seven." Except she was twenty-eight.

"Lara."

"Fine. But he *is* cute."

"Let's focus on sorting out your work situation," I said, hoping that Lara would know better than to place someone so wholly unsuitable for her under her spell.

Chapter 21

"So what exactly is this thing we're going to?" asked Lara as we drove to Cate's. Cate lived on the other side of the Harbour Bridge now, on the North Shore—very different from solidly suburban Maroubra, where I lived.

"It's a housewarming party," I told Lara.

Cate knew it wasn't the sort of thing I'd ordinarily go to, but she'd assured me no one would be getting blind drunk, and as it seemed to mean so much to her, I'd agreed to attend.

"I think I need to get a place of my own too," Lara said. "This morning I caught my mum doing that evil eye thing while I was still sleeping."

"What evil eye thing?"

"You know . . . The melting-the-lead-in-the-pan-and-swirling-it-over-the-head thingamajig."

"Because . . . ?"

"Because I got fired and she's convinced someone put the evil eye on me. She says there's no way I'm naturally this wild and that all these bad things just happen," explained Lara cheerfully.

"I think this is the place," I said, pulling up to the curb. I checked the number and confirmed it was the correct address.

"Wait," said Lara as I was about to exit the car. "We need some sort of code."

"A code? For what?"

"For 'Get me the hell out of here,'" she said. "Ooh! I know. I'll wink, like so." Lara winked conspiratorially.

"Erm, maybe not. How about you just come up and squeeze my arm if it gets really bad and you want to leave?" I suggested.

Lara thought for a moment. "Okay," she agreed.

"You owe me for coming along, by the way," she said as we walked up the pathway to the flat.

"I owe you?"

"Yup!"

"Right. Never mind all the IOUs from you to me."

"I don't know what you're talking about."

"Of course you don't."

After we were buzzed in and had climbed two flights of stairs with Lara exclaiming, "Crap! Who doesn't have a lift nowadays?" I knocked on the door. A few seconds later, Cate swung it open, looking fabulous in a summery black and orange halter-neck dress. Her long hair ended in giant curls, and she wore gold and orange bangles up her arms.

"Samira, you came!" She smiled delightedly and hugged me.

The liveliness of the party, the music, and the penetrating hum of chatter, trickled into the hallway. I'd never been to a housewarming before, because Arabs never had them. We had crockery parties, and Nutrimetics and Tupperware parties. Mum had bought me enough Tupperware to stock a small outlet in anticipation of when I'd have my own home and would need airtight containers with a lifetime guarantee.

"Thanks for inviting me," I said, giving her a peck on the cheek. I handed her my gift—a Japanese tea set.

"Oh, Samira, thank you!" she said, squeezing my hand appreciatively. "I'd say you shouldn't have, but I guess that would sound a bit silly since it's a housewarming."

As we stepped inside, I looked around and took in my surroundings. The tiny flat was lovely. There were framed photographs on a brown feature wall, and tiny cabinets lined the opposite one. It looked lived in, despite being new. It was cozy, had character, and I loved it. I had a sudden yearning to have my own space. But I immediately snatched the thought back before it sprouted wings and made me feel crap. I wasn't going anywhere unless I got married. And lately, that was starting to frustrate me a little.

"I'm so glad you made it," Cate said, pulling me toward a spot near the kitchen, which was about the size of a toilet cubicle.

Lara cleared her throat.

Oh, right. "Cate, you remember my cousin Lara."

Cate gave Lara a dazzling smile. "It's so nice to see you again!"

"Thanks," replied Lara, returning the smile. "Likewise."

"Now, there's plenty of food on the other side of the room. Stay away from the sausage rolls and meat pies—they have pork—and you'll be all right," said Cate. "And the bar's open for mocktails." She winked and gave me a final squeeze on the arm before excusing herself.

I nodded and smiled, already thinking about what sort of mocktails were on offer. It was a bit exciting. Lara raised her eyebrows at me.

"What?" I said to her.

"Nothing," she said.

I waited.

"It was just thoughtful of her to think of our restrictions," observed Lara, amused.

"Yes," I agreed. "We don't have to stay long, okay?"

Half an hour later, Lara and I were ready to make a dash for it. I knew we were party poopers, but within fifteen minutes of our arrival, Marcus had cornered us. Not even my delicious virgin mojito could make up for it. Bewildered by Lara's lack of hijab, Marcus quizzed us about it for ten minutes, before moving on to the time two Jehovah's Witnesses came by his place and he fed them homemade Anzac biscuits.

"Samira, if we go now, we can still have a nice dinner somewhere," said Lara the moment Marcus got up to assist Cate with something.

"It's a bit rude if we leave now, though," I said.

Lara gave me a frantic look. "No, no, no. It would be rude of us to stay! I mean, what with us not being raging alcoholics and all!"

"Right, okay. Well, let me just say goodbye to Cate. I'll have to make something up about why we're leaving so soon."

"Good girl, thank you!"

Although Cate seemed disappointed, she was busy with her guests and in a celebratory mood. Another half an hour and she'd be three sheets to the wind.

She let us go without any guilt. We could have handled it, of course, what with our familiarity with Arab Guilt and Muslim Guilt and the fatal hybrid Arab-Muslim Guilt. But as Cate wasn't Arab, nor of any other similar ethnicity, she sent us off with a sincere regretful farewell and some chocolates.

Lara and I went for dinner at a nearby Thai restaurant. It was simple, small, and intimate. It was also quite busy, which was to be expected on a Saturday night.

As though she'd been waiting to pounce, Lara began quizzing me about Jamal the moment the waitress placed our plates before us.

"So how old did you say Jamal is?" said Lara, spooning chili onto her noodles.

I wondered if I should caution him that he was featuring on Lara's radar, sort of like a storm warning. "Lara, what are you doing?"

"I'm putting chili on my noodles."

"No," I said. "Why are you asking me about my cousin?"

"I'm just curious. You said he's younger, right?" said Lara, taking a bite.

"Yes," I told her.

"Okay," said Lara. She shrugged and continued eating.

When she hadn't said anything else ten seconds later, I felt satisfied that we were done with the subject. I was a bit protective of Jamal. He was such a lovely boy and I didn't want anyone to mess with him.

I eyed the curry puffs. Then the spring rolls. I was so hungry. I'd managed a Snickers bar (full-size) after the dress fitting, but besides some tea and fried halloumi cheese for breakfast (after Mum had yelled that I had to "Eat something! Your body is young!"), I hadn't eaten a proper meal all day.

Just as I was taking my first bite, Lara said, "What I'm saying is, it's only a couple of years. It's not that big of a difference." She looked at me innocently, her mouth full. I was sure she got away with so much because she was so beautiful.

"Yes, Lara. It's not a big difference," I said.

"Is he very strict?" said Lara, oblivious to my disapproval. I began to eat, realizing with each bite that I'd much rather be here than at Cate's housewarming.

"Yes, Lara. He's quite strict. Whatever that means," I said.

"Well, are we talking Hakeem levels of fundyness?" she persisted. "Because if we are, I should probably forget it altogether." She bit into a spring roll and looked thoughtful.

"I don't know," I said slowly. "What are Hakeem levels of fundyness?"

Lara rolled her eyes. "You know! Controlling. Obsessive. Everything has to be in order. His wife will need a permission slip to go to the shops. That kind of fundy."

"I think you're exaggerating, don't you? Hakeem isn't like that. And if he is any or all of those things, it's nothing to do with his fundyness. That's just his personality."

I didn't ask Lara why she was in such a rage for me to get together with someone she considered obsessive and controlling. Better not to open that treasure chest of Lara wisdom.

"Speaking of whom," she said between mouthfuls, "are you guys talking again?"

"I guess. I don't know."

"Samira, just tell him to get on with it and propose already."

"Lara!"

She laughed so loudly that the people next to us looked over, a little annoyed by the disruption. I sent them a conciliatory smile before turning back to my cousin.

"*You* are crazy," I told her.

She nodded, unperturbed as she dug into her food. "He acts like your husband."

"He does not."

"What about wimpy brother?"

"He has a name."

Lara stuck out her tongue. "Sorry. Have you seen *Menem*?"

"I've seen him a few times here and there," I confessed.

Lara scrunched up her face. "No!" Because she knew. I had no poker face.

"Lara, leave the poor guy alone," I said.

"No, I won't leave him alone. This is how you got hurt the last time with The Boy."

"That was a bit different."

"How so?" She tilted her head and gave me a look.

"Well, I was stupid."

"You weren't stupid. You were just trusting and let him lie to you about his intentions! I don't want to see that happen again." When I didn't respond, her expression softened. "Seriously, if he's interested, he should get a move on."

It dawned on me how ridiculous it was that my fairly non-religious cousin was saying a guy should be proposing to me when we'd known each other less than a minimum lease period. Marriage surely deserved greater care.

"I still think you're being a bit harsh."

"And what kind of name is Menem?" said Lara, placing her chin on her hand. "Please, he's left himself right open with that."

"He didn't pick it!"

"I don't care. He should get it changed by deed poll."

"Well, if he shows interest 'the right way,' you have to back off," I said.

Lara paused mid-bite. "You wouldn't seriously consider him, would you?"

"Why not? He's a nice guy. He seems good and successful," I said matter-of-factly.

All true. And, well, I *liked* him. It was that simple. More important, he seemed to like me. Not that he'd said as much. It wasn't a *Bridget Jones* I-like-you-just-as-you-are thing so much as a feeling I got whenever I was around him.

Lara put aside her fork to assess me. "Okay, well, I don't want to influence you, except to say you'd be crazy to consider him, period. But even more so when you have someone like Hakeem."

"I don't *have* Hakeem in any way, shape, or form. You need to let that fantasy go."

"Do you want to see me cry?"

I smiled. "If you can't stop yourself from mentioning my name, promise me you won't try to initiate a conversation with Hakeem," I said.

"Why do you have to ruin all the fun?"

"Lara."

"Fine. Be that way."

I shook my head. "You need to find a job."

"Agreed," said Lara.

"Menem's actually very sweet to me."

Lara looked like she wanted to object but thought better of it. "In what way?"

"Well, he's always polite. He's interested in me but doesn't overdo it. He always tries to pay for coffee and sweets. He's active and adventurous. Should I continue?"

"Well, I'm sure he's not awful," conceded Lara.

"Besides, if it's his way of communicating with me that's bothering you, why don't you care that Hakeem emails me but still hasn't made a move?"

"Hakeem's different."

"How so?"

"You know him."

"Isn't that worse?"

Lara twisted her mouth and sighed. "Fine."

"The council is merciful!"

Lara took a sip of her Coke. "I'm thinking of getting a job at a clothing store. What do you think?" she said, swiftly changing tack.

"You're not going to look for another nursing job?"

"I don't know." She looked thoughtful. "I wasn't terrible at it. But it was a lot of work and a bit depressing at times."

I never understood how she did it. I thought she had the right personality to work in such a place. Very little could shake her. She'd probably make illness nervous. But I guessed not.

"I wouldn't mind working in a fancy shop somewhere," she said, brightening up. "Just think of all the good I could do for girls who come in looking crap!"

After dinner, Lara begged me to drive to an eatery nearby she'd been to recently. "They make a sticky date pudding to *die* for!" she assured me.

We were halfway there when my car signaled a complaint. I heard it before I felt it—a flat tire. It'd probably been there for ages, waiting patiently for its moment of glory, choosing the most inopportune time to leave me stranded.

"Oh gawd!" said Lara helpfully. She kicked the tire and let out a monumental sigh.

"Do you have any idea where we are?" I said.

"Of course I do! We're in . . ." Lara looked around and pointed. "Well, that shop over there looks familiar."

"Health Barn?"

"Okay, maybe we're lost."

I blamed myself, really. I should have known better than to listen to her on a matter such as an eatery location, or even eatery recommendations.

"This is not my fault," announced Lara.

"No, of course not, it's mine."

I called roadside assistance and worked my way through the automated prompts. Eventually I was talking to an actual human, who requested our location.

I looked around and spotted a street name, which I supplied to the lady. She typed it all in, then said, "Great. The current wait is approximately two hours."

"Pardon me?" I said, my heart diving into my stomach. "Did you say two hours?"

"Yes, we have a huge backlog. It's Saturday night."

"Oh, I see. Is there any possibility at all of someone coming sooner?"

"It's possible, but I can't guarantee anything," she said apologetically.

"All right, well, thank you." I hung up and looked at Lara. "They're not coming for at least two hours."

"Crap," said Lara. "Your mum's gonna kill you."

I nodded. Mum still imposed a curfew. Tragic, but as I was reminded so often, as long as I was living under their roof, and as long as there were "nutsos" on the streets, I was to be home before midnight.

Of course, the days of Arab-style discipline were long behind us—meaning there was no more shoe throwing and ear pulling. Nevertheless, no one dared cross my mother when she was in a temper. Even though a flat tire was not my fault, my desire to go to a housewarming party and not factor in the possibility of a delay would land squarely on my shoulders.

"Well, sodding call someone else," said Lara. "Omar?"

"There's no way I'm calling Omar." I'd never hear the end of it. This was all Mum needed to keep me coming in at a reasonable hour: *"Remember that time you broke down at night in the middle of nowhere?"* Health Barn, despite being in a shopping district in the leafy North Shore area, would become "the middle of nowhere" forever after, and a flat tire would be the breakdown of the century.

Mum and I had already had this fight before. The worst had been a couple of years ago; we woke Dad up with the yelling. I'd come home half an hour late from a wedding, and she wouldn't let it go. Finally I'd told her that she couldn't control me, I was in my twenties. Then Mum had come back with this little gem: "I don't care if you're forty! As long as you live here, you won't come home late. It's not safe."

She might have had a point on the safety, even though it pained me to admit it. I wasn't exactly fond of driving late at night, particularly on my own. I had an overwhelming fear of carjacking. That and the plastered loons yelling, "Go back to your own country, [insert colorful term]!" tended to put a damper on things.

"Okay, so call . . . oh . . . Hakeem!" Lara did a little jump, pleased with her own genius. "Yes!"

"Ah yeah, that's not gonna happen!"

"What? Why not? Just call him!" she pleaded.

"Lara, I'm not going to call Hakeem! Don't be ridiculous!" I replied, my voice getting a little high-pitched. He'd almost be worse than my mother—more silently fear inducing.

"Do you have any better ideas?"

I paused. *Damn. It.* "Well, we could just wait for roadside service to come. They might turn up earlier," I said.

"Okay, honey, I'm not waiting two hours for roadside assistance. It's cold, and your mum killing you will also seriously bum me out. On top of that, even though my parents are much easier about this stuff than yours, they'll hear it from your mum and things will get messy. If you don't call him, I will!"

So she did. She grabbed my phone and called him and without pause asked him to come to our rescue. It was more of a demand, and I could almost feel the disapproval through the phone waves. This was all kinds of annoying.

While we waited for Hakeem, I cancelled the roadside request then listened to Lara rattle on about everything from mad cow disease (at one point she'd thought she was experiencing symptoms) to the time she'd dated a boy in high school. We were on a quiet, not terribly well-lit street, sitting opposite Health Barn, a name that was now etched into my mind. The only other noise came from an occasional passing car and an orchestra of crickets nearby.

"Of course, what stopped me from dating him properly," she said, "was the thought of my parents finding out and then doing something awful. Then the BBC would make some crappy biopic about me, and that alone put me off. I really didn't like him enough to risk it."

I stared ahead, mentally whimpering, not wanting to open the present-day-dating can of worms.

"Of course, they'd get some B-grade actress to play me," continued Lara.

"Lara, you've never had a boyfriend, right?"

She paused. "Technically . . . no."

"You've just had a bit of fun?"

"A very little bit," she offered, albeit grudgingly. She was silent for one blissful moment, then, "I don't feel bad, you know."

"About?"

"Having some fun. With boys. I have my limits. It's harder when they get you with the guilt, though."

I shrugged. "I don't know what to say."

"Would you really go your whole life without ever kissing a guy if you don't get married?"

It wasn't the first time I'd thought about it, of course. It did seem unfair, sometimes, that it was a matter of naseeb. Fate. You were either destined to get married or you ended up a spinster like a supporting Jane Austen character everyone liked but pitied. I hadn't thought about it much, though, because a loveless, sexless life wasn't what I wanted for myself; it was better not to let the idea of never being kissed take root.

"I don't know, Lara," I replied. "I'm not the same person I was a few years ago. Who knows where I'll be five years from now?"

My response surprised me, but it was an honest answer. I knew enough about life to understand that it was a bit hilly. A few years ago, I wouldn't have been so easygoing about talking to guys, let alone having regular coffee catch-ups with them. I didn't see anything wrong with it now, but I'd have felt crap about it in the past. Perspective could be such a beautiful thing—like hindsight, just more useful.

"What about you?" I asked Lara. "Guys don't just want to kiss. Would you ever go all the way?"

"Oh Lord, no," she said easily. "That introduces too many issues. Stuff you can't bounce back from. And I don't mean the mental drama."

I didn't say it, but I was amazed by her response: it sounded like Lara wasn't worried about being ghosted; she was concerned about pregnancy and STDs. I couldn't see myself going there, because I'd been taught to think about sexual intimacy differently, and that way of thinking wasn't going anywhere. Still, I envied Lara's ease a little. She understood Arab-Muslim Guilt, but it seemed to bounce off her before it could penetrate. She thought for herself but still cared about the basics. I admired the truthfulness of it, though I could never tell her this because her head would explode.

As with all serious matters, Lara didn't linger on the topic, and a few minutes later she was singing to me. To be fair, she had a beautiful voice; I could get goose bumps listening to her. It was one of the few times she didn't act like a complete loon. She knew some Arabic songs, including a famous one by a popular Lebanese artist named Nancy Ajram that she was singing now. It was a playful song about courtship and treating a girl right. She moved her shoulders in time to the melody, her arms half raised elegantly, her facial expressions flirty and cheeky like the singer's in the video clip. In Arabic, she urged her love to come closer and look, look, look. She cautioned him to not be angry, to be careful or else he will be the loser.

Arabs have always been poetic.

"I wanted to be a singer, you know," Lara said wistfully when she'd finished the song.

When I didn't say anything, she continued. "I know, you're thinking, 'What's new?' It's just one of my 'things,' right?" She cocked her head to the side. "Singing was different, though."

"You've never told me that," I said.

She shrugged. "Nothing to tell. I was in every choir in

school. I did a solo once at the Royal Albert Hall for some school spectacular thing. Dad wouldn't even come to hear me sing. He was all like, 'Sure, go for it. Who's going to be there anyway?' Then on the night, he got into a fight with my mum about it and wouldn't go."

"That sucks," I said, frowning.

She gave an exaggerated sigh and a small smile.

Hakeem arrived not long after, and twenty minutes later, he was wiping his hands on a towel as he crouched beside my back left tire. He was ticked off—I was sure of it. I didn't think it was so much that he had to change a tire for me than he was wondering why on earth I was where I was when I was.

"You really should learn how to change a tire," he said, straightening up.

"Yes, yes, of course," said Lara, who had her arms wrapped tightly around her. "Are we all done yet?"

"Yes, we're all done. Samira, you'll need to get a new tire, okay?" he said, glancing at me. "This one's just to get you home."

I nodded obediently as Lara rushed to the passenger's side and jumped into the car.

"You'll be all right getting home from here?" Hakeem said.

"Yes," I replied. "I have maps."

Hakeem studied me, his expression eventually softening a little, and I met his gaze. I was reminded of his impressive height. It was, of course, a blessing from Allah. But, praise Allah, he was brilliantly tall and manly.

"Thank you," I said, turning away. "Sorry for disturbing you."

"It's fine," he said. "Just be careful."

"It wasn't my fault," I mumbled. But everything seemed different lately. I felt immobilized. Defenseless. It was totally irritating.

"I didn't say it was your fault. I said you have to be more careful."

"Sorry," I said, feeling deeply embarrassed. I almost wished we'd called Omar now.

"Next time don't leave it so long," he said. "Call me straight-away. I know you can't call your brother."

Lara popped her head out the window. "Samira! Come oooooooon, I want to go home!"

Hakeem smiled tightly and started to back away.

"Wait," I said without thinking.

He stopped.

"Um. How are you?"

"I'm okay. Alhamdulillah."

I nodded. "That's good. And work is good?"

"Work is fine. How about you? Still tackling the world of weddings with ease?"

I smiled awkwardly. "Yes. So I just wanted to know if there was anything new with you," I said.

"Things are same old, Samira. For me, anyway."

I hesitated. "Yeah, same."

We stood there stupidly before my car horn pierced the silence.

"Samira!"

"Okay, okay!" I shook my head at Lara disapprovingly. "One second!"

She pouted formidably and sat back in her seat.

"You should probably get going," said Hakeem. "You don't want your parents to worry."

"You mean my mum."

"She's pretty scary when she's mad."

I nodded and smiled. "Okay, well, thank you again."

"Do not send me anything!" he said as he walked away.

"I wasn't—"

"No!" He waved a hand in my direction. "I know you! You're already figuring out what to get me as a thank-you gift."

"But—"

"Samira," he said, turning around, his tone growing more serious. "If you want to do anything for me, you will go home now, and drive safely. You will also stop taking directions from Lara."

"Okay, but before I go, have you watched *The Princess Bride* yet?"

"No, not yet," he said. "I will, though. I just want to watch it when I know there'll be no interruptions, and when I'm feeling fresh. It looks intense."

I rolled my eyes. "Very funny. I'll have you know *The Princess Bride* is one of the greatest parody-spoof comedies ever made." I realized he must have assumed it was some cockamamie love story set in medieval times, all slow motion and sweeping music.

"Hence my comment about intensity," he replied, smiling.

I crossed my arms and looked away, embarrassed. "I know you don't take me seriously, but believe me, it has depth. It's clever."

"Why would you say that?"

"Because I've watched it so many times," I said, now looking straight at him.

"No. Why would you say I don't take you seriously?"

"You know, the usual: Samira's an airhead. 'Studied' communications. Works as an assistant." Not even Lara had the same professional reputation as me. While her high school results had been less than stellar, she'd majored in the science strands. I was the artistic humanities grad. I might as well have been a hippie.

"Don't be ridiculous," said Hakeem. "I can't believe you would even think that."

"Right. Sorry?" I offered feebly.

"You should be. You're too hard on yourself, Samira."

"I'm not. I just know what everyone thinks about me."

"Obviously, you don't. Do you have any idea how proud your parents are of you?" Hakeem said. "You should hear the way they talk about you."

"Really?"

"Yes, really. I wouldn't make that up. If you feel inferior, it's because you let people make you feel that way."

I was dumbfounded. I had absolutely no idea how to deal with this information. My parents were proud of me? It was practically a new concept to me. They'd certainly never shown any signs of it. Then again, while they'd mastered Arab Guilt in most areas, they'd never made me feel like a failure.

"Stop spending time with Zahra. You know . . . until you can master detachment," said Hakeem, interrupting my shiny new realization.

I scoffed. "I don't do it voluntarily, believe me."

There was a pause and I looked at the ground and kicked a pebble about. For reasons unknown to me, I wanted to ask Hakeem if he was proud of me. But even the thought of it was shameful. I felt like the student who'd brought in the shiny apple to suck up to the teacher. Or did that only happen in old-timey American TV shows? We'd never done that in Sydney. My primary school teachers would have looked at us like we were mad if we'd brought them apples, shiny or otherwise. Although they'd never seemed to mind the tray of baklawa Mum would always make me take in at the end of the year.

I decided not to ask him. Instead, my brilliant response was "Anyway!"

Lara beeped the horn again and I hurried back to the car.

"I'm coming, I'm coming!" I said as she let out a deluge of self-pitying complaints.

Chapter 22

It was a Monday afternoon and I had an appointment with Menem. We generally saw each other on Mondays (routine coffee break) and, well, yes, on other days too. Today, however, I had a list of tuxedo-hire shops that he needed to collect from me, so it was a completely legitimate meeting.

Wedding plans were a frequent feature in my life now. The weeks were flying by in a mishmash of orders and requests from Zahra, dress fittings, and weekend expeditions to find this and that. And then there was Menem, who didn't seem to be going anywhere.

Of course, I could have messaged him this list, but he'd asked if he could get it directly from me. I was surprised and a bit nervous, because although we'd meet up, it was unusual for him to be so specific about seeing me.

Cate was with me, as she wanted an afternoon coffee. While we waited for our order, and for Menem, she updated me on her recently discovered medical condition—in great detail.

"So it turns out I may have psoriasis, which is just a shitter!" she said, waving around her coffee card dramatically.

"Gosh, that's awful," I replied. Just as I was about to, reluctantly, ask her more about it, Marcus snuck up behind her, his long legs moving in comically elongated strides. He motioned for me not to say anything as he did so. Then he pinched Cate on both sides of her waist and she jumped in fright.

I laughed despite my skittish mood. It was rather cute. I still didn't quite get it. But it was cute nonetheless. They had a little cuddle and Cate took Marcus's hand before he pecked her on the cheek.

"Samira."

I turned around and Menem was standing before me. Then I looked back to Cate, who raised her eyebrows at me and barely suppressed a smile. Marcus's eyebrows were slightly raised too.

"Hi," I said to Menem, my face warming up.

Cate reached over to take her coffee and passed me mine. "I have to get back to the office," she said meaningfully, before giving me an exaggerated wink. One for subtlety, she was.

"Bye," said Marcus. "By the way, I like your scarf today, Samira! Ow!"

Cate had kicked him in the shin. She winked at me again, then took Marcus's hand and they walked off together.

"Interesting guy," said Menem.

"You could say that."

By now I had my coffee and was trying, and failing, to nonchalantly pour some sugar into the cup.

"It helps to take the lid off," said Menem.

Oh. That was embarrassing. I smiled, now blushing furiously, wondering how I'd managed to become such a bonehead in the space of a few minutes.

"Look, is it all right if we sit for a second?" Menem asked, his voice soft. He seemed quite serious, and for a moment I wondered if he was about to reveal something awful about himself. I knew I had bad instincts when it came to people. I just knew it. He was a spy. No, he was already married. Wait. No. He would have struggled to hide that in his circle.

"Sure!" I replied, a little too loudly.

"Okay, good. Let me just grab a coffee first, okay?"

"Sure!"

Oh, for goodness' sake.

Five minutes later we were seated in the park behind my building, on the same bench we had shared—when? It felt like an eternity ago, but in reality, it had been only a couple of weeks. Nearby, two old men sat at a dirty concrete table and played chess, and not far behind them, a couple sat on the grass, looking intimate and as if they had no awareness that they were in public.

"How's your day going?" asked Menem politely.

"Yeah, you know, busy."

Lie.

"Yeah, me too."

Before Menem could say anything else, I produced an envelope containing the list and handed it to him. "Enjoy," I said, doing my best to project calm.

"Thank you." He took it off me and put it aside immediately. "Look, I have to ask," he began purposefully, "how are you still single? Is there something I should know? Do you secretly have a husband stashed away somewhere?"

I laughed, feeling shy. "No. I think you're being too generous there."

He shook his head, looking a little nervous and uncomfortable too, so at least I wasn't alone in that.

"In any case," I continued, "I'm not sure why. Maybe it's

because I'm a dreamer," I said, biting my thumbnail. Not in a coquettish way, though—it was purely to fend off the nerves.

"Or maybe no one worthy enough has come to you yet," Menem ventured, but not in an insulting way.

I was blushing even more now. "No, that's not it," I assured him. I could have said more, but the nerves were overtaking the blushing, killing all possibility of a snappy comeback.

"Look, is it okay if I come for a visit?"

I'd been holding my breath. The whole conversation was a swirling morass of . . . confusing weirdness. Yes. And there I was, right there at the bottom of the bog, looking up at Menem, who was more comfortably positioned above, looking suave and sophisticated.

"Okay, that's not a good sign," he said, looking down at his cup in embarrassment.

I was mortified. I'd completely forgotten to actually answer his question.

Oh God.

"No, no," I said, flustered. "I'm sorry. It's not that." Door-knocks were never like this!

He nodded, seemingly relieved and pleased. "And so the answer is?" he prompted. "I like you, Samira."

"Yes," I said finally. "I think that would be just fine."

A visit. A declaration of interest that was clear and unequivocal. All I could think was that at least he was doing things The Right Way now so everyone could get off my back about it.

Menem let out a sigh of relief and set aside his coffee cup.

"Okay." (Menem.)

"Okay." (Me.)

I was feeling a bit light and silly. A hundred emotions pulsed through me. Annoyingly, I couldn't pinpoint a single one of them.

Never mind. I held back a squeal of excitement.

Wow.

Wow, wow, wow, wow.

We left it at that, our coffees barely touched. His mother was going to give my mother a call. Probably in the next ten minutes if the look on his face was any indication.

I smiled like an idiot all the way back to the office, feeling thick with excitement. But the moment I stepped into the elevator in my building, I fell abruptly back to earth. I had immediately agreed to the visit. What did that mean? I hadn't agonized over it. I was flattered and excited at his confession. All of which I presumed was a good sign.

Yet I'd never experienced this before. That is, knowing the door-knocker beforehand and—very important—liking him already.

By that evening, a Saturday night appointment had been settled upon. It was only a few days away.

I told the girls the news. Lara was surprised he was coming ("Bloody hell! He's got guts!"), probably shocked that Menem was not turning out to be a copy of The Boy. She didn't seem very pleased, but she didn't launch into a Hakeem advertorial either. Sahar was quietly optimistic (several short prayers were invoked).

But the nerves remained. Maybe it was confusion. I was managing to convince myself that it was all too good to be true. Which was a bother, particularly as I was doing such a spectacular job of it.

Why couldn't I be one of those self-assured, never-second-guess-yourself types you'd see on the back page of city weekly magazines? You know, those women who started a business with little more than a coat hanger and a phone line and were now multimillionaires and such?

Work was a good distraction. I had two shoots this week with Gabriel. As usual, he got me to assist with setting things up. He asked me how I would compose the shots, describing the theme of the spread in detail. Happily, I managed to tear my thoughts away from Menem for a good three hours.

After we were done, I sat with Gabriel on the slope beside one of the Harbour Bridge pylons. It was early evening, my favorite time of day. Daylight Savings would set in shortly, and I couldn't wait for the long, balmy days of summer.

We could see Luna Park in the distance, and I was content watching the lights flicker across the water while Gabriel smoked a cigarette. Oddly, the smell was comforting. It reminded me of my father, who used to be a smoker when I was a child.

I tried to imagine what it would be like on Saturday. Mum and Dad would undertake their usual shopping expedition to stock up the fridge. We'd be frantically cleaning and dusting and putting away any unsightly pieces of furniture. The usual. The only difference was that I wouldn't be nonchalant and curious, I'd be sick with nerves.

All of this made sense in my head. But I didn't want to say it out loud and explore it with anyone, even Cate, who kept asking me if everything was all right. What if she told Marcus? He'd be coming up to my desk every day, asking me questions like, "So, Samira, when you get engaged, can you be in love with the person first?"

I shook my head.

"You okay?" said Gabriel.

"Yeah," I sighed. "I'm a little distracted, I guess."

"I noticed."

"Sorry. Don't mean to be rude. I just have a lot on my mind."

He smiled and held up his camera. "There's never a better time." He handed me a Nikon, a lesser model than the one he used at shoots. "This one won't give the full-frame effect," he explained.

I had no idea what that meant, but as I wasn't shooting a photo spread for a glossy magazine, I decided it wouldn't matter. It was a good camera either way, and I knew my way around this model pretty well. The menu wasn't too complicated, and while the camera was a little heavy, it was manageable.

"I want Luna Park," Gabriel said, putting out his cigarette in the dirt. "For your portfolio."

"I don't have one."

"And now you get to start one."

I began making adjustments, but I felt challenged by the task. "Everyone shoots Luna Park," I said.

"Exactly. Now make it different."

The next day at work, Jeff walked frantically past my desk and asked to see me. He was carrying a stack of folders and had his Very Important Person expression. I abandoned what I was doing (doodling).

"I need to talk to you," he said when I entered his office. He motioned to the chair opposite and leaned back into his own.

"Is everything all right?" I sat down, notebook and pen at the ready.

He looked very grave. God, maybe I was in trouble. Was this about the Facebook conversations? The personal emails?

I scanned my mind for other possible offenses. To be honest, if he did fire me—not that it was likely—I would have almost welcomed it.

Awfully reckless thinking. Totally unlike me too.

"Samina. I'd like to talk to you about the cadetships."

The bloody ads. They were running already, so what could be the problem?

"What about them, Jeff?"

"Are you going to apply for one?"

"Pardon me?"

"You should apply for a position," repeated Jeff.

"But I tried to tell you—"

"I've been meaning to say something for a while now, but there's too much to bloody do around here. Anyway, I think *Childhood* is right up your alley." He looked at me and I sat mutely, waiting for him to continue. "It's a magazine for parents," he added when I didn't respond.

"Yes, I know it," I said.

Childhood resided in the same publications stable as *Bridal Bazaar* but had much higher circulation figures—people had more children than weddings. It was also a quarterly magazine, but that was about as much as I knew.

"I'm not sure if I'm the right fit for that," I told him.

Jeff sighed. "Do you not have a master's in communications?"

"Um, actually, no. But I graduated with honors."

Jeff raised an eyebrow. "Do you not have a *degree* in communications?"

"Yes, I do."

"Have you not worked at this magazine for just over a year? Is this not magazine publishing? Have you not written for us, dealt with correspondence, and edited copy?"

I'd written a couple of feature articles for *Bridal Bazaar*. While they were adequate enough, I was surprised Jeff remembered them. After all, he still hadn't gotten my name right.

"Yes, Jeff," I said finally. "I am qualified, but I don't have actual reporting experience, which I'm sure would limit my chances."

"It bloody well won't. I'll recommend you."

It took a moment for this to sink in, and I felt a tiny ripple of anxiety. Jeff seemed serious; he'd be a referee, and as editor-in-chief of a cash cow, a recommendation from him was extremely valuable.

I wasn't sure how to respond.

"Take some time to think about it," advised Jeff. "But you can't be my assistant forever, as much as I'd like you to. You are very good to me."

I smiled and nodded slowly. An actual junior reporter's position? It sounded rather professional and intriguing.

Samira Abdel-Aziz, junior reporter. Breaking news, Samira Abdel-Aziz reports!

Well, that would be more on television really, but nevertheless, junior reporter was a step up from editorial assistant.

"I will. I'll think about it," I assured Jeff.

Enthusiasm aside, even if he recommended me, there was no guarantee I'd get the job. I dimmed the excitement bulb a little. Back to reality and all that.

As I got up to leave his office, I had to acknowledge a gnawing sense of unease, though the exact reason for it eluded me.

Chapter 23

Menem's visit was my first door-knock appeal where the guessing was minimal. Of course, there were things I didn't know about him or his family. But blissfully absent were the horrible thoughts about what he looked and sounded like.

Basically, I could tick off any potential manga issues. I was pretty sure Menem didn't use hair gel. And I knew he didn't have an issue with me having a career, even in the most elastic interpretation of the word.

But the nerves were still about, and having great fun at my expense. They'd brought a newcomer, a love guru: "Where is this relationship headed?"

Menem and his family arrived at 6 p.m. Arabs may not always be the best of planners, but when marriage is involved, the ability to get things done increases exponentially. And as a little extra, many cease operating on AST (Arab Standard Time)—meaning they don't arrive two hours fashionably late. Still, an arrival on time was surprising, as we'd been expecting them to arrive at 6:30.

Never mind. The house had been cleaned to within an inch of its life, the collection of shoes by the door and the slippers we used for ablutions relocated out of sight. The snacks were on standby, as were abundant supplies of coffee, tea, sage, and juice.

I was in my room, getting ready and still completely nervous. I was wearing a simple short black dress over trousers, which I was going to pair with a pale blue headscarf. I ran the fabric through my fingers. It was soft and voluminous. I decided to tie it back, positioning it so that my earlobes were exposed and then slipping on a pair of small hoop earrings.

As I assessed my look, my stomach curdled with nerves, but there was something else: a flicker of excitement. I liked this look. I realized I should wear it like this more often.

I moved on to makeup: I applied some kohl eyeliner on my bottom lids, followed by some mascara, then a light brushing of blush on my cheekbones.

Downstairs, everything about the visit sounded familiar: Dad's bellowed greeting, the light murmurs and chatter. I could hear Menem speaking to my father, polite as always.

Oh God, I can't do this, I thought. I had no idea why, but I felt scared. Was it because this was a bona fide possibility? That perhaps Menem and I could be heading toward, well, an *actual* engagement? And then *marriage*? Egads.

I'd been expecting texts and calls and emails from Lara, warning me against Menem, but she was unusually quiet, which made it easier not to think about what she might have to say on the matter. Sahar was encouraging. Cate had sent me a message earlier, dispensing her advice:

Cate: Make sure you wear blue! xxx

I took a few minutes to calm myself. Closing my eyes, I recited a short prayer and recalled my first meeting with Menem. The memory immediately calmed me.

Eventually, I garnered the courage to get up from my bed. I

straightened my dress, took a deep breath, and went out to greet our guests.

Menem had come with his parents, who both smiled at me warmly as I entered the room, interrupting the lively conversation.

"Assalamu alaykum," I said, and I felt a bit shy.

Menem smiled as soon as he saw me, and although I glanced his way briefly (I could *not* make eye contact), I went straight to his mother and greeted her.

Nervously, I sat down, trying my best to project calm and confidence.

Thankfully, our parents were getting along smashingly. The more they spoke to each other, the better I felt, because I didn't have to field questions and worry about speaking in Arabic. I just sat and listened as respectfully as I could, pretending that I wasn't wholly aware of Menem's presence. But I knew he was discreetly glancing at me. I would occasionally take a quick look back, and our smiles were very tight and polite. It was awkward, not just because we were in company but because this was like a demotion from our usual interactions. My face was warm, and I was already willing the evening to be over.

A moment later, Mum got up. Escape! *I could help Mum,* I thought ingeniously. But she shooed me away when she saw me about to follow her.

Crap. I sat back down, then slowly turned to Menem. As Mum had been sitting between us, we now had uninterrupted views of each other.

"This is kind of weird, isn't it?" said Menem, breaking the tension smoothly. He was like James Bond, I decided. Full of charm and confidence.

My remaining nerves swiftly scattered and I laughed. Not

too loudly, of course. The usual door-knock-appeal rules applied, after all.

"Yeah, kind of," I agreed. "Especially since I know I'll probably run into you next week." I had no idea why I'd said that, but I immediately regretted it.

"Yes. And things might be different then," replied Menem.

I'd walked into that one. Oh, it was pathetic: I blushed, I actually *blushed*.

"How's work?" I ventured, moving past my faux pas.

"Good," he said. "Really good. I might be relocating permanently to the next floor up."

"Nice. A promotion?"

"A small one. How's your green-wedding-that's-white story coming along?"

"Fine. You know. There was lots to talk about but not enough space," I said. Creative genius at work here. *Everyone clear the way—make room for my stunning conversational skill!*

Menem's father then interrupted with a question in Arabic about a car auction they'd gone to the other week. Oh God, give it a month and Dad's new hobby would be attending car auctions. While I began formulating a plan to get out of attending a car auction when the time came, Menem responded to his father. He spoke in Arabic, fluently.

It wasn't the first time he had spoken Arabic in front of me, but it was the first time I'd taken notice. His pronunciation was perfect. Much, much better than mine.

To begin with, I had difficulties with some of the letters. There were two different types of *h*'s, differentiated by how you positioned your tongue. Aside from that, a couple of the letters had very guttural elements that weren't found in English.

Arabic was a very complicated language. For example, there

was no word for "cousin." In Arabic, I'd have to say, "Jamal is the son of my aunt," to explain our relationship.

And there were different ways to refer to an aunt and uncle. An aunt from Mum's side was "khaltee," but an aunt from Dad's side was "a'mti." An uncle from Mum's side was "khalee," while an uncle from Dad's side was "a'mmi."

Besides that, older people—family friends, acquaintances, spouses of your aunts and uncles, the man in the furniture store who came from the same village as your father—were also given an aunt/uncle title, out of respect. And these ones had rules of their own. To a man, we'd say "a'mou" (derived from "a'mmi"), and to a woman we'd say "khaltou" (derived from "khaltee").

I loved the Arabic language because it was poetic and lyrical and not at all as scary as those homemade videos on the news made it out to be. After all, it was the language of my prayers. What wasn't to like? I was just thrown by Menem's response.

"You speak Arabic fluently?" I said to him.

He looked surprised. "Yeah," he said, nodding. "Of course. I read and write fluently too. Why? Didn't you have to go to Saturday school too?" He grinned.

"I was just curious because I've never really heard you say much in Arabic. And yes, we did have to go to Arabic school." We just didn't really learn anything, unless you counted how best to shove your snobby cousin into a garbage bin without getting caught.

"No problem. Wala himmik," he said. He was telling me not to worry. I rather liked the way he said it, and my stomach agreed with a tiny flip.

We recounted our Saturday school days: for me, two hours of Arabic and Quran lessons every weekend. The first teacher we had couldn't speak any English. We were a bunch of brats.

You can pretty much guess how well that panned out. Eventually the poor guy packed up his chalk and duster and stalked out, vowing never to return. He kept his word. That was one of the few occasions when we beat the system: our parents couldn't administer disciplinary action because there were just too many of us. Power in numbers. So Sahar's dad filled in until they could find another victim, which changed Saturday school dramatically because he was a total fundy.

Menem laughed in all the right places, then explained that he'd been the studious type when he was younger. "I know I don't seem it, but I wanted to be better than Malek," he recalled.

"And are you better than him in Arabic?"

"Yeah." He laughed.

"I'm impressed," I told him.

"Ask me anything you want," he said.

"Right," I said. "Well, I've misplaced my list."

"Oh God, there's a list." Menem feigned feeling hot and suffocated, fiddling with his collar. He looked very nice, in tailored black trousers and a simple white shirt.

"Well, yes. You know, questions are important, some of which are in multiple choice form," I said, beginning to relax and have fun (but not get too relaxed, and not have too much fun). "This means," I continued, "there is a best answer and quite possibly no *incorrect* answers."

"Is there a high chance you'll find this list anytime soon?" said Menem.

"It's okay, I have it memorized."

"How is the boredom cure coming along?" inquired Menem after we'd served the fruit.

"Pardon?"

"You told me once that you're bored and that you're a hermit," he said.

"Well, I've been pretty busy, which solves the boredom problem. And there's also Zahra's wedding to think about." And dream about. And never stop hearing about.

"She's really got everyone on board with that, hasn't she?" Menem laughed. "I love my brother, but if he puts me on the phone to her one more time without warning, I'll hurt him and hide all the evidence," he said, although without a hint of malice in his tone.

"Why does he do that?" I said, crinkling my forehead.

"Zahra doesn't want to ask him to do anything, so he tells her I don't mind. And I don't, really. But there are only so many deliveries and pickups I want to be doing in my off time."

"That's very generous of you," I observed.

It hit me once again how placid and easygoing Menem was. I'd never seen him upset or angry. It was a little unnerving. Surely he had some hang-ups waiting in the wings? Did he ever brood? I wondered if he ever took offense to anything. Meanwhile, he managed all of that without being vanilla. Easygoing and baggage-less as he was, he was great company.

Menem leaned forward and met my gaze. "Well, we both know she's been making good use of you too."

"Yes. Well, I help out where I can."

"Somehow I get the feeling that you're generous in most ways." Then he took me by surprise with an expression that made my heart go into free fall.

I looked down, blushing, feeling suddenly overwhelmed, then relieved when I saw Mum return from another visit to the kitchen. She was carrying a tray of chocolate biscuits, and I realized I hadn't met with her yet as per our usual procedure. I was desperate to know what she thought of Menem.

When she went off again, I got up and collected the fruit plates to take them back to the kitchen. Mum was pouring peanuts from a massive jar into small glass bowls—the woggiest ones in her collection—straight from the West Bank warehouse, and decorated with apples and strawberries all around the sides. She put them on a tray and took a Turkish coffeepot and matching cups and saucers from the cupboard.

"Remember, if you're not interested, just excuse yourself and leave," said Mum in Arabic.

"Okay, Mum," I said, opening the pantry door and taking out the tea and sage jars.

"He seems very nice. But don't be too friendly," she continued as she opened up the Turkish coffee bag.

"Okay, Mum." Then I dared to ask, "So you like him?"

Mum assessed me as she spooned the coffee into the pot. "He seems like a nice boy," she said finally.

An hour and a half and a three-course light menu later, Menem and his parents rose to leave. Menem and I had spent the last half hour talking without interruption, all the while observing the rules of the door-knock appeal: we were polite, not overly friendly, interested but restrained. Basically, the lite version of our usual interactions.

"We're having a barbecue tomorrow," said Menem's father in Arabic as we all stood up. "You have to come."

This was a highly unusual development. This being our first meeting, there was no way of knowing if (a) Menem would still be interested after tonight (okay, I knew he would be, but what about his parents?), and (b) I was interested in Menem (okay, I knew I was, but what about *my* parents?).

So I was quite surprised they were asking us along before we knew where this was heading, particularly given tomorrow would be the day the obligatory follow-up call would come.

Dad politely refused, one hand outstretched, the other on his chest.

Of course. We were Arab. This was only part one of the invitation. First came the initial request, which was politely refused. Then came the entreaty that we "must come" because they wouldn't take no for an answer. This was met with a response of humble offense. "Of course we'd love to come, but really we have so much to do tomorrow!" Then the third and final demand (no longer an invitation) was put forth, at which point my father conceded defeat and agreed to attend the barbecue.

"Bring any friends you want, Samira," said Menem's mother with genuine warmth in her voice.

"Thank you," I replied, excitement working its way up to my throat. I had to stop myself from smiling like an idiot, which was so hard at that moment. I settled for a friendly smile, even though it seemed inadequate.

We followed them outside (a totally new experience for me at a door-knock) and waved them away, much like, I felt, the Bennet sisters as they farewelled the soldiers from Meryton in *Pride and Prejudice*.

When they finally left, I went straight to my room and called Lara.

Chapter 24

While I had several weighty objections to barbecues in the park, this one was different. Menem would be there, and after last night, I was looking forward to seeing him again.

I'd been unable to sleep properly, and just the thought of where this could be heading was keeping me in a semipermanent state of anxiety—but not in a completely unpleasant way. I realized that this time the outcome mattered to me.

Lara had agreed to come along after much cajoling and several You-owe-mes, although I wasn't entirely sure there was any point in that since trying to keep track of the "favors" Lara asked of me would be like counting the grains of sand at Bondi, or any beach, for that matter.

But I needed Lara to meet Menem properly. I was sure that if she saw him, she'd change her tune. More important, she'd stop petitioning for Hakeem, who'd never asked to have his name put on the ballot in the first place.

When I picked her up, I could tell she wasn't in the best mood. But I decided to put it down to the fact that we were going to a barbecue in the park and not doing something glamorous like going out on a sailboat. We didn't say much as we drove to Centennial Park. It took ten minutes to find a suitable parking spot, then another ten to find my family. When we finally located them, I couldn't see Menem with them. I was fairly sure he was coming.

Oh gosh, what if he wasn't coming? Wouldn't that just be fantastically embarrassing?

Lara and I gave our obligatory greetings, went through the awkward introductions—singledom radars going off and the like—then dumped our things on the picnic blanket. I told my parents that we were going for a walk and would be back to assist shortly.

We walked off in the direction of the duck pond so that our departure wouldn't seem suspicious. As we neared the water, I spotted Menem in the distance.

"There he is," I said to Lara, motioning discreetly with my head.

He was getting closer, a cooler in each hand. There was no missing him, but Lara practically yelled, "Which one?"

"Be quiet!"

"What?" she said, lowering her voice. "I'm just asking—"

"He's right there! The tallish one with the dark blondish hair."

Lara finally homed in on Menem. "Ah, the wimpish one. Okay." She pouted.

"Lara," I pleaded.

She sighed. "Okay, sorry."

"So. What do you think?" I said anxiously.

Lara hooked an eyebrow, which I couldn't help noticing made her look rather exotic and mysterious. "Well, he doesn't *look* Arab, does he," she said, although it was hard to tell if she saw that as a good or a bad thing. She hooked the other eyebrow and pursed her mouth. "Fine," she said in resignation. "He looks okay, I guess."

Sigh of relief.

"Which is of course only more reason to be suspicious," she added.

I gave her a look and she attempted a smile.

"Hey!" said Menem as he reached us.

"Hey," I replied. I gave him a simple, librarian smile in the hope it would subdue the excitement rising in my stomach. Lara pursed her lips again and greeted him.

"So this is the famous Lara I've heard so much about," said Menem.

He was being so nice, but I felt sorry for him because it was obvious that Lara was already freezing him out.

"Yes," I replied. I kicked Lara in the ankle.

Lara fake-smiled. "Yes, I'm her cousin. I know everything there is to know about Samira, and I look after her and make sure she doesn't do anything silly."

I felt as though I'd been sucker punched, and I smiled uneasily, a humiliating blush spreading across my face.

"Right," said Menem uncomfortably. "That's good to know. Although I'm sure Samira can take care of herself."

"You'd think so. But you'd be surprised at how innocent she can be. Honestly, she's always on the phone to me needing advice," continued Lara. "Like, how many times, Samira, have you called me because some guy's asked you out on a date? She can't even lie to them; she just says she doesn't date."

Menem nodded slowly, a bewildered expression on his face. "Right," he repeated. "Well, like I said, I think Samira is smart enough to know what's best for her. And I think it's good that she's always honest."

I smiled appreciatively at Menem, then, deciding I needed to put a stop to the discomfort without delay, I told him we were needed elsewhere.

"Tabbouleh emergency," I joked, realizing immediately that I could have come up with something more plausible than that.

But Menem laughed. "Okay, I'll speak to you soon." He gave me a meaningful look.

"Right," I said, smiling at him. I felt a tickle of excitement. A frisson, if you will. He was just so dashing and lovely and comforting to be around.

Menem nodded to Lara and said goodbye before making his way to our group. I turned to Lara, my mouth in a tight line that expressed my disappointment.

"What?" said Lara.

"What the hell was that? You look after me and make sure I don't do anything silly? I'm always on the phone to you? I'm a total moron when it comes to guys?"

Lara rolled her eyes. "Samira, it's not like that."

"Oh my God. Lara. I can't believe what just happened."

"Chill, Samira. It's not a big deal."

"Not a big deal?" I fumed. "You don't even know the guy and you've already deemed him unworthy. Worse, you can't just keep it to yourself. Not only were you rude to him but you humiliated me at the same time!"

Lara obviously realized I was truly upset because she went from careless to contrite in a matter of seconds. "No," she said. "It's not like that, Samira. I'm so sorry! I wasn't trying to humiliate you!"

"I would have expected that from Zahra!" I said, struggling to get the words out. I felt like crying, I was so embarrassed.

"I'm used to her bitchiness, but the one person I never would have expected it from is you."

"I'm so sorry, Samira," Lara repeated. "Please forgive me. I didn't mean it that way." She did seem upset, but I couldn't help the uncharitable feeling that she was the thief who was sorry to have been caught, not at all remorseful about the crime committed.

"You know what? I don't even care," I said, waving her away. I was not going to cry, even though my throat was a bit lumpy and my voice was getting thick.

"Samira, wait," said Lara, looking a bit panicked.

"I can't talk about this right now."

"Crap." Lara stomped her foot once in frustration. "Look, we'll talk later, okay?"

"Yeah, sure," I said. Then I walked off without looking back.

At the end of the day, Lara left with my parents. Mum raised an eyebrow, clearly suspicious, but we explained that I needed to make a couple of stops on the way home and Lara didn't want to tag along.

I did feel a nudge of guilt as I watched her leave. Particularly as I knew, while she didn't, that Dad would be telling her his post-9/11 stories on the way home, as he always did after leaving barbecues at the park (exact reasons unknown).

But disturbingly, Lara and I were now officially in a fight. We never fought about serious things. Or maybe we argued, but as sisters do; in the same breath Lara could call me a cow, then tell me she loved me. This was different.

When I got home, I helped Mum put everything away, before taking a shower, then performing the last prayer of the day. After that, I texted Menem so that I could apologize for Lara's behavior. Just as I hit send, Hakeem messaged me.

> Hakeem: Sorry to disturb you.
> Samira: I'm already disturbed. What's up?
> Hakeem: Lara sent me a message. She seemed upset.
> Samira: How so?
> Hakeem: Well, there was a lot of %^%*&%&*, something about death to family BBQs, and I think she mentioned a wimpy brother.

Oh gawd. Wasn't Lara venting to Hakeem on a par with conspiring with the enemy? Surely this was breaking some sort of code. Then again, she hadn't said anything explicit so perhaps it didn't count. I wasn't up to scratch on the sisterhood rules. Nevertheless, I was feeling a little like a schoolchild being sent to the principal's office.

> Samira: OK.
> Hakeem: What's going on?
> Samira: Nothing. She's obviously upset about something.
> Hakeem: Look, I wouldn't interfere, but Lara messaging me is a cry for help so it must be dire. I'm not sure what she's trying to tell me is all.

I stared blankly at the screen in disbelief. I was sure that once upon a time my life had held no excitement or intrigue. Nowadays it had more drama than a telenovela. Well, minus the skimpy outfits and the bitch slaps.

Hakeem: Samira?

Samira: I don't know what to tell you.

Hakeem: OK. Obviously it's none of my business, but I'm
guessing her state has something to do with you. Am I
warm?

Oh bloody hell.

Samira: We had a fight.

Hakeem: You and Lara had a fight?

Samira: Yes. Not just an ordinary one. This was a proper fight.

Hakeem: About what?

I paused. I had no idea what to tell him. Or rather, how
much to tell him.

Hakeem: Samira? If you don't want to talk, just tell me.

Samira: We had a fight about a guy.

There was a pause.

Samira: Menem. Zahra's fiancé's brother. He came for a visit.

Hakeem: I see.

Samira: Yeah, so anyway, she doesn't like him, so she was
rude and made some humiliating comments about me.

It was a full minute before Hakeem replied, enough time for
my face to heat up and for me to think about telenovelas again.

Hakeem: I'm sure Lara didn't mean to humiliate you.

Samira: It doesn't matter. Look, I don't want to say anything

bad about her. She's my best friend and you're a boy, and
I can't betray her for a boy.

Hakeem: Right. Well, you should fix things with her.

Samira: I will.

More cyber silence.

Hakeem: So he came for a visit then?

Samira: Yes. Last night.

Hakeem: So things are getting serious?

Samira: I guess so. Maybe.

Hakeem: OK. Be careful.

Samira: Yes, thank you. I'll be sure to enroll in a Relationships
for Dummies course.

Hakeem: Samira . . .

Samira: What is wrong with everyone? What do you want
from me?

Hakeem: What are you talking about?

Samira: I finally meet a decent guy and everyone is acting
like he's an ex-con or something. Why? Am I missing
something here?

Hakeem: Well, I don't know how "everyone" is acting, but I
care for you, so I am just telling you what I would tell you
no matter who the guy is.

Samira: Sure, OK. Well, thanks.

Hakeem: What have I said wrong here?

Samira: Hakeem, please.

Hakeem: I'm sorry you're feeling frustrated.

Samira: Why are you always so formal?

Hakeem: What do you want me to say?

Samira: Nothing.

Hakeem: You want me to say nothing?

Samira: What do you want from me?

Hakeem: I don't want anything from you, I just want things for you.

Samira: Why?

Hakeem: Is that even a question?

Samira: Yes. Why are we having this conversation? Would you say this to Lara?

Hakeem: You seem upset, so I think I should go. I'm sorry for upsetting you.

Samira: You're not upsetting me!

Hakeem: OK.

Samira: Sorry.

Hakeem: Lara is worried about you. She knows you deserve the best. She can't hide her feelings well is all. Just give her time.

Samira: OK.

Hakeem: All right. Take care.

Samira: You too.

Hakeem: Sorry again.

I threw down my phone, crawled into bed, and shut my eyes extra tight. It took ages for me to fall asleep.

Chapter 25

The next day I awoke to a text from Menem.

> Nothing to apologize about, Samira. You're the one I'm interested in. Yours is the only opinion I care about. You are the only one I see.
>
> P.S. Check your email at work. :)

As I logged on at my desk, I could barely breathe. The nerves skidded in as I found the message at the top of my inbox.

> Subject: Hi
> Hi Samira,
> I haven't stopped thinking about you. Yesterday, all I wanted to do was to find a spot away from everyone so we could talk alone.
>
> Just so you know, I've asked my mum to call your mum. But I didn't want you to hear about it all from your parents. Am I wrong? I hope not.
>
> I guess I could tell you all of this to your face, but I know you're not always comfortable when we meet. So I want to make this easier on you (and OK, I won't lie, this isn't the easiest thing I've ever done).

I really like you. You're constantly on my mind. If you have any doubts about how I'm feeling, you can put them to rest.

The question is—and this is where it gets really hard for me—how do you feel about all of this? Do you feel the same?

I know it's a lot to take in. But if you can reply soon, I'll be able to breathe again.

Menem

P.S. No pressure.

I really should reply to that, I thought. Once *I* could breathe again.

I was probably on version forty-one of my reply when Gabriel dropped by my desk in his usual uniform, a camera bag slung over his shoulder. We exchanged some pleasantries and then he handed me a list of back invoices of which he needed copies.

"Bloody accountants" was all he mumbled. He leaned against the partition and glanced around the office.

As I began searching for the financials server on my computer, he turned around and slouched over the wall of my cubicle. He mentioned the cadetships, asking if I had applied for one yet. "Competition for them is always strong so you should take advantage of my current position," he explained. I told him Jeff had recommended me.

"Great. If you need me for a reference too, let me know," Gabriel said. He fiddled with a Homer Simpson bobblehead, which Marcus had put on top of the partition ages ago.

"It's a journalist position," I said, biting my lip.

"What?" I looked up at Gabriel, who looked supremely confused.

I quickly turned back to the screen, continuing to click through various menus.

Gabriel straightened up and brushed a hand through his messy hair. "What's this bullshit about journalism? The photography cadetships are right there." He now looked very annoyed with me, but he didn't raise his voice.

I could see Cate glancing over, trying to get a view and quite possibly listen in. She'd hound me later for details.

"I can't just apply for that—I don't know enough," I said as I scrolled through Gabriel's invoices. "They'll want someone who's done a course, someone with an actual portfolio."

"You have done a course. You've been schooled by me. And I can put together your portfolio."

I looked up from my screen and his blue eyes bored into mine. I gave him a conciliatory look. "Gabriel, seriously, it's not a big deal."

"Look, let's cut the crap for a second, okay? I really don't know what your life is like outside of work. You seem pretty happy, generally speaking. Well, as happy as anyone can be working in this hellhole." He gave a cursory nod toward the rest of the office. "But I'm kind of amazed that you're not even going to try. I mean, what the hell, Samira?"

He looked genuinely frustrated as he yanked out his phone and unlocked it. I wasn't sure how he'd had room for them because they were the tightest jeans I'd ever seen.

"I'm not sure I'd be cut out for it," I said.

"Cut out for what?"

"I don't know what they'd expect of me. There are a lot of things I can't do."

His eyes widened. "Like?"

"What if I have to take photos of inappropriate things?" I said, my voice low.

"Inappropriate? The magazines are for brides and parents."

"You wouldn't understand."

"Ah, hello? Catholic school upbringing," he said, pointing at himself with his phone. "My dad still hasn't forgiven me for not getting a 'proper' job." Gabriel rolled his eyes and jammed the phone back into his pocket.

"Okay, fine. I'll think about it," I said, hoping to get him off my case.

Gabriel stared at me, shaking his head slowly. "You could make people fight to the death for these opportunities. You probably have a better chance than any of them, but you're not even going to try."

I felt terrible when he put it that way.

"Later, girl." He sighed and walked away.

When I'd completed the invoices for Gabriel, who was now nowhere to be seen, I placed them in an envelope, wrote his name in black marker on the front, then handed it in at reception.

I was a little rattled by our chat, but I had a more significant task on my mind. So far, all of my responses to Menem had been lackluster. I was completely lost for words and I saw no improvement in sight. So I finally acknowledged that there was no clever way to respond and kept it simple.

Subject: Re: Hi
Hi Menem,
Sorry it's taken me so long to get back to you. It's been crazy

here today. If you're saying that you'd like to see me again, the answer from me is yes. :) I can think of nothing else I'd like more. And yes, I do feel the same.

Samira

P.S. Thank you for your message.

The postscript really was an afterthought and the only thing I reconsidered. Then my gut instinct told me to leave it, so I did.

I didn't even pretend to be occupied with work. I sat biting my nail, watching my inbox uneasily. I only had to wait two minutes before Menem's name appeared.

Subject: Re: Hi

When can I come over? ;)

If I had my way, he'd be over tonight, but that would be too soon, even in our Austen-like universe.

That night, Mum came into my room and reported the "news," and I pretended not to know anything. I simply said I wouldn't mind seeing him again. Mum said okay with a shrug and that was that.

By midweek, we'd arranged a meeting for Friday night, and I couldn't think about him without my internal organs doing somersaults.

Of course, we met for coffee the next day, and the day after that. And because official interest had been declared, we were "free" to communicate now. Our parents weren't going to be the third wheel. They would expect the courtship rules to be observed: propriety and all of that. But it was relatively guilt-free and, well, exciting.

Even though I heard from him every day, phone calls and messages and emails didn't seem like enough. He was all I could think about, and it was exhausting. I wanted to see him, more than for a quick coffee break. I wanted to touch him, to know what it felt like to be held by him.

To distract myself, I paid Sahar a visit after work on Thursday. She was baking, as usual, and I was helping her. I realized how much I'd missed her company and felt terrible for neglecting her.

Today we were making strawberry chocolate muffins, and the smell was as delicious as the final product promised to be.

"Does he pray?" inquired Sahar as she stirred the batter.

"Um, I think so, but I have a feeling he's not obsessive about it." I didn't look at her as I said it, focusing on the strawberries I was chopping up. "He's not really strict," I added reluctantly. It didn't bother me the way it might Sahar. Truth was, I'd never asked him about it directly.

"Samira, maybe you shouldn't think of him as being unreligious per se," Sahar said, staring thoughtfully at the batter. I looked up in surprise, and she shrugged. "Maybe he's in your life because you're supposed to help him. Why assume marrying someone more religious is the way to go for you?"

"Well. I don't know what I think," I answered, not even sure what "more religious" meant and if it was necessarily a good thing. After all, doing more didn't make you a better Muslim, let alone a better person. And if I was being completely honest, it wasn't the first thing I thought about. I wanted connection.

"Right," said a bemused Sahar. "I'm just saying, Allah is the best of planners. You never know who might enter your life and why. Even if the method is not so good, the outcome is what's most important." She didn't look me in the eye, but this was her way of telling me that Menem should have gone straight to my door from the moment he felt an interest in me. Sahar had always done things The Right Way.

I pondered it all. Maybe Sahar had a point about religiousness. I didn't give it much thought nowadays, but I'd always felt I needed improvement when it came to nurturing my, erm, spirituality. It followed, naturally, that were I to marry, I'd need a husband who could assist with said nurturing. It would be a sorry situation if I were the one providing the guidance. In fact, I was about to tell Sahar this when she stopped me short with her next remark.

"If you were to marry Hakeem, he would be the guide, true."

"Huh? Who said anything about marrying Hakeem?"

"Sorry. No one said anything about him. I was just comparing him to this other man." Sahar took the bowl of sliced strawberries and tossed them neatly into the batter. She stirred the mixture around, then began pouring dollops into the cupcake tray in precise, even amounts. She was so casual, not at all behaving as though she'd just gone Mills & Boon on me.

I nodded in bewilderment. "Don't you start now," I warned. "Have you been talking to Lara?" I wondered if everyone had secretly met behind my back at some stage to discuss my love life, and previous lack thereof. While Hakeem was annoying me with the overly protective vibe, I was beginning to feel a bit sorry for him now. Everyone presumed to know what he was thinking and feeling.

"Yes," Sahar admitted. "She's around more often since she lost her job. She's actually been very helpful with orders. Never knew she had such an eye for colors. She's still a little easily distracted, though. Anyway," she said, shaking her head. "Just so you know, it is possible to be conflicted over men."

"Sahar, do you have a secret stash of romance novels I should know about?"

She smiled shyly. "Just because I'm, well, you know, quiet, doesn't mean I don't know about these things."

"I didn't mean—"

"I know. Anyway, my point is, who knows what's right for you? Maybe it's Menem, maybe it's Hakeem. Maybe it's the guy down the street. Have you done istikhara?" she asked, seriously.

She was talking about the Islamic prayer for guidance, a special prayer to offer when making an important decision because it, in essence, truly leaves it up to Allah. Of course, if you were Lara, you did istikhara before going shopping.

"The guy down the street is missing two teeth," I said.

Sahar nudged me aside, then opened the oven door. "I stand by what I said. Allah knows best. You can't do any better than that." She placed the tray inside, then wiped her hands on a tea towel. "I don't think you give yourself enough credit, by the way." She grabbed a notebook from the counter and began scribbling something on a blank page.

"Credit for what?"

"For who you are. If anyone can make a go of things without a man, it's you. Maybe something more worthwhile is around the corner. Have you ever really given yourself a chance?"

"Is that a trick question?"

"No," she said with a laugh. She placed the notebook on the kitchen bench and crossed her arms, turning to face me. Then she launched into a story about the Barbie games we'd played as kids and how I'd kept changing careers. I'd have thought that made me a little indecisive and flighty, but apparently not. "It showed an incredible desire to experience life and achieve great things," concluded Sahar. "What happened?"

Bloody hell, I thought. I grew up.

As I walked home, I thought about my conversation with Sahar. I hadn't been expecting it to go along those lines. She'd given me good advice, but I was a little taken aback by what she'd said about me and my life direction. I wasn't a desperado, trying to get married for the sake of it. I knew what I was hoping for, and it was a connection.

That and I'd never been kissed. I really wanted to see what the big deal was with that, and what exactly was involved. Did the man lead? Did he hold her face between his hands, deepening the kiss, hands twisted in the woman's hair? Would it feel as lovely as it did in my imagination?

And that was just for starters. I'd imagined more. My mind had wandered in ways my body could not in reality.

It was as basic as wanting to experience something adolescents took for granted. Unfortunately for me, it came with a whole set of rules.

Marriage, no matter how easily it could be undertaken by adults, was always a big deal, a life shaper. I only knew being single. I had no idea about relationships or intimacy, and it was an experience for which I was yearning—especially now that I had someone I liked who stirred these feelings within me.

The mention of Hakeem had also taken me by surprise. I hadn't spoken to him following our last conversation, during which I had, admittedly, challenged him to explain his strange behavior toward me. I still didn't think he was jealous; he was just brooding and sullen, as per usual.

Worse, though, Lara and I hadn't spoken either. Both absences weighed heavily on me, but I was too caught up in everything else happening in my life. And my life was becoming Menem-centric, but not in a pathetic way. I wanted to know everything about him. In our first few conversations we'd talked about religion (of course), politics, and history. We'd played the "If you could go back to any era, what would it be?" game. When I hadn't been able to decide after half an hour, Menem said, "It's just a game. There's no right or wrong!"

I still hadn't been able to decide.

Over the phone, we'd taken stock of our respective musical tastes (mostly different) and movie preferences (some commonality). He had seen *The Princess Bride*, and could recite a line or two, but I'd played it cool. Then I'd regaled him with my movie premiere adventures with Lara. He clearly didn't care about actors, but he'd indulged me when I told him about the time we met Matt Damon and we were on the evening news.

"My mum wasn't impressed," I said.

"Did she bring out the shoe or the wooden spoon?"

"She gave me a look, then said, 'Do you think Matt Daymoon cares about you?'" I said to Menem's gentle laughter. Of course, I didn't think Matt Daymoon cared two straws about me, but Lara had declared her undying love for him, which lasted about a week.

"Well, I hope you have time for us little people now. I'm not sure I can compete with Matt Damon," Menem had said, but I'd heard the smile in his voice.

I spent generous portions of my workday thinking about Menem. I couldn't remember the last time I'd had a reason to daydream about anything but sleeping in, and it made for a nice change. One minute I'd be sending off quarterly reports to executives, the next my mind would be on Menem and me, married and riding horses on an exotic beach somewhere. My headscarf would billow dramatically as we thundered (none of this galloping business) over the sand. But shortly thereafter, the daydream would crumble. Reality would wearily tap me on the shoulder and politely remind me that I'd never been on a horse before. And since I couldn't recall a time when my headscarf had billowed dramatically (unless you counted driving along the motorway with the windows down, which I didn't), in my little daydream my scarf would always end up on my face, blinding me. This would then cause me to fall unceremoniously off my horse while Menem continued along the beach, all dashing and heroic.

Before Menem came over on Friday, I spent two hours trying to find the right outfit. I finally settled on jeans, a white Boho top, and a light green scarf.

Mum and Dad left us alone in the sitting room, but we sat on separate sofas. We were still close to each other, though, and I could smell his aftershave.

Thoughts of a physical embrace floated into my mind. I needed to stay focused, so I shook them away.

We happily chatted away over chocolate biscuits and tea, made by yours truly (the tea, not the biscuits).

"You're the only girl in your family. You must've been spoiled," Menem observed.

"Indeed I was not!" I actually said "indeed," though I wasn't sure why exactly.

"Hmm, I'm not sure I believe you," said Menem, in the closest he'd come to being outright flirty.

"I only have one brother," I said, followed by some hmmphing, even though I enjoyed the teasing a little. Then Menem said something about spoiled girls being high-maintenance. All the while, he sat drinking his tea, completely nonchalant.

The nerve. But I forgave him when he assured me that he was only joking. That and he gave me a box of Lindt.

I studied his face, taking in the angles and lines of his cheekbones, his nose, his mouth. I noted the stubble on his face.

I thought of Gabriel and how he'd once told me that in portraits there was always a characteristic that became the focus of the shot. With Menem, it would be his cheekbones—he had such an elegant face. Hakeem would be all about the intensity of his eyes. Lara projected bubbliness—she was all about the smile.

There was something about Menem, though, about that moment when he pulled out the box of chocolates and handed it to me. I thought about just how much I liked him already. I wanted so much to move closer and touch his cheek, to hold his hand. I found myself wishing he would offer his hand to me, all the while knowing I'd completely freak out if he did.

I felt, for the first time in my life, the desire to be with the man sitting in front of me. And as God was my witness, it had nothing to do with the chocolates.

Chapter 26

The next week whizzed by in a circus of emails and phone calls. Menem had come over on Sunday with his family, then booked in another visit for Wednesday. Even though he was coming to our house, I still felt the need to check that my parents wouldn't mind.

So I asked Dad, but received a surprising response from him.

"Of course, Samira! Why do you ask like a child? You're a mature young woman!"

I realized then how deeply embedded the guilt was; I was feeling it even when Menem and I were openly "courting."

I told Menem that I'd be spending Friday night with Lara, who had called me early in the week to set up a date.

When she arrived, Lara peered hesitantly through the doorway of my bedroom. "Hi," she said.

"Hey."

Lara entered and closed the door behind her. She attempted a smile, looking a bit tired and nervous and not at all her usual bubbly self.

"I'm sorry," she said, her hands in her jeans pockets. She sat down on the bed, flipped off her slippers, then rested her legs sideways. "I was being a bitch. And you're mature and ugly enough to take care of yourself," she said with a half smile.

"Cow," I replied.

This time she nodded. "Friends?"

"Of course. But Menem deserved better when you met him. I would never have acted that way toward someone you liked."

"I know you wouldn't. But it came from a good place. Honestly."

We were quiet for a moment. Lara looked truly repentant, almost a little shell-shocked that it had come to this. I understood how she felt.

"About Menem," I began.

"Maybe he is a good guy," interrupted Lara. "Fine. But you're special, so you deserve special."

"You think that way because you're my cousin. And my best friend."

"No," she said emphatically. "I'm crazy. I have no balance. I don't even think I could ever get married because I'd drive him batty. And that's all right. You're different, though."

I shook my head.

Lara grabbed my hands. "It's not an accident that you're single. You deserve the best and that takes time."

I sighed. "Lara—"

"Look," she said. "You've got two great guys wanting to be with you."

At least she'd said two. If she'd said one, there was no way she'd be referring to Menem, and we'd have to restart this entire conversation.

"I know I behaved badly," she continued. "And I probably was unfair in judging Menem. I admit it."

I could tell it hurt her to do it. Lara admit to being wrong? Look out the window to catch the flying pig show.

She leaned over and hugged me tight.

"You're being too generous," I told her.

"No. I'm not." She hugged me tighter.

When she finally pulled away, I said, "Okay, but will you give Menem a chance?"

"I don't need to give him a chance. You'd be the one living with him."

"You know what I mean."

Lara paused. "Yes. Even though I stand by what I said—it's just my opinion. I think Hakeem cares for you in ways *he* doesn't even realize."

"Stop watching movies! I thought *I* was bad!"

"He shows it with all the little things he does for you. Whenever you need something, does he even hesitate? What about that time we got stranded and he came and changed the tire at a moment's notice?" she said hopefully.

"Yes, he's very kind. But did you not see how disapproving he was?"

"He's not the easiest guy to deal with," conceded Lara.

I didn't know what to say, but I suddenly felt deflated. Lara wasn't the only one to romanticize things. We all did it in some way or another. Was it meant to be this hard? Could someone please sue Hollywood? And book publishers? And anyone else who'd ever messed with women's heads?

"Lara, I need to think about my future. It's fun to hypothesize that Hakeem and I have this amazing connection. Maybe we do. But that doesn't mean we should get married."

"Would you consider him, though? If he asked?"

"No. I really like Menem. Now can we please change the subject?"

"I'm sorry. It's just that if I'm going to lose you to someone,

I'd much rather it be Hakeem. At least I know him and what his issues are. And Lord knows Hakeem needs someone who'll make him lighten up a bit." She sighed.

"He's not *that* bad," I said. For a moment, I wondered about my bond with Hakeem. He had for so long been a fixture in my life. A friend who could be tetchy and annoying, but also amazingly kind. We cared about each other—I knew that much for certain. But love?

"Whatever," said Lara. "I love you and that's all that matters." She reached over and hugged me again. "Now let's get something to eat and prank your cousin Jamal," she said, mid-embrace.

"Lara, be careful with him," I warned, pulling away from her.

"What on earth do you think I'm going to do?" she asked, startled.

"Oh, I dunno. Make him fall for you, then reject him when he wants to marry you?"

"Oh my God, that only happened, like, twice!"

Chapter 27

Zahra was staring into space. I stood biting my thumbnail, trying to figure out how to deal with what was rapidly turning into a saga of Bollywood proportions. Lara waved her hand up and down in front of Zahra's eyes, but she didn't even flinch.

We were assembled in a spacious dressing room at Livvy's Bridal, Zahra in her spectacular wedding dress, Lara and I in ankle-length lavender chiffon dresses. They were, incidentally, very pretty and flattering, with a sparkly dark purple belt and ruffles along the hem.

Zahra had been quiet on the way over, but it was only after she'd put on the dress that she went comatose.

"Bloody hell," said Lara. "She's lost it."

"That isn't helping, Lara."

"He's going to see," said Zahra suddenly, still staring straight ahead. "One day he's going to find out who I really am and he's going to look at me the way you do."

Lara and I glanced at each other. She made a cuckoo sign with her hand and shook her head. I gave her a reprimanding look and crouched down next to Zahra.

"Zahra, honey, what are you saying?"

She looked at me and shook her head slightly, tuning back in to reality. "I'm a bad person," she said.

Lara gasped, but I cautioned her with a wave.

"I know it," Zahra continued. "You think I don't know how much you hate me?"

"You started it!" Lara said.

"Just calm down, will you?" I looked up at Lara beseechingly from my spot on the floor beside Zahra. Lara rolled her eyes and started pacing, her heels clicking against the wooden floor. It was a large room, with three floor-length mirrors on one side. Claustrophobic and we needed air-con.

"What she's trying to say, Zahra, is that we don't hate you, but there's more to the equation. If you *think* we hate you, doesn't that make you wonder why?"

"Yes. I know why. I know I am a bad person!" she said pitifully. "And Malek is going to see it, and that will push him away and he'll hate me." She started to cry.

Lara stopped pacing and shook her head in disbelief. "You're a bad person because you choose to be. You're jealous and manipulative and—"

"Lara!"

But she continued. "No, Samira. Let her know what she is. I mean, she's treated you like crap since *forever*. What, she says this and now we're supposed to forget everything?" Lara stood her ground, arms crossed. She was genuinely upset, while suddenly Zahra looked like she'd taken a few too many drowsy antihistamines.

"Now is not the time for this, Lara." I had yet to understand why Arabs were always so dramatic. I didn't want to imagine what family events would be like if we were drinkers.

Lara walked toward us. "Why are you defending her?"

"I'm not. But this isn't the time," I reprimanded. "Zahra's not herself, and we're her bridesmaids. Her wedding is in a week."

"By the looks of it, there may not be a wedding," said Lara, her eyebrows raised.

"You, I don't like you anyway," said Zahra, pointing at Lara.

"Why, you little . . ." Lara looked like she was about to lunge for Zahra, but by then I was standing beside her.

"Stop it!" I grabbed Lara's arm and dragged her away as she tried to kick at Zahra, who rose from her spot and hobbled into position, her big white dress swishing against the floor.

"Let me go!" Lara cried.

"You're just as bad as me," said Zahra. "You're so distrusting and rude."

"Both of you calm down!"

"Stay out of this, Samira. It doesn't involve you," said Lara.

"Yes, it does. I—"

Zahra started to cry again. Oh *gawd*.

"Now look what you've done." I stood between them, Zahra crying into her hands, her makeup cascading down her cheeks like tiny waterfalls, Lara pouting and miserable.

"Pardon me, ladies, but is everything all right?" chimed in a sales assistant, her head peeking through the curtains.

"Yes, everything's fine, thank you," I said.

"Well, could you kindly lower your voices?"

"Of course. We're very sorry," I replied politely.

The sales assistant left. Lara was a little calmer now.

"Will you just stop crying?" she said to Zahra, exasperated.

"Zahra," I began. "We're not going to pretend we're best friends. We know you don't like us, for whatever reason, and in return, we haven't liked you back. If we can heal all of that, great. But right now, I'd just like to see another day, because God knows my mother will kill me if I let your wedding get ruined."

This was our final dress fitting, having been through three of them relatively drama-free. Since tonight Zahra was having a party, now wasn't the time to tarnish that impressive track record.

Lara had gone back to pacing. "This is so not your fault," she muttered.

"I know. But Zahra isn't exactly in a good headspace. So please, help me out here."

Lara stopped and looked at me thoughtfully. She seemed slightly appeased. "Fine," she said. "But only for you, not for snot face here."

Zahra was still weeping. I sighed and put my arms around her, rubbing her back. "Sit down, Zahra. We're going to listen. Just tell us what's wrong." I helped her spread her dress out so that she could sit properly on a chair. She hiccuped and looked up at me. "Zahra, Malek loves you," I said. "And he is marrying you because he sees the good in you, not the bad. Besides, we all have horrible sides."

Lara snorted, and I gave her a stern look.

Zahra was still crying, but she wasn't hiccuping anymore. She looked at me like a wounded puppy dog. "He told me that I'm selfish."

I looked at Lara and shook my head. She was doing her utmost not to say anything. I could tell it was a true effort, though, her face crumpled with the pain of not being able to squeal.

"Why did he say that, Zahra?" I prompted.

"We had an argument."

I wasn't going to ask about what, even though Lara was bursting to. I was sure I didn't need to know the details. Before Lara could prod for more information, I said, "Well, you'll have to get used to that, Zahra. I'm sure it's just the first fight of many. It's not the end of the world."

"No, it was more than that," she said, crying in earnest. "I was talking to him about the wedding and some of his family members, and he got into a huff because he thinks I don't like his aunts."

The belly dancers. Lara would need to be physically restrained in a moment.

"I don't want his aunts stealing attention at the wedding! Did you see what they did at the engagement?" Zahra said, a touch of hysteria in her voice.

"Yes, briefly," I replied. Before I'd escaped to the kitchen and binged on Arabic sweets, anyway.

"He's just so loyal to his family. He hates looking bad in front of anyone." She sniffed. "Although, I'm sure his parents would agree with me. And I was telling him that when he started calling me selfish and saying that if I was going to be like this over such a small matter, maybe I wasn't worth the trouble." Fresh tears spilled out of her eyes while I tried to formulate a reasonable response.

"Zahra, you just have to speak to him and compromise," I advised.

"You might have to define that last word for her," said Lara.

"You just can't help yourself, can you?" I practically snapped.

Lara shrugged. "I'm just saying. Little Miss Weepy here has always got her own way. This isn't even a big deal and she thinks her life is over."

I fished a tissue from my handbag and handed it to Zahra.

She blew her nose noisily. "I understand the meaning of compromise," she said. "I'm realistic. I just want my wedding to be *perfect*."

"Okay, well, Lara is sort of right, Zahra. On any scale of things, this is a minor blip. You've got to be yourself with

Malek. If you try to be perfect all the time, these arguments are going to happen with increasing frequency."

God, I sounded wise. Giving advice to other people was always so much simpler than figuring things out for oneself.

"In other words, stop pretending you're sugar and spice and all that's nice," said Lara bluntly.

"Oh my God, he's going to run," wept Zahra.

"Zahra, he's not going to run. You need to talk to him!"

She nodded frantically. "Yes. And I'm sorry," she said, turning to me. "I promise I'll try to be nicer."

I looked at her with sympathy. In all the years I'd had to deal with her bitchiness, I'd never stopped to consider why she behaved as she did. I nodded and rubbed her back, grabbing more tissues with my free hand.

"I'm so scared he'll hate me," she said, taking the tissues from me and blowing into all of them. "Sometimes I hold back saying what I feel."

"I don't think you should do that anymore." It sounded pretty awful. Limited in experience as I was, I wondered if I had ever done that too. I was only just getting to know Menem, but what about Hakeem? My brother? My parents? How many times had I kept my feelings to myself to not rock the boat?

"You're right," Zahra said without a trace of sarcasm.

"Don't start out hiding your feelings, Zahra. He already knows you enough to be in love with you. No matter what you've done to us, you're nice to *him*. And that's not an act. He brings out the good in you. I've seen you together."

Lara snorted. We both looked at her, and she put one hand over her mouth and gave me an apologetic look. I suppressed a smile.

"It's different with guys anyway," said Lara eventually,

dropping onto a plush stool. "The good ones almost always end up with cows."

Surprisingly, this seemed to be of some comfort to Zahra, who nodded as she examined her tissues. "Thank you," she said, placing a hand on my knee without looking at me.

I put my hand over hers and squeezed it gently. "No problem."

"But what am I going to do? I want to dance at the wedding, but it'll only lead to disaster if his aunts take over," Zahra said.

"Look, the dance floor is going to be so crowded at your wedding, you won't even notice his aunts. Besides, they'll have plenty of opportunity to get the belly dancing out of their systems tonight at the party."

Lara's eyes widened. "Oh Lord, they're not going to be there, are they?"

When we got back from the dress fitting, we had to set up Zahra's living room for her layleeya. This was a traditional party with dancing and food and good company that Arab women commonly have before their weddings. Sort of like a hen night, minus the alcohol and antics. Sometimes Arab girls would also opt for a henna party, an evening spent getting intricate tattoos of swirling vines and flowers over hands and arms. But for whatever reason, Zahra had decided to forgo the body painting and stick with dancing.

We didn't have to do much; we just set up some chairs and put out finger foods and drinks. Even Lara seemed excited about the party, and she helped without complaint. I had a sneaking suspicion her mood had something to do with her blossoming "relationship" with my cousin, but I didn't want to think too deeply about that. In fact, I preferred not to ask her about it at all, in case she revealed too much, and then I'd have to become all mum-like. Frankly, I didn't have the energy for it.

We'd intentionally asked people to arrive at 6 p.m. because they'd all be operating on Arab Standard Time. True to form, guests started trickling in at 7:30, just as we'd finished setting out the last plate of food. There were mini pizzas, homemade spring rolls, and, of course, sweets. Sahar brought with her pink-iced banana cupcakes and a trifle.

Lara and I were already dressed—me in a light blue sleeveless chiffon dress with a V-neck and Lara in a floor-length green satin dress. I wore my beloved silver Robert Robert heels and a silver ankle bracelet. I didn't skimp on the occasions when I could dress up. Lara had also straightened my hair for me with her fancy flat iron and lent me a pair of dangly earrings that practically dropped to my shoulders. I felt rather glamorous, and while I never cared about dressing up for men, I wondered what Menem would think if he saw me like this.

Sahar emerged from the bathroom de-hijabbed and met us in the kitchen. She'd come in an abaya and white headscarf, and the transformation was striking—her sparkly bronze dress hugged her curves, and she'd curled her wavy hair. She looked amazing.

Zahra was yet to come out, and I hoped she wasn't going to keep everyone waiting. She'd seemed a little better after the dress fitting, her bridal glow beginning to return. Surely she wasn't obsessing over her looks?

"Is it even possible for a bride-to-be to look less than beautiful?" I asked Lara.

"Yes," she said as we went to check on our cousin. "There's only so much makeup can do."

We found Zahra alone, sitting on the edge of her perfectly made bed, her hands fisted at her sides.

"Are you all right, Zahra?" I asked. She nodded, but she looked terrified. There was certainly no bridal glow now. She looked as pale as a ghost. Not that I'd ever seen a ghost. Nor did I ever hope to see one. But I assumed they tended to be translucent, in any case, not pale.

"You're not going to lose it again, are you?" said Lara over my shoulder.

I sent her a reprimanding look and she held up her hands in mock defense before rolling her eyes and heading back to the sitting room.

I went to sit beside Zahra. I grabbed her hand and she squeezed it tightly. "It'll be fine. You look beautiful. Mashallah."

She wore a gorgeous vintage-style dress, beige and beaded, similar to the one she'd worn at her engagement.

"Thanks," she managed, letting go of my hand to adjust the straps.

"Are you ready?"

"I can't believe this is happening," she said.

"What? That it's your layleeya?"

"Yes. It's surreal. Like . . . It's like I'm up on the ceiling looking down and watching myself." She shook her head. "I know that sounds crazy."

"Well, getting married takes its toll," I said.

Zahra made a face. She looked like she was about to say something, so I waited patiently, expecting her to tell me that she'd sorted things out with Malek (she'd spoken to him on the phone for an hour). But she didn't, and I couldn't let her go into such an important night like this.

"I know Lara and I weren't your first choice for bridesmaids. I'm sure you're under a lot of pressure to make everyone happy."

Zahra shook her head, then turned to meet my eyes. "You weren't. But Najwa booked a trip overseas knowing I was going to get married. I don't know . . . She doesn't like Malek. She thinks he's controlling, but I think we're just into each other."

"Is she coming tonight?"

Zahra shrugged. "Don't know. Maybe."

I was surprised, but then Zahra let out a big breath, and her whole body seemed to loosen up. I decided not to pry further. I felt a little hurt on her behalf. Lara had caused me grief with her protests against Menem, and I wondered if this was just what happened when someone you were close to found a romantic partner. But I knew that Lara would always be there for me.

Zahra smiled and stood up.

"Let's go party," she said.

And party we did. The music was loud, the food was delicious, and we danced like crazy. Lara led the dabke—the Arab equivalent of *Lord of the Dance*—all stamping feet and enthusiastic kicks as we moved around in a circle holding hands. She tied a glittery scarf around her hips and held a hanky in her hand, which she twirled frantically above her head. She was mistress of the dance, so good at it that no one dared try to take her place at the head of the line.

Eventually, we dispersed and congregated in small groups. Lara removed the scarf from her hips and placed it around mine, dragging me to the center of the sitting room. After my shyness subsided, I succumbed to Amr Diab's voice as he sang joyously about the love of his life. "Habibi, ya nour el ain"—

literally, "sweetheart, the light of my eyes"—was a must at every party, even if it was an old song. As it blared through the speakers, the small room pulsed, full to the brim with dancing children and young women, while mothers sat on chairs along the walls chitchatting and no doubt scouting for potential wives for their sons/nephews/next-door neighbors.

Lara and I twisted and turned as seductively and cheekily as belly dancers, shaking our hips whenever the music called for it, arms outstretched. The more we were egged on, the more adventurous we became, sparring and staring each other down. Lara was a much better dancer than me, but I could hold my own. She wouldn't leave her spot in the center of the room, even dragging Zahra toward her a few times. She clapped for the bride-to-be and swept around Zahra, who danced happily but in her usual proper, subdued way. Thankfully, the belly-dancing aunts (once again clad in sparkly outfits) didn't attempt a dance-off with Lara, apparently content to stick to one-half of the makeshift dance floor.

It was here we could let loose and dance without worrying about anything—no concerns about how we were dressed or the appropriateness of our behavior. We just let our hair down, literally in some cases, and danced and danced and danced.

Chapter 28

We'd all been recruited to assist Zahra and Malek on Sunday in setting up their new apartment (the men) and putting together 250 bonbonnières (the women). Even Lara was coming, without being asked, because she was "bored to tears and sorta curious." I knew she was really coming in the hope that Jamal would be around.

"I need Hakeem," said Zahra the night before, as we were leaving after the layleeya.

"What for?"

"We need more men!"

"Very true. There really are so few men in the world."

"Samira!"

"Well, ask Hakeem then, Zahra. Why are you telling me?"

"I need you to ask him because he won't say no to you."

"But it's your moving day."

"Look, can you just help out?" she said, exasperated.

"It's a bit last-minute, Zahra." I wasn't purposely being difficult. Honestly. I just couldn't understand why this task was being appointed to me.

"What is *up* with you, Samira? Sheesh!"

"Fine," I relented. "I'll ask him, but there's no guarantee that he'll be available."

"Whatever. Thanks, cuz," said Zahra.

Cuz? Oh Lord. What next? A secret handshake? Genuine three-cheek kisses?

"Why are you moving so many things in the first place?" I asked.

"Our apartment wasn't ready when we bought some of the furniture so it got delivered here," explained Zahra. Her glory box—or, as Zahra would quip, her "glory garage"—alone would probably require a few trips.

"Okay, see you tomorrow, Zahra."

I sent Hakeem a message when I got home.

> Samira: Zahra's moving day is tomorrow. Tall, swarthy types required. Are you available?
> (By request of Her Highness—sorry about the short notice.)

He responded ten minutes later.

> Hakeem: Address and time?

I wrote back with instructions. Hakeem wrote back with a quote.

> Hakeem: "Be men, or be more than men. Be steady to your purposes and firm as a rock."

I hazarded a guess.

> Samira: Paul Newman.

I imagined Hakeem at home, brooding in the half dark, a glass of whiskey—oh wait, we didn't drink—a cigarette (he didn't smoke, but it would have to do) perched between his fingers as he stared at the screen, the smoke wafting dramatically about him.

Hakeem: Why do you do it?

Samira: Do what, pray tell?

Hakeem: It's from *Frankenstein*, a book I know you've read and loved.

Samira: Very true. But hard to say why, really. Anyway, I have one for you!

Hakeem: OK.

Samira: "It's amazing the clarity that comes with psychotic jealousy."

Hakeem: I told you I rarely watch movies.

Samira: Who says it's from a movie?

Hakeem: Isn't it?

Samira: OK, yes, it is.

Hakeem: So what is it?

Samira: What's what?

Hakeem: The movie?

Samira: *My Best Friend's Wedding.*

Hakeem: Ah yes. It's on my list of movies to watch. I know I have the list somewhere.

Samira: I can lend it to you if you want.

Hakeem: I'm good, thanks. I finally watched *The Princess Bride* btw.

Samira: And you're only telling me now?!

Hakeem: Apologies. Little things get in the way sometimes. Like a full-time job, spiritual commitments, etc.

Samira: Lol, spiritual commitments?

Hakeem: :)

Samira: So what did you think?

Hakeem: It was a good movie.

Samira: Good? You thought the movie was good.

Hakeem: I've said something wrong, haven't I?

Samira: It was "good."

Hakeem: Remember that I have very limited knowledge of
films and therefore no reasonable means of comparison.

Samira: Whatever.

Hakeem: Look, it was very humorous, I agree.

Samira: Uh-huh. Don't try to fix this now.

Hakeem: No, look, in all seriousness, I can understand
why you like the film. It's very clever and has a lot of
memorable moments.

Samira: OK. Well, that's better. Anyway, how's things?

Hakeem: Alhamdulillah. You?

Samira: Alhamdulillah.

There was a pause. I was smiling like a fool. Balance had
seemingly been restored to the universe by a quote.

Hakeem: How are things progressing with you and that guy?

Samira: They're progressing.

Another pause. Then typing.
Then nothing.
Then more typing.

Hakeem: Insha'Allah everything goes well.

Samira: Knowing me, it'll all come to nothing.

Hakeem: Don't say that. Trust in Allah. He knows what's best
   for you.
Samira: I know.

But I supposed the reminder didn't hurt.

We arrived at Zahra's house to find Jamal standing in the
driveway beside a utility truck. Lara practically flew over and
I soon joined her, albeit at a more orderly pace.

"What's wrong?" asked Jamal when he saw my confused look.

"That's not your ute, is it?" I said.

"I borrowed it," he explained. "A buddy of mine owed me a
favor so he hooked me up."

Now, rest assured, my cousin Jamal was an honest, God-
fearing young man. I knew there'd never been anything untoward in his dealings. But someone always owed him a favor, and
I had yet to ever figure out why.

"It's so cute." Lara giggled.

"It's a ute," I said.

"Come on, Samira, where's your sense of adventure?" said
Lara.

"See that?" said Jamal. "I like her style!"

"Lara," she offered demurely.

Jamal lowered his gaze. "I know," he responded, blushing
profusely.

For goodness' sake. I wasn't like that with Menem, was I?

We'd barely stepped into the hallway when we were met by
Zahra, hands on hips.

"Come on, lots to do! Is Sahar still coming?" asked Zahra.

"Yes, later," I replied.

"Welcome to the working bee," said Zahra in her syrupy tone.

As we followed Zahra into the dining room, Lara looked at me in desperation and made choking motions.

Everything I'd collected for Zahra was neatly arranged on the dining table, still in the cartons. There were flat cardboard sheets in a lovely sheer silver ready to be constructed into little boxes for the bonbonnières. We had chocolates (each box was to have four), and there were yards and yards of organza ribbon (forty centimeters per box, to be tied into neat bows).

I felt like an air hostess as I gave instructions. I'd always wanted to do one of those demonstrations they do before the plane takes off—the ones where they point in a fancy way at the exits and explain what to do in the event of an emergency. However, as that bore no relation to bonbonnières, I stuck with what was relevant to the task at hand.

Half an hour later, Lara threw down her box and pouted. "This working bee sucks." Never mind that she'd spent half the time so far texting and checking Instagram.

Zahra rolled her eyes. "So go home then," she said, finishing off a box. She looked at it and smiled before delicately placing it in the "done" pile.

I was actually starting to enjoy myself even though none of us was doing an outstanding job. My bonbonnières were serviceable. Zahra's were fine too. Lara had managed two and they were lopsided.

Sahar joined us half an hour later, armed with cupcakes. She took her place at the table and got to work without instruction. That woman was like a Muslim version of Martha Stewart. She just needed to start a YouTube channel or write a book, and she'd be one of those "I'm Muslim but I'm just like you" spokespeople. Sahar was squeaky clean. Her biggest challenge in life to this day was to determine the most suitable halal substitute for white wine. So far she'd settled on apple cider.

Totally terror-free.

Sahar was soon followed by the male contingent: Malek, Menem, Jamal, and Hakeem.

Menem smiled at me as he entered, looking relaxed in chinos and an old business shirt and not at all as though he'd been lugging heavy furniture for the last three hours or so. He was growing a beard and it suited him.

I smiled back, a ripple of excitement working its way up my throat. I couldn't help it. The man just seemed to have that effect on me. I'd never had someone look at me the way he did, or if I had, I hadn't cared enough to notice. I felt special, and not in a bad way. But most important, he made me feel as though there was no one else he cared to look at or think about.

I really had no idea how anyone ever managed to get together with another human being. It seemed so complicated and difficult. So many elements needed to be in sync. The feelings had to be mutual. The emotions needed to be high. And, well, lots of other things needed to be just right. Chemicals and whatnot. That was all before even getting to physical compatibility.

I really should have been preparing myself for some nasty shocks, like a previous marriage—or a current one, for that matter. But I doubted there'd be any with Menem. I knew he wasn't conservative and that he'd had some fun in his twenties, but most people had. Besides, he'd volunteered that information himself.

Lara had told me not to believe him. "He's probably one of those guys who's fooled around and just wants to 'settle down' now," she accused.

To which I'd thought, *Yikes*, and said, "The whole madonna/whore complex, you mean?"

To which Lara had replied, "No, what's Madonna got to do with anything?" before looking at me as though I was daft.

But Menem's past did temporarily freak me out. What if I had him pegged completely wrong? He could have spent the last few years attending wild parties on the Greek islands. He may have been a complete Casanova, like a lecherous Arab man Lara had once flirted with, who preyed on innocent girls, and the sweetness was just all an act to capture the hearts and minds of unsuspecting young women. How was I to know?

But my gut instinct popped by unannounced, just when I almost had myself convinced. Nothing about Menem suggested I had the wrong idea about him. I knew in my heart and soul and every fiber of my being—and anything else you could throw in there—that Menem wasn't a playboy or Casanova.

Okay, he obviously wasn't fundy—he'd definitely had more experience with the opposite sex than, say, Hakeem. I knew this, but for some reason it didn't bother me. There were no double standards at play, and that mattered to me more than a couple of former girlfriends. Let's face it: completely observant types like Hakeem were rare.

Menem was respectable. More important, he attached value to things. He enjoyed life, which was sort of new agey when I thought about it. Oh, and he still lived with his parents without feeling a shred of embarrassment about it, which I felt deserved some cool points.

Anyway, when I wasn't feeling anxious about things or listening to Lara throw out convoluted theories, I was on top of the world. Menem and I clicked. There was a spark—a chemistry—and I couldn't stop thinking about him. The courtship rules were frustrating, and we were both exploring what we felt and how to show it. Messages were lovely. Our meetings always felt too brief. When I was alone, my imagination started to soar and I'd find myself yearning more deeply for things I couldn't yet have. My mind was in overdrive, and I'd begun to wonder how anyone could survive being in love.

Lara was soon missing in action. She'd slipped away unnoticed. As she'd barely done a thing, it wasn't a great loss to the working bee. She was probably outside pretending to be interested in Jamal's ute.

I was aching to get up and speak to Menem, but now a few of our parents had arrived, which made this difficult. Too chummy and I'd get lectured.

Mum was pretty stern in these matters.

I chose life.

Menem also knew better than to approach me. We were still in the pre-engagement getting-to-know-each-other stage, so we had to be extra proper about everything. It was getting to the point that he would have to officially propose if he wanted to continue seeing me, meaning I'd have to either accept or refuse.

He'd hinted on more than one occasion that he was ready to do so, but I'd changed the subject to something less frightening, like the old Greek lady who sat next to me on the bus and showed me pictures of her grandkids.

I *really* liked him. But I'd never visited this Serious Suitor place before. While the view was great, it was taking some time to settle in. I didn't want to rush, but I realized there were high school kids more experienced in relationships than I was, and that left me feeling embarrassed rather than stoic about my restraint. I was disappointed in myself for letting it get to me, but the rules all seemed too restrictive now that I actually had an interest in someone and he happened to want me.

Lara reappeared at lunch, plopping down beside me at the dinner table looking chirpy. We'd bought, amongst other things, barbecued chicken, fries, and cauliflower bake. Zahra's mother had also made fattoush, a tangy cucumber and radish salad with slivers of fried Lebanese bread, and Mum had made fried rice with pastirma, a cured beef packed with flavor.

"Hakeem wants you," Lara said, reaching over to grab a plate. I watched as she began furiously scooping food onto it, then after a moment's consideration, she opted for more salad too. "Did you hear what I said?" She looked at me expectantly.

"You're not going to start on that again, are you?" I frowned.

"No, I mean he actually asked for you. He's outside. He asked me to tell you to come out," she said.

"Really?" I said, a touch doubtfully.

"Yes, really. He's with Jamal. Go," she ordered. Then she began shoveling food into her mouth as though she'd just returned from an exhausting trek and hadn't eaten real food in weeks.

"Now?" I protested. "I haven't even finished my lunch."

Lara punched me in the thigh.

"Ow! What was that for?"

"Go, otherwise he's going to think I didn't pass on the message," she said with her mouth full.

"Okay, well, don't let anyone clear away my food," I said, getting up from my seat. Lara waved a yes with one hand as she continued to attack her plate with the other.

I went outside as Lara had instructed, maneuvering my way around a dressing table and sofa. I padded my way down the driveway and located Hakeem by Jamal's ute. My cousin was nowhere to be seen.

"Hey," I said as I approached.

Hakeem was roping up some furniture—what appeared to be dining table chairs. He was dressed in a pair of old jeans and a T-shirt, and wore a faded baseball cap turned backward. He turned to face me when I reached him.

"What's up?" He seemed a little tense.

"Lara said you asked for me?"

Hakeem's expression was one of confusion. "No," he said.

It was my turn to look confused. Then I felt embarrassed and foolish. My face flushed as I folded my arms awkwardly. Gawd, he must have thought I was lying.

"Oh," I said feebly. "I must have misunderstood her."

I was going to physically harm Lara. Actually hurt her. What on earth could she have been thinking, sending me out under false pretenses?

"She might have overheard me saying to Jamal that you'd need to wrap up some of the smaller things we're moving," said Hakeem. I wondered if he was trying to cover for Lara, but I doubted it. Besides, she had explicitly told me that Hakeem had asked for me, which had little connection to what Hakeem had just said.

"Sure, no problem," I told him.

"If you don't mind, that is," added Hakeem. "We're pretty tied up lugging this stuff back and forth." He shook his head. "They're not making things easy, doing it this way."

I nodded. "Yeah. Anyway, we'll be done with the party favors soon, so I'll help with the packing."

Hakeem shoved his hands into his pockets and looked away. But he didn't move. I smiled politely, about to leave, when he turned back to me.

"Will you be making party favors for yours next?" he said.

I looked up at him in shock, a little taken aback by the question. It wasn't what he'd said so much as how he'd said it. There was something in his tone.

"Um, I don't know," I managed, realizing I truly hadn't given it any thought.

He looked away again, a little broody, then went back to fixing the rope on the truck. I turned to go but stopped when I heard him say my name. Facing him again, I waited for him to say something. But before he could, Lara's voice crashed through the moment.

"Oh, there you are!" she said, coming down the driveway, acting oblivious to what was going on. Not that I actually had a handle on what exactly *was* going on here. But it seemed pretty obvious that Hakeem had wanted to say something important.

I looked behind me and my heart stopped when I saw that Menem was a few paces behind Lara. He slowed down as he got closer and smiled tightly at me. I had no idea what had just happened, but I knew he'd seen something he didn't like.

Lord, I hated weddings and all manner of wedding-related preparation.

By 5 p.m., the last bonbonnière had been constructed and Zahra's smaller pieces of furniture had been boxed. We'd separated into two teams because the bonbonnières were nearly done. Zahra and Sahar had finished them off, while I took care of the furniture. Lara supervised.

I would have much preferred continuing with bonbonnières, as it kept me safely within the dining room, but I wasn't as efficient as Sahar and there was no way Zahra was going to opt for manual labor. Since she was the bride, I figured that she was owed a free pass. I did the lugging, and kind of got stuck with the wrapping too. In any case, Zahra seemed rather pleased with the work we'd done. *And so she should be*, I thought. We'd done a great job, even if I did say so myself.

Still, I was feeling a bit crap after what had happened. I did my best to not show it, but I was also a little miffed at Lara. Ordinarily, I would have been furious, but I was more concerned about Menem's reaction than what had led to it. Playing on my mind was the look on Hakeem's face and the way he'd said my name. He'd clearly been about to reveal something significant. Or so I thought. I really had trouble reading the signs these days.

Menem didn't say anything to me about it, obviously. But I could see he was, well, upset? Annoyed? I wasn't quite sure. He was definitely *something*.

So my afternoon had gone to pieces. But I'd speak to Menem and sort everything out—I was sure of it. *Will it and it will be so*, I decided, in a moment of self-inspiration.

The bonbonnières were neatly placed into several boxes, ready for deployment next week. All the furniture had been moved to Zahra and Malek's new apartment. Everyone was present and accounted for. It was time to go, and not a minute too soon. It had been an exhausting weekend of hysteria, dancing, and drama.

Just as we were leaving, Zahra motioned me over to where she was standing in the hallway.

"Samira, um, thank you for helping out," she said, standing awkwardly with one leg crossed over the other. "Not just today," she added. "You've been very helpful the whole time."

I could see that it had been a bit of an effort for her to say it, but I did think it was rather good of her to have done so.

She produced a fancy paper bag from behind her. "This is for you," she said magnanimously.

It wasn't just any fancy paper bag. It was that distinct, signature robin's-egg blue.

Oh, my heart. Tiffany!

My mood lifted a tiny bit as I snuck a peek: a 'Return to Tiffany's' silver bracelet. "Thanks, Zahra," I responded in surprise, still not sure how to deal with my New and Improved cousin. "It was my pleasure to help out," I added, and not just because of the Tiffany gift. Although I had to stop myself from reaching out and saying, "The darling thing!"

I'd always wanted to do that.

The last three months really had been quite strange. Life altering. At times, wonderful.

Chapter 29

As it turned out, Menem was a very accomplished brooder. I'd have never put him down as one, what with star brooders like Hakeem about. But he wasn't happy. Placid, easygoing, patient Menem was showing signs of discontent.

I couldn't blame him. He was used to dating, I guess. Actual relationships, not courtships. And despite my depth of feeling for him, I was holding back, and he knew it.

And now he'd seen me with Hakeem and gotten completely the wrong idea. Or at least I thought he had. I wasn't sure exactly what Menem was thinking, what he must have been imagining about Hakeem and me.

I was doing my utmost to shut out any Hakeem- and Menem-related thoughts as I did the obligatory Monday-morning tasks: checking emails, running through the week's location shoots, confirming conference schedules, etc., etc. I just wanted to shove them way into the back of the closet. Remember them next summer and bring them out again.

I wished I could. But Hakeem's face was boring into my mind, as was Menem's as he'd approached us on the driveway yesterday.

I didn't want to live in a world where Lara could be right about affairs of the heart. But—and there was always a but—

recently Hakeem's behavior had graduated from unsuspicious brooding to outright questionable. And it was affecting me. I couldn't deny that. I had no idea what any of it meant, though. But I was quite sure it most definitely wasn't because I was in love with him.

I would have known.

Perhaps I needed him. I was certainly used to him. But surely I would have known if I wanted to marry him. Don't even get me started on *Anne of Green Gables*. Gilbert Blythe had to be on his deathbed before Anne realized she loved him. Which was just silly.

As if you wouldn't know.

Anyway, I didn't want to overreact. Menem had looked *something*, but it wasn't as if he'd come storming down the driveway and challenged Hakeem to a duel. (It would have been a striking moment if he had, to be fair.)

Instead, Menem had spent the rest of yesterday afternoon moving furniture, unable to speak with me. I hadn't heard from him in the evening—no phone call, no message, no email. I'd expected accusations to be flung my way. Even a public denouncement wouldn't have surprised me, although I did concede later that that was a little fanciful.

Then came the email at work: Menem asking if I was ready to move on to the next step. Just like that. It was barely civil, and I didn't know how I felt or how to respond.

When I summoned the courage to email him back, I wrote that I honestly didn't know if I was ready. I thought I had more time—which I did, until Hakeem had given me that strange look yesterday and asked me that strange question about whether we'd be making party favors for me soon, making me all confused.

Of course, I wrote an essay, but somewhere, probably around the fifth sentence, I mentioned that I was afraid. I studiously avoided any mention of the moment at Zahra's house. I hit send, feeling completely anxious. His response didn't help matters.

> Subject: Re: Going forward
> Samira, I'd like to see you. Can you please meet me outside your building in ten minutes?
> I won't leave the office until you let me know.
> Menem

Approximately ten minutes later I was pacing outside my building, my heels clicking against the pavement. The lovely weather was an affront to my mood and I fought the urge to rush back inside and sulk. I further toyed with the notion of taking up smoking since drowning my sorrows in alcohol was not an option and I already had too much sugar and caffeine in my diet.

I stopped pacing when I saw Menem approaching, a knot forming in my stomach. I took in the blue suit, the white business shirt, his tie. He looked beautiful as he crossed the courtyard outside my drab building.

"Hi," I said. I was fit to burst with emotion, but I kept my expression neutral. Menem looked slightly stunned.

"Hi," he replied. He indicated the park behind my building and we walked toward it in silence.

We found a bench to sit on, and for a moment we were both quiet, only the sound of traffic and pedestrians walking along the footpath intruding.

I was the first to speak. "I'm so sorry, Menem."

"Maybe I'm daft, but what's going on?" He looked hurt and frustrated, and I just wanted to cry then and there.

I studied my shoes. "Nothing. Nothing has changed."

"I thought the feelings were mutual," he said after a pause.

"They are. Look, it's not that simple. We don't know each other that well yet. This isn't easy for me. I don't want to rush."

It might have sounded like an excuse, but it was the truth. I mean, clearly we were both interested, but we'd barely scratched the surface of getting to know each other. There was none of that instinct you share with someone you've known for ages.

"I might not be religious, but I'm not a player. I don't make it a habit of befriending women and pursuing them for kicks," said Menem.

"I never said that you're a flirt."

"What's going on then?"

"There's nothing going on!"

"Samira, that guy I saw you with—your family friend . . ." He stopped when he saw my look of mortification.

I felt so cheap all of a sudden, as though he'd caught me in a wild embrace with Hakeem. Meanwhile, Menem actually looked hurt. I'd never seen him like this. Could it be that he was just jealous? I wouldn't like that, and until now, he had shown no signs of such insecurity.

"Samira, look, is there something I should know? Do I have competition?"

I shook my head. "No. Menem, I don't know what you think you saw, but there's nothing going on. Hakeem's just my friend. I've known him all my life."

Menem shook his head. "Samira, please. I saw how he looked at you."

"It's not like that," I said, flustered. Amazing. Hakeem barely ever made eye contact with me, such was his piety and respect. Of course, the one time he did, Menem had seen it and blown it all out of proportion.

Menem studied me. "Modest to the end."

There was another moment of awkward silence. I shuffled my feet, biting my lip, unable to sit still.

"Samira, if you don't want this, I'm not going to push you," said Menem.

"Why are you saying this?"

"Because I don't think I'm what you want," he said, and I detected hurt and frustration in his tone.

"How would you know that?"

"I would marry you tomorrow if I could. Can you say the same for me?"

"I'm not you. This doesn't come so easily to me. And forgive me if I don't really want to say yes to you via an email."

Menem looked startled. Then, placing his hands on his lap, he took a deep breath. "Do you just need more time?"

"Yes," I admitted. "I'm afraid."

"What are you afraid of? I know I don't deserve you—"

"Please don't ever say that. You're a wonderful man. You really are. I'm the messed up one here." Positively and categorically screwed up. I considered projecting, but I'd be spoiled for choice on who and what to blame.

Menem shook his head. "You're not messed up," he said, more gently this time. "You obviously just know what you want."

"That's just it, I don't." I really didn't. I'd thought I did. But I'd gotten so used to dud door-knockers, it had never occurred to me to prepare for what could follow. I supposed I'd always expected it would come naturally to me; I'd always thought marriage was a given. How could I have any chance of a normal relationship when the options were marriage or being alone, with nothing in between?

Menem stared at the ground, his hands between his knees. "Samira, I'm not going to pressure you," he said, resignation in every syllable.

I wanted to say, "No! I do want this!" But I couldn't get the words out. Instead, I said, "Whatever it is you think is the reason for my doubt, it has nothing to do with you, and there is no one else I'm considering."

"I understand," he said, in a tone that suggested he didn't understand at all. "I know we don't know each other the way we would if we could just date normally. But I've fallen for you, completely. I would take care of you," he added quietly. "I don't want to drag this on. We both know it's better to move things along."

"I'm sorry," I said. Everything was slipping through my fingers and I was frozen, unable to stop it.

"Don't be. It's fine," said Menem, rising from the bench. He buttoned his jacket and looked around him. "I have to get back."

"Wait, Menem, don't go. Please, don't leave like this."

"Samira, you know how much I care about you. But you're making this really difficult for me."

I shook my head, ready to defend myself, but I had nothing to say. I barely registered the tears brimming in my eyes.

"We all have hang-ups," he said. "But the woman I met on that team-building day . . . What happened to her?" He turned to face me, and I looked up at him. "You were different. You were feisty. I mean, don't get me wrong. I love being with you. But you seem like another person sometimes."

My face was burning. What, now I had two personalities? Well, I was glad I was finding this out now. I wouldn't want to marry someone who felt like he was getting two for the price of one.

I now refused to look at him, instead directing my attention to a couple of pigeons pecking about on the grass, inspecting the remains of someone's lunch.

"I'm not saying you have two personalities," said Menem, reading my bloody mind, just as he'd done that first time I met him (apparently as Samira version 1.0).

"What are you saying then, Menem?"

"I feel like the person I met at team building is you. But when you're around others . . . My God, your family, they're like—"

"Hey!"

He backed off, but not without shaking his head once in frustration.

"I had a fight with my best friend because of you," I said, feeling a little peeved. "She was rude to you and we didn't speak for over a week! I have never done that in my life." I fidgeted on the bench, wishing I was anywhere but on this grotty old seat.

"Samira, can't you see what I'm saying?"

"No, I can't." I crossed my arms against my chest.

"The constant demands, the way your mum watches every move you make. Let's not forget the running," he said.

"What are you on about?"

"Weren't you, like, a champion runner? I saw the trophies in your house."

"I was in primary school!"

"You downplay it, but I know you were good, so something made you stop."

"Does it look like I can be a runner, Menem?" I lifted the edge of my headscarf.

"Oh, whatever. That's just an excuse." He began pacing, hands jammed into his trouser pockets. His sweet face was overtaken by angry lines, and I didn't like it one bit. For as long as I'd known Menem, he'd been a soothing presence, and it was hard to imagine any negative energy around him.

"You know what, I think *I* have to leave now," I said, amazed at how badly the conversation was going. I stood up, arms crossed at my chest.

"What do you want, Samira?"

"What kind of question is that?" I stared at him, sizing him up as though he was a dodgy cop nosing about my affairs.

"A really simple one. What do you want? Imagine you can have anything in the world right now—anything. What's the first thing that comes to mind?"

I had no idea what my expression was, but Menem nodded.

"All right then."

I shook my head. "What's your problem with hijab anyway?" I said.

"Excuse me?"

"You make it seem like me quitting the running thing is a cop-out, but it's not that simple," I continued.

"Wait a second, don't even go there. Your hijab is about you, not me. Why are you even mentioning it?"

"Because I think it bothers you," I replied.

"Why would it bother me?"

"You asked me if I'd ever thought about taking it off, and—"

"It was just a question," Menem said in frustration.

"But why would you even ask that?"

"Curiosity, Samira. That's all. Obviously, I have no idea what it's like to be in your position."

"But—"

"But nothing. You know I think you're beautiful; you could be wearing a sack and I'd feel the same," he said. "But I don't think hijab is the be-all and end-all, and I wouldn't blame you if you didn't want to wear it. I'm Muslim too, remember? I have nothing against it. If I didn't like you the way you are, I wouldn't be putting myself through all of this." He shook his head, and I could see he was calculating the monumental mistake he'd made in showing interest in me, and I wondered at my own ability to make the situation deteriorate even further. A moment later, he said, "I really have to get going."

A little dazed, I faced him, my arms still positioned across my chest. I could have told him I was sorry for underestimating him, but the words wouldn't come.

We said nothing. He walked me back to my building, then politely farewelled me. A huge part of me didn't want him to leave, but I watched him go.

Thankfully, the next few days at work positively sped by. I had two location shoots, one with Gabriel, who didn't seem terribly pleased with me either.

I didn't care. I was busy, and pressure equaled distraction. If it had been a slow week, I'd be thinking and worrying about Zahra's wedding on Saturday. And that small matter of my own possible engagement to Menem. Not forgetting Hakeem's role in this whole sorry affair.

Naturally, a few random thoughts crept in here and there, even when I had a temperamental model to deal with, unexpected humidity and showers, and a busload of Japanese tourists smack bang in the middle of a location at Rose Bay Wharf.

But yes, distractions helped. As did caffeine and sugar. I was better at getting my prayers done too, which was also something positive to come out of it.

And I had one more thing to focus on: my cadetship interview with *Childhood* magazine. I had sidelined it amid the wedding duties and Menem. But I had to write a pitch for a feature article in advance of my interview next week. I was stuck. What did I know about raising kids?

Chapter 30

Saturday, November 22—the day of my cousin Zahra's wedding—finally arrived with a generous amount of fanfare. The sun burst out, hinting at the summer that was to come. Despite the great excitement, there was an atmosphere of calm. I was pleasantly surprised at my own serenity. No more stress to be found here, thank you very much.

Well, perhaps a few remnants.

I should have felt energized about the day ahead, but I was dreading it because Menem would be there and things would be uneasy between us. And, well, Hakeem would be there and things would be uneasy between us.

Lara and I were assembled at Zahra's place, waiting for Malek to arrive and for the hire cars to collect us.

I'd totally forgotten that we would have to trail along while Zahra and Malek had their wedding photos taken, incidentally by a photographer that I, anointed wedding expert, had recommended.

And then followed the terrible realization that I'd have to be in some of the photos, which I absolutely had not signed up for. I'd been hoping that Zahra would be so self-absorbed and so deeply "Zahra" that Lara and I would barely get a nod.

By three in the afternoon, we were all ready to go. Lara

and I were dressed in our lovely bridesmaid gowns, frilly and fabulous all around. Lara's hair was curled, hanging loosely except for a tiny knot at the back. I had my headscarf tied back with the ends rolled into a small bun at the nape of my neck. I wore stud earrings that glinted in the light. The bridesmaid dress itself was actually quite flattering and not too tight.

I found Zahra sitting alone in her bedroom, just as I had on the night of her layleeya. Once again, she had her hands at her sides and her eyes shut tight. She looked tiny in the voluminous dress, which she had spread all about her, covering three-quarters of the bed.

"You okay?" I asked her. I carefully repositioned a section of Zahra's skirt and took a seat beside her.

She nodded and took a deep breath. Perhaps this was her calming-down ritual. Maybe this was what lawyers did before their court appearances and meetings with major clients. I'd no idea, but I realized that she needed some reassurance and hoped I could provide some (unofficial counselor and all).

"It'll be just fine once you're at the reception," I told her. Of course, I had no idea if that was true, but what else was I supposed to tell her? It seemed to me like the hard part was over. After all, they were Islamically married already, and they seemed to have worked things out after the selfish episode the other week. But what did I know?

"You look really beautiful, Samira," said Zahra with a brief smile.

"Thanks," I said, surprised. "You look amazing."

She really did.

"It's difficult, you know," said Zahra.

"What is?"

"Being married. I mean, I know I don't live with Malek yet. But just being in a couple is hard. It's not just you anymore."

"I can imagine." That was all I could do, really.

"Malek is very protective," Zahra said slowly. So slowly in fact that she seemed to be regretting the words the moment she uttered them. Her face turned a little red. "Najwa made a big thing of it. It bugged her that I would tell Malek where we were going when we went out. Like I said, he's protective. But also, why shouldn't I tell him? I expected the same from him when he went out."

"Protective in a good way?" I said.

Reading between the very tight lines, Zahra seemed to be suggesting that she had to answer to Malek. A lot. Granted, it would be an adjustment for Zahra to listen to anyone. But I could sense there was more to it, and I was worried.

Oh God, what was I supposed to say? Was this one of those You-don't-have-to-go-through-with-this-if-you-don't-want-to moments? That always happened in the movies. People did nikah then called it off. It was hard on the women more than the men, but there was a way out.

Instead, I opted for, "Are you sure everything is all right?" Hang the expense, I would have added, but since I wasn't paying for the wedding, it wasn't really my place.

Zahra didn't answer immediately. "I think so. It's different. I'm not answering to him, but I can't just act like I'm single. Najwa doesn't get it."

I waited, wondering if there was more, unsure if what she was telling me was really just a case of losing some threads of independence and her best friend roasting her about it because she was feeling neglected.

"It must hurt not to have Najwa be supportive," I said.

Zahra nodded and smiled. "Yeah. But I'm fine."

But she wasn't exactly fine. Five minutes later we were still sitting on her bed, Zahra with her arms stretched out behind her as though she was on a picnic blanket.

"Marry someone you can be yourself with," she advised, settling in for a chat, apparently unaware that this was her wedding day.

"Inshallah," I replied, invoking the response that never failed to work in any awkward situation.

"Menem is a good guy," continued Zahra. "Hakeem is too. Even if they're both very different."

I laughed, confused. "Okay, I don't—"

Zahra smirked. "Please. Just because we're not close doesn't mean I don't know things."

"What things exactly?" I was genuinely curious.

"Well, obviously Menem's into you," she said. "He's been to your house and you're getting to know him. But Hakeem is a different story."

"And what do you know about Hakeem?" I asked.

Zahra smirked again. "He's only liked you for the last five years."

"He's been engaged before. Don't you think he would have asked for me if he liked me?"

"You'd think so. Look, Samira. I never told you, for obvious reasons, but I was interested in Hakeem once."

I had no idea what my facial expression was, but Zahra hastily continued.

"It was a long time ago. But he wasn't interested."

"What happened?"

"Nothing. I just tried to chat with him online, I'd find excuses to email him—that kind of thing." Zahra laughed and straightened up. She brushed away a loose curl, a thoughtful expression on her face.

"And he didn't respond?" I held my breath in anticipation, feeling an unidentifiable twinge all of a sudden.

"Oh no, he responded, but it was always so formal, and, well, it was very clear he wasn't interested. So I backed off."

"Well, that doesn't mean he likes me," I told her, feeling a bit relieved.

"Samira, he likes you. I can't believe a person of your intelligence thinks he'd waste his time unless he didn't."

"Don't look now, Zahra, but you're paying me compliments," I said lightly.

She grimaced. "Don't get used to it." She might have been joking, but I pretended she wasn't. Much safer that way. We'd come a long way from snarky conversations about marinated olives and television shows, but I wasn't sure Zahra and I would ever be close.

"You'd make a good lawyer," she said a moment later.

"Why's that?"

"Because you demand indisputable evidence for everything."

I thought I'd make a terrible lawyer. I'd get all flustered and probably start crying if things were going badly. "But it's all circumstantial!" I'd wail as they carted away my innocent client.

I rose from the bed and patted down my dress, taking a quick look around to make sure everything was in order. The carpet was littered with bits and pieces—the box from the florist, some plastic bags, and a nightie—so I gathered them and placed them in the corner by the door.

"For what it's worth," continued Zahra, "it's not enough to have a connection and like someone. You really need to be on the same path. If Malek and I didn't want the same things, it could never work. You know?"

"I guess so," I said, not sure what else to say.

She looked at me a moment. "Menem really is crazy about you."

Thankfully, just as my stomach was about to turn in on itself, Lara interrupted the heart-to-heart. "Your husband's here in a fancy car. You ready?"

Zahra cleared her head with a little shake. "Yes, I suppose it's time to get going."

"Wait," I said to Zahra. "Are you sure everything's okay?" I couldn't let her go without asking again if she was all right. I looked her directly in the eyes and she nodded, biting the inside of her bottom lip.

The noise levels in the house rose as more family entered, all calling out for the bride. Zahra listened, her face lighting up. In an instant, she was more relaxed, and she smiled as she rose from the bed. "I love him. I'm just not used to making decisions with someone else," she told me. "It's an independence thing. You wouldn't—" But then she saw my look and stopped. "Thank you for everything," she said.

Zahra's mum came into the room then, tears gushing down her face, and Zahra looked as though she was about to lose it too. But, remarkably, she kept her composure as she hugged her mother tightly. I got a little teary myself as I watched them.

Someone had commandeered a duff, a hand drum Muslims favor for music, and was playing it in the living room. The beat was accompanied by several male voices and clapping. The music filtered through to us as Aunt Shaimaa took her daughter's hand and led her out to the waiting guests. Aunts and uncles and cousins were all gathered around, Zahra's father standing to the side, his eyes also full of tears as he clapped and sang.

I spotted Menem just as I was wiping away my own tears, clapping enthusiastically with a grin on his face. He looked, of course, extremely handsome in his suit and he was clean-shaven again. He nodded once at me, then turned his attention back to the bride and groom.

That was it. Even though I was hurt and disappointed, I was going to force myself not to worry about it. I was at a wedding, after all; a celebration. Smile and say, "Cheese."

By now, just about everyone was clapping in time to the music, and I joined in. Zahra and Malek stood together by the couch, happy and excited, while my father and my uncle Hamza danced in a circle in front of them, stamping their feet, their hands in the air. I watched as Zahra clutched her husband's arm and looked up at him, beaming.

Shortly after, the women in the room let loose with the zaghroota, that high-pitched ululation heard at every Arab celebration.

True to her word, Zahra hadn't organized a cardboard cutout wedding reception with the standard trimmings. She'd done her homework (with my help, I conceded), and the hard work had paid off because the hall looked beautiful.

White linen cloths and smaller silver satin pieces covered the round tables. Each featured a simple but elegant white cake platter holding a bouquet of off-white flowers. There were small candles in little glass holders, and the bonbonnières we'd made for each guest sat beside place cards with calligraphed names.

This wasn't a big woggy wedding, but it was far from a simple Islamic one; it was somewhere in between. That seemed a fitting notion: life had always involved a struggle of some sort, really, trying to connect two very different things.

It was nice to be sitting down following a tiring afternoon outdoors. I'd begged Zahra not to have her photos taken in the standard places: by the Harbour Bridge and along the Nurses Walk at The Rocks. I gave her the gift of my location shoot knowledge. I knew of a lesser known but just as beautiful spot in Watsons Bay, about twenty minutes from the city. I generously offered the tip to Zahra, but she didn't want to listen.

"The Nurses Walk, Samira!" she said pseudohysterically as we set off in the hire car. I remained calm, even while the men looked on in amusement.

"No, we're not going to the Nurses Walk. You'll have to get in line if we do. There'll be other couples there. Driver!" I said, shouting over Zahra. I'd always wanted to say that. Of course, I'd always envisioned it along with something more exciting, like "Driver! Follow that car!" not "Driver! Watsons Bay and take the Cross City Tunnel!"

"Where am I going, ladies?" said the exasperated man after another thirty seconds of bickering. Sydney whooshed by as he drove along, unsure which direction to take.

"The Nurses Walk!" said Zahra, leaning forward.

"The photographer won't be there! I told him to go to Watsons Bay!" Which granted was sneaky, but I'd been left in charge of organizing it, so it was tough luck.

I gave the driver precise instructions and he nodded. After several minutes of pouting, sighing, and "It's my wedding—shouldn't I decide where I have my photos taken?" Malek reached over to take his bride's hand.

"I think you should leave it to Samira," he said, amused.

Obviously, he couldn't care less where the photos were taken, but it was going to be a long drive if things continued this way.

When we arrived and she saw how amazing the hidden spot was, she shut up pretty quickly, actually looking grateful at one point.

Menem still hadn't said a word to me. I'd go so far as to say he seemed indifferent. There were no discreet looks, no signs of silent longing. If it weren't for the acknowledgment back at Zahra's house, I'd be wondering if he knew I was there at all. I couldn't allow myself to think about how that made me feel, though (still terrible, for the record). At least not right now. So I kept my feelings to myself. Lara hadn't broached the subject. The most she'd ventured to say about Menem was, "Bloody hell, he *is* dashing."

Back at the hall, Lara and I were seated at the same table as the bride and groom, with Menem and the parents from both sides. The best thing about the wedding reception was that it was the first time in years we—meaning assorted family members with whom I'd spent my earlier, somewhat formative years—were all gathered together. Just like old times. Zahra's brothers had also come to Sydney to attend the festivities. It was hard to believe that once upon a time I'd attended Saturday school with them. Even my brother, Omar, was here, and he'd given me rare praise about my appearance when he'd seen me earlier. Sahar was missing, though. She'd declined the invitation when the wedding went from small and modest to cirque du spectacular.

I spotted Hakeem sitting beside his father in the center of the hall and felt a little rumble of anxiety as I waved at them. Hakeem's expression was unreadable.

Chapter 31

By the time the third R&B dance song began blasting through the speakers, I was ready for an intermission. I watched the teeming dance floor, where even my father and Uncle Hamza were joining in. Embarrassing, particularly as they had no idea they were dancing to suggestive lyrics.

Menem was also there, dancing with his brother, and for the briefest of moments we caught sight of each other. Our eyes locked and I felt a sweep of nerves rush through me. For a second, I was breathless, then he turned away and I smiled scathingly to myself.

I needed to get out of the hall and get some fresh air.

"I'll be outside if anyone wants me," I told Lara as I placed my napkin on the table.

She barely looked up, preoccupied with a message she'd just received. "Okies. But wait, there's dancing!"

I exited the hall, breathing in the crisp, clear night air. After walking around the parking lot for ten minutes, I still didn't want to go back inside. My wanderings led me to the side of the building, where I found a set of steps I could sit and rest on for a few moments. There were some cardboard boxes beside a dumpster, so I took one and flattened it before placing it on the step. I sat down, careful not to stain or damage my dress, then stretched out my legs. I admired my shoes: they had pretty diamanté across zigzag straps. My feet were freshly pedicured—Zahra had treated us to some pampering yesterday.

I turned my attention to the few people milling about, most of whom I didn't recognize. I people-watched for a few minutes, the sound of the bass coming from the entrance to the hall.

"Hey," came a man's voice.

Hakeem.

I straightened. "Hi," I said, that anxious rumbling in my stomach returning.

"Some wedding, huh," he noted without commitment. Hakeem didn't like these gatherings in general; add music and dancing, and he was ready to leave. Lord knows why he even came—probably for his father's sake more than anything.

"Well, Zahra wanted a fancy wedding. At least we're being spared the belly dancers," I said lightly.

Hakeem kicked around a small bottle beside the dumpster. He had his hands shoved in his jacket pockets and he looked sullen. He continued kicking the bottle around until it landed meters away, the sound of glass rolling on concrete louder than the muffled music. I fought the urge to go and pick it up and put it in the bin. Instead I sat mutely on the steps, unsure whether or not I should get up and leave or stay and try for more conversation.

Just as I was about to go with the former, Hakeem turned and looked at me, kind of in the same way he had the other day at Zahra's house.

"Samira," he said, but that was it.

I waited for more. When he still hadn't said anything several seconds later, I started to get annoyed. For God's sake. What did he want to say? What was with the high drama levels? Should I just put the bottle in the rubbish?

Still nothing.

"May I speak plainly?" I said at last.

I'd always wanted to say that. "May I speak plainly?" was so much better than "Can I be honest?" It didn't exactly fit in the context of this conversation, but never mind.

"Of course," said Hakeem. He moved closer to me.

How was I going to say this? I could deal with quotes and being lectured and annoying him. Messages were easy enough. But any sort of face-to-face confrontation demanded a movement beyond my comfort zone. Besides all that, I wasn't quite sure what I was even thinking, or if I wanted to know what Hakeem had to say.

"Were you going to say something to me the other day? At Zahra's place?" I said, a thrill rushing through me.

"Yes, I was," said Hakeem.

I felt a little sick. I hadn't expected him to give in so quickly; I thought I'd have a few minutes of buffering. My heart thumped.

"Okay," I managed. "What did you want to say?"

Hakeem didn't reply. He studied the wall while I waited, patiently, all the while feeling as though a paperweight was squatting in my stomach.

Finally, Hakeem looked at me again and said, "You're not dumb."

I almost laughed. God, his behavior was odd. I had to rule

out drunkenness for obvious reasons; I had absolutely no doubt that Hakeem had never touched a drop in his life. *Maybe he's on meds*, I thought, a little alarmed.

"Thanks?" I said.

Hakeem shook his head in frustration. "No, what I mean is, surely you know what I want to say to you."

"Actually," I stammered, "I don't."

Hakeem looked deeply uncomfortable.

Out with it, I wanted to yell. The suspense was killing me!

"You know I care about you," he said.

I felt another thrill slide through me. "I care about you too," I said, a bit nervously because this was Hakeem and I didn't want to freak him out. Propriety and so forth.

"I never asked for you," he continued.

"No, you didn't."

"Should I have?" he said.

I fixed my eyes on the ground, feeling embarrassed and out of place, as though I'd stepped into someone else's strappy heels for the evening. "Why would you ask me that?" I said. "Of course not."

"Of course not," he said, his voice low.

"I never expected you to," I told him. Well, apart from that awkward adolescent period, before the door-knocks. More silence. "Hakeem, what are you doing?"

"I want you to marry me," he said quickly. Just like that.

"Excuse me?"

He hesitated. "I want you to marry me."

I stared at him in disbelief. "What?"

Hearing Hakeem say this was *not* something for which I'd prepared myself. I'd been half expecting him to come out with a logical explanation for his behavior of late. Alien abduction.

Lack of sleep. Brotherly concern that I might not have a big, fancy wedding like Zahra. That sort of thing.

"Would you? Would you marry me?" said Hakeem, as though he was asking if I'd seen his misplaced wallet.

"Why are you asking me this?" I said.

"Because I should have asked you a long time ago," said Hakeem.

"Why didn't you then?"

"I had my reasons, I suppose," he said mysteriously.

"And they no longer exist?"

"No . . . they do."

It was a riddle that for the life of me I couldn't figure out. Was it my job? My penchant for *The Princess Bride*? My inability to cook anything that required measurements? Objections to my family? (Obviously, a ludicrous proposition. Who wouldn't like my family?)

"And those reasons would be what exactly?" I asked.

"We know each other well. But I wasn't sure if our relationship would translate well to domestic life."

Well, wasn't he just a ray of bloody sunshine? I felt a bit wounded. And hurt. Stunned all the while, but nevertheless hurt. He was proposing, but he was reluctant. I'd not seen this coming. The good news, it quickly occurred to me, was that I had a new category: The Reluctant Suitor (glass half full and all that).

"Right," I said, my face burning.

"Don't get me wrong," said Hakeem, "I want to be with you. But we're so different."

"No kidding." He was about to say something more, but I interrupted with, "Are you just saying this now because there's someone else in the picture?"

"Well, I don't want to lose you," he confessed. He looked torn and a bit helpless.

"Why not before today then?"

"I told you why."

"But now that's different because it looks as though I may actually get engaged?"

"Samira, do you realize what marriage is? Do you realize it won't just be about banter and quotes?"

"Excuse me?"

"You'll have responsibilities. You'll have to adjust to a new way of life," said Hakeem.

My offense levels had capped. "Wow." I laughed. "I always thought you saw me as young, even when you said otherwise. But this is worse."

Hakeem looked frustrated. "I didn't say that. You're intelligent. And kind and funny. And you're a good Muslim woman. I care about you deeply."

"But? I'm silly and have no idea that marriage involves responsibility?" I replied, helping him along.

"Why are you angry?" he said, flustered. "If your answer is no, that's all you have to say."

I stared at him, swimming in disbelief and confusion. I knew he had a tendency to behave like a strict father, more so than my real one, in fact. I'd never really cared in the past, mainly because I could just ignore half of what he said and block him on Facebook until the waves passed. But right now, I couldn't do that. Everything I knew of Hakeem flew right out the window. He didn't seem stern; he seemed like another person. And I was so mad at him for it.

"Here's a little tip," I began brusquely. "When you're telling someone you want to spend your life with her, it's not a good idea to make her feel like an idiot."

I got up from the step and brushed myself off, ready to storm away. He'd managed to compliment me *and* acknowledge my sparkling wit (albeit in different words) *and* insult me at the same time.

"Samira, wait," said Hakeem.

"What?" I said, turning around. "What else could you possibly have to say?" I wanted to add more but I was suddenly speechless. I was on the verge of laughing—that horrible feeling of wanting to laugh when it's least appropriate to do so.

I didn't, though. Then—involuntarily—Elizabeth Bennet's diatribe against Darcy popped into my head. The one where she says that nothing could have enticed her to marry him even if he had behaved in a more gentleman-like manner. I would have thrown a line or two Hakeem's way, but given the mood, it would have gone straight over his head. That and I didn't think my Australian accent would have done it much justice.

"I don't mean to hurt your feelings." He looked truly upset. "I'm not good at this."

"No, you're not," I agreed.

"I'm not insulting you," he said. "You're a wonderful person."

"But you never proposed because you worried I'd be a bad wife?"

He obviously had no idea how seriously I took marriage. I wouldn't still be single, going through all this nonsense, if I didn't.

"I never said that you'd be a bad wife," he said, annoyed.

"You didn't have to."

Hakeem looked like his patience was due for a refill any

moment. "You drive me crazy," he said. His tone suggested that it was *not* in an adorable, lovable sort of way.

"I'm sorry I drive you crazy," I said flatly. "No one's ever forced you to talk to me. If it causes you so much grief, just stop."

Hakeem gave an exasperated sigh. "You want different things than me, Samira. I'm keenly aware of it. I'm not even sure I'd be a good husband to you."

"Fine. So why do this now? Why ruin it all?"

Hakeem flinched. He looked, I imagined, as one might when a sword slices through them. "Because I had to try."

I softened a little. Then a lot. I suddenly felt terrible. He looked so miserable and vulnerable now, not angry. I could have easily cried right then and there.

I cared about Hakeem. He obviously cared about me. So what *was* it? We were like two magnets, resisting each other.

And in a flash, it hit me like a sales stampede at Kmart.

"Hakeem, this is us when we're not on Facebook," I said. "This is us, period. We argue all the time."

Hakeem looked away, then he nodded. Neither of us said a word. I studied him. He still looked sad, but not so desperately miserable. Call me crazy, but I thought I sensed some relief on his end, and that I understood.

There were too many emotions to sort through, and the tears that had been on standby were raring to go. I did my best to contain them, which of course only made them more desperate to break free. A few managed it, sliding neatly and fiercely down my face in an act of mutiny.

"Would you have said yes? If I had asked before?" said Hakeem tentatively.

"How can I answer that?"

I had no idea what I would have said. Most likely, had he approached me, I would have considered him. If I let the Mangas and the Metrosexuals in, of course I would have let Hakeem in. I had liked him for such a long time. It might not have led to anything in the end. We seemed to be a case of sounding great in theory, but not being so great in practice, something this proposal would only cement for good. But I would have let him in. And served him tea and Turkish coffee and fruit, and maybe for a moment it would have seemed possible.

He just never tried. He didn't ask. He never even hinted. Not until a Serious Suitor came into my life, someone I now genuinely cared about.

Menem. God, I had messed this up.

"I'm sorry," said Hakeem.

Tears all over the place. I pulled out a tissue I had tucked into my belt and wiped my eyes, feeling horrible and confused. "Why are you sorry?" I said.

"I've only ever wanted the best for you. You know that, right?"

I did. He wanted "more" for me; that's what he'd told me in the kitchen what seemed an eternity ago. I hadn't forgotten. So I nodded, my face frozen from the effort not to cry even more. "Ditto."

We were both quiet. Then I said, "Lara's been on my back about you, you know. She said you were jealous. I thought she was just being Lara." I sniffed and laughed.

Hakeem nodded. "Well, not my finest moments, I suppose." He sat on the steps, his movements slow, his head down, and I sat back down beside him. More quiet, still crying because this felt like goodbye. "Samira," he said. "I'm sorry. Please don't think I meant we'd be wrong for each other because of you."

"It's okay. You want something else. So do I."

"In a way, yes," he admitted. "But I've liked you for so long. I just couldn't bring myself to do anything about it."

"Hakeem, there's a reason for that," I said. "You said it yourself."

"How? I feel like we're connected. But then I see a glimpse of what it would be like and I think, *I can't do that to her* . . ."

This was Hakeem and I without banter and quotes, perhaps looking in the same direction but arguing about which road to take to get there. And I couldn't help it, but I was still bothered by his estimation of my partnering abilities. I may have helped Blockbuster reach its annual budget when I was a teenager, but I wasn't a completely delusional half-wit. Only a mild one. For starters, I knew that all of this shouldn't be such hard work; life was going to be difficult enough. As if I didn't realize there was more to marriage than banter and quotes. Of course I bloody well did. I'd had many conversations with Menem that didn't involve either. Thoughtful, deep discussions about life and joy and, well, serious things.

Menem. Patient and adoring and ready to make things happen within a week of his first visit because he'd felt certain. I'd known Hakeem my entire life and he'd never once had the courage to give it a try.

"I'm sorry if I've hurt you with my response," I said.

"I deserve it."

We shared a look.

"That *was* the worst proposal I've ever had." I laughed again, still all sniffy.

Hakeem smiled. "I'll know better for next time."

"Maybe check with me first."

"You'll be spoken for by then, I'm sure."

"Maybe not. Things aren't going too well. I might have messed everything up."

"Kulshi qismeh wa naseeb," said Hakeem. In everything there is your share, your destiny. "Did you ever think of me in that way?"

"Yes," I said. "When I was younger."

"And after?"

"Well. Around first-year uni," I confessed. "But after that I never really allowed myself to. You got engaged a couple of times. You never showed interest. I guess part of me wondered, but I kept it out of mind." The boat had set sail on that front long ago, and there it was, melting into the horizon. I wasn't going to call it back.

Hakeem nodded. "Yeah."

"I wanted you in my life, though," I said. And that was true.

Just then, I wanted so much to get up and go find Menem to speak to him. But I didn't move despite the ache lingering in the pit of my stomach. I couldn't leave Hakeem alone and I wasn't ready to say goodbye to him.

We sat side by side for a little while, a load lifted. Things felt less intense, despite an overwhelming sense of loss. Whoever said that nothing in life is ever simple wasn't joking. All of that conjecture, all the drama, all this love between us, and it came down to this: a heartbreaking "what-if." Hakeem seemed better, but the look on his face still broke my heart.

"You know," he began, "even though we both know it wouldn't work, I just don't know how to live without you, Samira."

"You don't have to."

But his look said the complete opposite. Marriage, for either of us, would change everything, and we both knew it.

I found myself reaching out my hand to him. After a few seconds, he took it in both of his and squeezed it tight. My heart hammering in my chest, we locked eyes and stayed that way for a while. I nodded and he understood.

It would be okay.

Chapter 32

After the wedding, I prayed istikhara. I was feeling grief-stricken about everything and I realized I needed Allah's guidance and assistance. I was in a complete state of unrest. It was time for some damage control, and a little faith. I always had that, after all.

I knew I liked Menem. Hakeem's proposal only confirmed it for me. And I missed Menem terribly. But the cadetship was also pressing on my mind. I had an interview lined up for a position I felt zero excitement about. I didn't want my existence to rest on what everyone else thought about me or wanted for me. I wondered how long I had been this way: not really moving forward but sideways.

I wanted to progress. I *needed* to have something more fulfilling to look forward to in the mornings than being a world-class instant-coffee maker. But I wasn't sure writing for *Childhood* was it. In my heart of hearts, I wasn't sure I even wanted to write at all.

These scattered thoughts filled my mind as I prayed. I focused, doing my utmost to concentrate.

"Don't necessarily expect some major dream or signal," Sahar had advised once. "Just keep going as you are right now once you've done the prayer, assured in the knowledge that whatever is right for you will happen, inshallah."

I did dream that night—a lovely, comforting dream. Warm-towels-straight-out-of-the-dryer lovely. Only to then have the warm towels ripped viciously from my grasp and replaced with soggy, freezing cold ones when I realized it wasn't reality.

In the dream, I'd been in a nice car with Menem. He was driving, I was happily observing the rolling hillsides. Yes, they were rolling. It was magical. I'd never felt such peace and comfort, never felt so safe. Even I was a bit taken aback by this sudden spiritual awareness. It might have just been my subconscious talking, but I figured that was a sign in and of itself.

I didn't have the courage to contact Menem, despite my lovely dream. Instead, I went out for coffee three times on Wednesday, hoping I might run into him. I didn't. Nor had I even caught a glimpse since the wedding. He wasn't posting anything on Facebook. What if, rather than giving me my space, he was planning on avoiding me forever? I was a little fearful that I was too late, that he'd already moved on.

I knew I was being pathetic. Not even two full weeks had passed since our conversation. But after the way we'd left things, I couldn't blame him if he wanted to erase me from his memory.

Was I . . . ? Could I be . . . ? No, I couldn't say it.

Well, all right.

Was it possible that I was *lovelorn*?

I would survive this. Yes, I'd made an unsightly mess of things. But who knew, if given the chance, what I could manage were another spiffy suitor to come along? I'd be better prepared. Or better yet, maybe this was my opportunity to embrace a new path, sans suitors.

The relationship wasn't even cold yet and here I was already looking for the upside. There was no upside just now.

On the weekend, I reported my dream to Sahar and Lara. I hadn't told them what had happened with Hakeem, or even Menem, for that matter. I'd need to let Lara down gently, but I tried not to think about any of it too much. It was all too strange. Too . . . I didn't even know.

I'd hoped an afternoon with the girls would distract me from everything, and Sahar's cooking and assorted baked goodies usually helped.

We were sitting at the kitchen table, Sahar rolling stuffed vine leaves—dawali—while Lara and I tucked into quiche and muffins. The tangy aroma of rice, mince, and spices filled the tiny kitchen, mixed with the scent of freshly baked goods.

"That's a good dream, Samira," said Sahar. "Khayr inshallah. Try not to focus too much on it, though. It doesn't necessarily mean anything. Do the prayer again if you have to."

Maybe that would be a good idea. I had some clarity now, which was great except that I'd sort of lost the guy I was seeking clarity about. I nursed a cup of tea and bit into my third raspberry chocolate muffin. Don't judge me. They were fresh from the oven, and sugar hits always helped my thought processes. Besides, they weren't the monster-size muffins you buy at the shops; they were more cupcake-size, so two were really like one.

"Maybe I should do the prayer too," said Lara, licking her fork.

"For what?" I asked.

"Your cousin Jamal," she said, too nonchalantly for my liking.

"Lara, are you really serious about him? Remember that he's younger than you."

"I don't know. He's a lovely boy," she responded. Then a moment later, she said, "Oh my God, am I Demi Moore?"

Sahar was shaking her head again, but she smiled as she scooped out some rice and meat and placed them in the center of the vine leaves. I'd offered to help, but she'd insisted that I relax. Which was just as well, because I always ended up mutilating the leaves. Not surprisingly, Mum never asked me to help on these kinds of dishes.

"The Prophet, may peace be upon him, married an older woman, remember," said Sahar.

We looked at her, unsure what to do with the information.

"I'm just saying." Sahar shrugged. "A couple of years' difference isn't such a big thing."

"I never said age was the issue! Just maturity. He's young at heart," I told her.

"Samira, he's actually really smart. Just because he doesn't use fancy words doesn't make him dumb."

"I never said that. When did I ever say he's dumb?"

"It was implied. You're prejudiced against him because you think he's too woggy," said Lara matter-of-factly.

"Right, thanks, Lara!" I got up and went to the bathroom. I could hear her defending herself to Sahar, who was murmuring a reprimand.

Sighing, I stared at my reflection in the mirror, looking for answers. I looked a little sad. I had terrible bags under my eyes; they'd popped by unannounced and I couldn't get rid of them for anything.

On Friday morning before my interview for the cadetship, Cate had handed me a tiny bottle of a top-shelf eye gel that cost as much as a deposit on a nice apartment. "Trust me," she said, "your bags will disappear with this stuff. They won't know what hit 'em."

The miracle cure had worked for most of the day, but by the afternoon I'd looked even worse. Not that it had mattered. I was more concerned about looking less like a zombie and more like a human for my interview, which, thankfully, had gone very well.

At least I thought it had. Jan, the managing editor of *Childhood,* was lovely. We got along well, and I was in the interview for an hour. This, Cate assured me, was a good sign. And Jeff came by later in the afternoon and nodded as he stood before me. "You're the best assistant I've ever had," he said to me, not for the first time. "But on to bigger and better, Samina." Then he'd walked off. I wasn't sure if he'd been trying to say I'd gotten the job. I'd have to wait until next week to find out for sure.

I should have been optimistic and excited, but I wasn't. The job would be perfect for me content-wise: children wouldn't present problems, although interviewing doped-up pop singers might. All that aside, I did appreciate that *Childhood* wouldn't involve weddings.

No weddings. I took a moment to imagine it. Then I sighed. I was getting ahead of myself.

I made my ablutions for the next prayer, doing my utmost to block out all the negativity in my mind and making a mental list of urgent Things to Do. First task: banish damaging thoughts forever, or at least for an extended period of time. Second task: rid myself of horrible eye bags.

I concentrated through my repetitions, the water running soothingly over my hands, my arms, my feet. I felt better, cleansed.

As I left the bathroom, I heard my phone ringing. I ran into the kitchen and grabbed it, then went straight into the hallway to answer it.

I might have been hoping it was Menem. Or not. No biggie. It was a wrong number.

When I returned to the kitchen, Lara looked contrite.

"I'm sorry, Samira. I was out of line."

"It's okay," I said. "But how long have you thought of me as a snob?"

"Don't be silly! I'm just sensitive about this." Lara crossed her legs and picked at the tablecloth. "I know you think I'm corrupting him." Before I could say anything, she continued. "Which I sort of am doing, I guess. He's very innocent."

Sahar, who was still rolling the vine leaves, was quiet.

"I'm just asking you to be sure he's someone you can see yourself with," I explained. "Jamal is a pure soul. If he's interested and nothing comes of it, he'll be crushed."

"Well, I wouldn't want to hurt him," said Lara. "You're right, Samira. I'll back off."

"Thank you." We were all quiet for several seconds before I continued. "I think you need to find a job, but something you actually like this time."

"Maybe. I'd rather travel, if I'm being honest. My folks freak out when I bring it up, though. They already think people talk shit about me. A single woman traveling alone?" Lara made a face, then reached for a muffin.

Sahar offered no input. Instead, she fired up a burner on the stovetop to cook the dawaleh while I dropped my head onto my arms on the kitchen table, shutting my eyes tight.

"So can we expect an update anytime soon?" said Lara.

"About?" I mumbled.

"What do you think?"

"It's Sunday afternoon and I'm OD'ing on muffins and quiche. What do *you* think?" I replied, sitting up again.

"Leave her alone," said Sahar unexpectedly and with more force than I'd ever thought her capable of. Even Lara was stunned. "You're confusing her," Sahar said, placing the lighter to the side and turning to face us.

"I am not," protested Lara. "I'm just trying to show her why Hakeem could be right for her."

"Hakeem hasn't proposed to her. How do you know he's better?"

I would have corrected her if it weren't for her boldness. I hadn't seen Sahar this emotional about something since the time she'd found out her favorite brand of cooking chocolate had been discontinued.

"Samira, you don't want to marry someone who's going to be like a father," said Sahar.

"Ew!" exclaimed Lara. "Sahar, what in the bloody hell is wrong with you?"

"Lara," I interjected, "she doesn't mean it that way. Can we please change the subject?" I stood and walked over to the fridge, rubbing my face in my hands. I needed snappy, reasonable answers to my problems, not more drama. A say in my own life would have been nice about now too.

Then Lara spoke again. "He's not like her father. He's just very protective."

"She wants a *husband*, not a bodyguard," replied Sahar. "Why do you even care so much?"

"Because I want the best for Samira!" Lara crossed her arms, defensive and taken aback.

"How do you know what's best for her? She needs to be with someone who has the guts to step up and ask for her." Sahar tossed a wooden spoon into the sink. It made a loud clattering sound and we all looked at it. Lara and I stared at Sahar, whose attention was still on my wide-eyed cousin.

All that was missing was some popcorn. Perhaps some gladiatorial gear mightn't have gone astray either.

"Should I provide some mud?" I said.

They ignored me.

"Hakeem does want the best for her," Lara said. "He's always buying her books and whatnot."

"So what? If anything, he's just trying to make her into who he thinks she should be."

Sahar may have had a point there. I didn't mind Hakeem's gestures toward me; most of the time I appreciated them. But Menem was different with me. He wanted to know what I wanted; he didn't simply want things for me.

Besides that, Islamically, Menem had done the right thing in the end. He'd come to my parents and asked permission to see me. He hadn't cared how—supervised, in a basement, behind a curtain—he probably would have agreed to just about anything.

I coughed loudly. "Seriously, don't let me interrupt you, guys."

They didn't.

"It's like you're in love with him or something!" said Sahar hotly. Following this was a powerful moment of shocked silence. I leaned against the fridge, my arms crossed, my mouth residing somewhere on the spotless tiled floor.

Well, that was it. Sahar definitely had a pile of romance books stashed away somewhere in her house, maybe even in this kitchen.

Lara turned beet red. She was speechless, and I couldn't help but wonder at her reaction.

I broke the tension. "Are you quite finished?"

They both looked repentant as they turned to me.

"I wasn't going to say anything, but I suppose I have to now. Just for the record, nothing is going to happen between Hakeem and I, at all," I said unwaveringly, but not without a slight nudge in my stomach. "Lara, you have to let it go."

There was another stunned silence in the tiny kitchen.

"What happened?" exclaimed Lara. Sahar looked curious too.

"I don't want to be with Hakeem, Lara. I really don't. And I'm not in denial. I don't love him that way."

More astonishment.

"Neither do I, by the way," mumbled Lara. I smiled. Sahar seemed perplexed. "I was right about him, though. Wasn't I?" Lara continued, missing the solemnity of the moment. Think of a cat lapping up its milk.

I didn't want to tell her what had happened at the wedding. Feelings were involved—real emotions, not meaningless nothings for Lara to dissect. And what would I say? Yes, he does appear to have feelings for me, but he thinks we're wrong for each other? Never mind that he was right about that. Still, he was my friend.

I dropped again into a chair, but I really just wanted to curl up into a ball somewhere far, far away. "I think I've lost a perfectly wonderful man," I said miserably.

"I'm sure it's not too late with Menem," said Sahar.

"If he never spoke to me again, I couldn't blame him. He's

done nothing but be patient and respectful, and I've gone and thrown it in his face."

Lara was silently digesting my words, a guilty air about her. "I'm sorry for not being more encouraging and useful," she finally said. "I'm really sorry."

"It's not your fault," I replied.

We were all quiet again, the mood as deflated as a botched soufflé.

"God, adulthood is highly overrated," said Lara, studying the tablecloth thoughtfully. "One minute we're treated like babies, the next we're expected to make all these massive decisions." She frowned.

I nodded and felt tears well up in my eyes. *Bloody hell.*

"Oh!" said Lara getting up immediately. "Oh, sweetie!" She swooped over and put her arms around me. Sahar quickly joined in on the hug.

"Everything will right itself—you'll see," said Lara, rubbing my back.

"I know," I said. "I'm just being silly."

Lara tapped Sahar on the shoulder. "Quick, say something religious!"

Chapter 33

When I woke on Monday morning, I was still in my clothes from the day before. For a moment, I wondered if I'd been kidnapped, given that I wasn't tucked comfortably in bed in my pj's.

The panic subsided when I recognized my surroundings. I was definitely in my room. I registered my dressing table, the TV, then my wardrobe. My laptop sat precariously on my bedside table; I'd fallen asleep listening to music Lara had recommended last night.

"You need a soundtrack for this time in your life, sweetie," she'd said, pounding the names of several musicians into my phone.

I was in emo territory, so I had no qualms about listening to music that would make me cry.

I stumbled into work at 9:15—late but only just.

I didn't want to be there. I didn't want to be Jeff's assistant. I recoiled at the thought of instant coffee. I sat staring at my screen, reading but taking in nothing. I had thirty-five unread emails, the names and subject lines blurring into one another.

"Samina."

"Hi, Jeff."

"News."

"Pardon me?"

"Samina." He sighed. "I have news."

The job. Oh God. I was suddenly wide-awake. "What's the news?"

"What do you bloody think?" he said. "You're going to get offered the job. Just got off a call with Jan for the reference check."

"Oh my gosh! Thank you!" I said.

"Good pitch on that Muslim Barbie doll. They loved your ideas. Get me a coffee, please. Now." He stalked off.

I watched him saunter away, casting his eagle eyes over the editorial department and yelling out an indecipherable command to someone.

I remained seated, a little overwhelmed by the job offer. I'd won it, fair and square. I smiled, but a sick feeling snuck in, taking me by surprise. My excitement was evaporating. I had to remind myself what an amazing opportunity this presented. It would only be for a year, and it would lead to something better. I'd focus on the positives: I'd never have to think about instant coffee again; I'd be a bona fide journalist; I'd have respect.

But I couldn't ignore the negatives: I didn't like writing much. I much preferred taking photos.

When I took Jeff his coffee, I asked if I could speak with him for a moment. I couldn't believe I was about to do this.

He stared at me. Eventually realizing I was waiting for permission to sit down, he said, "Well, come on then."

I sat down and took a deep breath. "Jeff, I'm not sure how to say this," I began nervously, "but I think I'm going to move on."

"Ah yes, Samina, I think we just established that." He smiled at me like I was dim.

"No, I mean, I'm leaving altogether. Thank you so much for the job opportunity, but I'm afraid I have to refuse."

"Why in the hell would you do that? I know you like your job, but—"

I shook my head. "No, Jeff, it's not that. I need to explore other things."

"Such as?"

I toyed with the idea of being truthful with my boss. He had never behaved cruelly to me, so I didn't feel intimidated. But I wasn't sure there was any point.

"Samina?"

"I like taking photos," I told him.

"Photos?"

I nodded. "I've learned a lot while assisting at location shoots, and I prefer it to writing. I'm sorry, Jeff. I should have been upfront about it when you first spoke to me."

Jeff appeared at a loss. He swiveled about in his chair a bit before saying, "Get me your portfolio and I'll see what I can do."

"That's not necessary," I said, panicked, because I didn't have one.

Jeff sighed. "Samina."

"Okay."

"And I don't accept your resignation. Goodbye."

One frantic phone call to Gabriel later and I was looking better on the portfolio front. He was planning to extract my shots and put them together for me. All he asked for in return was a tray of baklawa and for me to "get over" myself. It seemed like a fair deal.

I felt better knowing I was in Gabriel's capable hands. Even so, I was fidgety and skittish. I needed someone to talk to about all of this work stuff.

The only person I could think of was Menem. Or rather, he was the only one I wanted to speak to. I decided against messaging him. It would seem odd for me to contact him out of the blue to ask for his advice. Much better to wait.

Okay. I know I'd said it would be wrong to message Menem. I'd said it and I'd meant it, but that didn't stop me from proceeding to do exactly that a few minutes later, sharing the news that I was getting offered the job, leaving out the fact that I didn't really want it.

Unsurprisingly, I was crushed when he didn't reply within a few minutes.

I didn't know exactly what I had been expecting. I would have been lucky to receive a polite reply from him. Yet there I was, hoping that he'd send me a meaningful text. Or call me.

Oh, I shouldn't have contacted him. I knew it.

My head drooped with disappointment and fatigue. I frowned and picked up my phone to check that the message had gone to the right person.

It had.

It was very unlike Menem not to reply. Even when he'd gotten very mad at me that day, he hadn't walked away without a polite farewell. So although it was unreasonable for me to expect a message in return, it wasn't stupid of me. I felt silly and small. Then I realized with no small amount of discomfort that I'd never let any man affect me this way. Obviously I hadn't known many men, which tended to decrease the risk of being affected. Still, that wasn't the point, was it?

A moment later the phone did a little dance on my desk as a message alert sounded. I grabbed it, my heart pulsing so hard in my throat I thought I'd swallowed it.

It was from him! He hadn't let me down. I opened the message with trembling hands.

> Menem: Congratulations on the new job, that's great news. Sorry for the delay in replying. My phone battery was flat.

Oh.

Well. That was nice. I wasn't sure what I'd wanted him to say. But I supposed I'd hoped for something *more*. Something that told me that he wasn't mad at me, and that we could repair things between us even after all of my shenanigans. I'd really only announced the job offer to him, I reasoned. Nevertheless, I felt deflated and sad. A bit annoyed, at him and then myself. His message told me that he was, in fact, mad at me. And a little smugly too.

I quietly said a brief invocation, best suited to times when you're feeling crap about everything.

So this was heartbreak, I realized. It *hurt*, and couldn't be cured by a tub of ice cream. It made me want to curl up and fall asleep and not have to deal with anything. Which, granted, was a little pathetic. I couldn't recall ever feeling this forlorn.

It was painful. And I couldn't do anything about it.

Or could I?

I had a light-bulb moment. Why was I conceding defeat? I thought about it: What else was Menem supposed to say to me?

We hadn't officially ended our "courtship." Close to, but not quite. Obviously Menem was far from pleased with me right now, but for all our parents knew, we were still working toward an official engagement. And Menem had left me to do some important thinking. And possibly link my conflicting personalities.

At least that's what I thought he'd done. I had to speak to him. I'd never forgive myself if I didn't.

Despite my burst of self-confidence, I was still preparing myself for the worst. The worst being that Menem had indeed decided I wasn't worth the effort and had moved on already. If he had, well then, I would have been well rid of him. How dare he move on so quickly just because I had some issues? We were both Arab, after all; surely he understood.

And if things didn't work out, I'd become a career woman. I'd learn how to cook too. I'd emerged from a life slump. A bit grazed and worse for wear, but I'd made it out of the wilderness. Head held high and all that.

Maybe there would be more love interests along the way, but they weren't going to be coming over with their mums. No more stats, no more awkward banter. No more chocolate biscuits to the undeserving.

I sent Menem another text and asked him if we could meet because I needed to talk to him. I was serious but exceedingly polite at the same time. And a few minutes of anxious thumbnail-biting later, I received a reply. He couldn't meet me now. Something about being very busy and that I was too late.

Okay, perhaps I made up that last bit. He didn't say I was too late, but I felt it.

I began tossing up whether to lock myself in a bathroom cubicle and cry my eyes out or write a strongly worded reply to Menem. Both seemed awfully tempting, but before I could do either, Cate arrived at my desk. "Ready to go?"

Chapter 34

The *Bridal Bazaar* staff were assembled in the lobby, ready to go out for a group lunch. Amy from sales was returning home to London, and Jeff had added in his email that I'd be moving on from *Bridal Bazaar*. Obviously that was before I'd cornered him in his office and offered my resignation.

Everyone was excited, but I suspected that was more to do with the prospect of a free lunch than Amy's departure or my cadetship. When they didn't whisk us up and carry us out of the building, cheering gaily, I knew I was right.

Cate swept up beside me, looking gorgeous in a summery off-the-shoulder maxi dress and gold stilettos. Her only accessory was a large plastic bangle.

"Hey, sweetie," she said, looping her arm around mine. "I forgot to tell you that this place has a bar. Is that a problem?"

"No, that's fine," I told her.

Cate smiled, relieved. "Okay, great, because I was worried you wouldn't come for a second." She pinched me, and we continued walking, arm in arm.

We converged on the brasserie-with-a-bar, chuffed that we had an excuse for a long lunch on a Monday. I was feeling a little better, happy to be distracted, and strangely optimistic.

When the food arrived, Cate began telling me a story about

her parents, whom she'd visited with Marcus in Melbourne. He wasn't with us, so I was getting the uncensored version of events.

"They loved him," she said, chomping into a cheeseburger, sauce dribbling down her fingers. "Now they're expecting me to get married!"

I laughed. "I happily pass the torch on to you," I told her, reaching over to steal some fries. I'd ordered a halloumi salad, but Cate's meal looked better.

"No thanks," she said, looking mortified.

"Isn't it the same as living with someone?"

Cate shrugged. "Marriage is . . . final. It's everything!"

That's what it seemed to ultimately come down to. No matter the culture or religion, marriage was of prime importance. It was not, however, everything. I'd managed so far without it. The world would not come to any sort of an end if I didn't get married anytime soon. Of course, I'd be heartbroken if Menem and I didn't work things out. Probably eat lots of ice cream despite my discovery that it didn't have true healing qualities in matters of the heart. But my life would not be over in any way, shape, or form.

"Well, you don't seem as freaked out about Marcus these days. That's an improvement at least." I smiled and Cate blushed.

"True."

"You never explained that, by the way," I said, still curious.

She sighed. "Oh, all right. He spent the night after our date. You can figure out the rest." She picked up her wineglass and took a sip.

"Oh, you mean . . . you and Marcus, on the first—?"

She nodded, embarrassed. "Look, I *never* do that," she said.

"You were so freaked out," I remarked.

Cate nodded. "I know! My instinct was to run, just get the hell outta there. But I don't know. He seemed different. I liked his honesty. He told me he'd liked me for ages but didn't have the courage to ask me out, and I was smitten."

"Okay, but why so uptight about it?"

"Because I liked him!"

"Right."

"I'm not good at emotions," said Cate.

Joanne from advertising tugged on Cate's sleeve, and as they struck up a conversation, I sat back and scanned the busy restaurant. It was noisy and packed. Lots of suits, business deals being dealt, a couple of group lunches like ours. Chatter and laughter competed with the sounds of pseudo–fine dining, and it occurred to me that we were all the same at a basic level. We just wanted to feel some happiness and to fill the gaps with good things, a nice meal, and some laughter.

Then I noticed him. Menem was at a table in the same restaurant, in the corner by the kitchen.

And he was with a woman, a very pretty one in fact.

I felt a little dizzy. And so stupid.

My God, what had I been thinking? He *was* too good to be true. Of course he was. No one could be that nice and lovely and adoring and speak Arabic beautifully. He *was* a Casanova!

Menem had told me he was busy with work. Couldn't fit me into his schedule. But there he was, sitting and chatting away with a pretty woman.

Cate finished speaking with Joanne and turned to me. She followed my gaze.

"Samira?"

As though he could tell someone was looking at him, Menem

looked up and saw me. More important, he understood the look on my face.

This would be the moment to make a dramatic exit. Fly out of my seat and run off crying. An extremely appealing plan it was too. Instead, I held back the tears awaiting their cue.

"Can we go, please?" I said to Cate, already gathering up my handbag.

She nodded quickly. "Of course."

We stood up, our chairs scraping across the hardwood floor. Most of our team were at the bar (free alcohol), but I didn't give them a second glance.

At first Menem just sat there, but as soon as I began moving, he leapt (well, hurriedly got up) from his seat and called out to me.

I increased my pace once I was outside, while poor Cate tottered after me.

"Samira, wait," she said.

I felt bad ignoring her, but I couldn't slow down. Oh, the humiliation. I wanted to scream at the top of my lungs. I picked up speed, grateful I was in ballet flats.

"Samira!" This time it was Menem calling out to me. He caught up with me easily and reached out to take my arm, but I yanked it away. "Samira, stop!" he said.

"I'm sorry, aren't you very busy right now?"

"Yes!" he said with energy. "I am."

"Well, don't let me keep you," I said, realizing just how unoriginal heartbreak could be. I could have said something unexpected and different, something terribly clever. But no.

God, I hoped we weren't attracting a crowd of curious onlookers. That was what always happened in movies, wasn't it? The crowd would slowly form, people smiling and pointing, waiting to see an outcome.

I looked around self-consciously. No one was looking at us. I didn't even know where Cate was by now. I realized we were in the same park where we'd had that terrible argument.

"What is wrong with you?" said Menem, and I finally stopped trying to escape and stared at him. He looked tired. Still dashing, though.

"Me?" I said incredulously. "What's wrong with *me*? I just saw you having lunch with another woman when an hour ago you told me you were busy. 'Sorry, Samira. Not today,' you said. I guess you meant never."

"She's a colleague!" he said helplessly. "And we weren't alone! There were three other people with us."

"A colleague!" This was not a question.

"I swear to God! Why on earth would you think I'd do something like that?" Menem said.

He wasn't lying, I realized. I guessed I hadn't noticed the other colleagues while I'd been busy fuming away at his betrayal.

"I'm sorry," I said, feeling embarrassed to the core.

Menem let out a sigh of relief. "You're unbelievable," he said.

"Well, I haven't heard from you. What was I supposed to think?"

"You told me you needed time!" he said, exasperated.

"Well, I didn't think you'd give it to me!"

Menem shook his head. "My God," he said, turning away in surrender.

"Do you hate me?" I said, my voice trembling.

Menem turned around, looking taken aback by my question. "What? Hate you?"

I nodded.

"Samira, what are you talking about? Why would you think that?"

"Because I just accused you of doing something awful. Because I've been so difficult when all you've ever been is kind and patient and lovely."

Menem shook his head. "Samira." He took a step closer. "I wasn't patient. I could have been better. I could have asked you how you felt, rather than focusing on my feelings as though they were enough for both of us."

A lump formed in my throat. He moved closer still.

"Do you have any idea how amazing you are?" Menem said. When I didn't respond, he continued. "I thought I was being clear about how I felt. I had no doubts about you. And I guess I was waiting for you to say the same. But it became obvious we weren't on the same page."

"No, that's not it. I'm new to this, Menem. I was wrong not to share things more openly with you. And I know it." My hands were shaking and even my lips were quivering by that point.

There was a tiny flicker of something in Menem's eyes. "What are you saying, Samira?"

Oh God. It was now or never. There was nothing to lose— except my self-respect and pride, both of which I'd deserted many times throughout my life journey so far. But I knew I would never forgive myself if I didn't attempt to fix this now.

"If the offer is still there," I said, slowly raising my face to meet his gaze, "I would like to get engaged to you. I want to marry you."

That was, quite simply, one of the hardest things I'd ever had to say. I'd mustered all my courage. Thrown caution to the wind. Put myself on the line.

A few tears tumbled down my face. I felt exhausted. Menem still hadn't said anything, but he was studying me, doubt marking his features. He obviously wasn't sure what to make of me just now.

I couldn't blame him. For all he knew, I was settling.

But I wasn't. Not at all. I was whatever the opposite of settling was. In another world, if we'd been able to just date like everyone else, this might have been a whole lot easier.

"Do you mean that?" Menem said at last.

I nodded. "I meant every word. I want to be with you. I should have said that weeks ago. It's just . . . It's partly your fault, you know. I've only just opened my eyes, and I'm not sure where to look." That was the half of it. I had work to do, yes. But who knows when I'd have gotten started if Menem hadn't entered my life. "You give me strength," I said.

Menem slowly brought his hand up to my face and wiped a tear from my cheek. More tears immediately followed and I could barely breathe. This was the first time he'd touched me properly and I felt an instant jolt run through me. I placed my hand over his and pressed my cheek against it. He moved closer and cupped my face. If I hadn't known any better, I would've thought he was about to kiss me. Instead, he pulled me in so that my head was resting against his chest and held me tight.

He exhaled. Our first proper hug, and I had yet to breathe. I didn't care if anyone was watching. I felt safe, and the feeling was electric. I took in his scent. I let him hold me, enjoying the comfort of a solid embrace.

"I still want you," he said.

Chapter 35

As with all marriage-related business (Arab Standard Time was tossed out the window), things were already on track for an engagement. This only slightly freaked me out, but I felt a scattering of genuine excitement too. I'd met a lovely man and it was a new experience.

However, I felt nervous about telling Hakeem. He'd have heard it from his father already, but I owed him a conversation. So the next evening I sent him a message, asking if we could talk.

I'd called Lara that afternoon to tell her the news. She'd cried, which had surprised me to no end because she only cried watching BBC productions, never in real life. She even got me teary. It was emotional. Then she'd promised to go shopping with me to buy a dress for my party, something I'd not given any thought to, mainly because I would elope if I could.

She was mortified to realize, however, that I would be marrying into the same family as Zahra. "Lord, who'd have thought it?" she'd cried. "I think you got the good brother, by the way. But gawd, it's bad enough being related to her. Now you'll have the same in-laws! Make sure they like you more!"

I promised her I'd try. Then she'd declared that she was going into cake making with Sahar while she worked on her parents regarding a trip to Europe solo: "She needs help with the business, she's busy, and daily lunch is included."

Perhaps Sahar and Lara could balance each other out—Lara did have creative flair. But she also had the attention span of a flea, so I wasn't highly optimistic on the longevity front.

When I spoke to Sahar (more tears), she'd praised Allah, in several variations: Subhanallah! Mashallah! Alhamdulillah! As well as a few obscure expressions I couldn't translate.

Then, of course, there were my parents.

It was bizarre telling Mum and Dad, almost like an out-of-body experience. I'd approached them when they were in the sitting room watching an Arabic program. I was probably beaming, about to burst, but I still managed to be the essence of composure.

I told them I had accepted Menem's proposal, prompting them to look away from the television and study me. Dad was the first to speak.

"Alhamdulillah. Very good, Samira. This is magnificent news!"

Then he changed the TV station and tuned in to the Lebanese version of *Who Wants to Be a Millionaire?* as though it was every day that his daughter announced she'd found a dashing man.

Mum, meanwhile, didn't say anything. She had a strange look on her face. Not her standard Look, but then she had probably heard from Menem's mother already.

I waited, expecting something profound to be sent my way. Mum and I had never really bonded, but she seemed to be in a peculiar mood, so I wouldn't have been surprised if she'd started quoting Keats.

"Mabrook, habibti," she said eventually with a tender smile. Congratulations, sweetheart.

I nearly died. Mum had never called me sweetheart. It might have made for a perfect moment too, had the heartfelt congratulations not been followed by "Now fold the washing."

It wasn't metaphorical, I'd quickly realized.

No matter. Current state: excited. About everything. No guilt to be found here. No nerves to be seen or heard, except for one little annoying thought. Something was beginning, but I was also facing an ending. And I wasn't quite sure how to deal with it.

Hakeem finally replied an hour later, just as I was imagining Menem and I doing fancy things like hot-air ballooning and taking long drives in the country. And all that other stuff people share on social media.

Hakeem: Hey.

I was so grateful he wasn't standing in front of me. This was so hard. How was I going to say this? I was never stumped like this. It should have been the easiest thing in the world. But of course, after everything that had happened, after our conversation at the wedding, it was anything but easy.

As it turned out, I didn't have to worry about telling him.

Hakeem: I hear congratulations are in order.
Samira: You do know already then?
Hakeem: Of course. Did you forget you're Arab? :)
Samira: No. But I wanted to tell you myself.
Hakeem: It's OK. I knew it was coming.

Samira: I suppose. Well, about time, eh?
Hakeem: I pray everything works out well for you, inshallah.
     You deserve only the best. I mean that sincerely.
Samira: Thank you.

Before I knew what was happening, a lonesome tear found its way to the corner of my eye. Just the one, though; there was no mutiny this time.

I was going to miss Hakeem. I was going to miss the friendship we shared, the conversations we had. I'd probably even miss his sternness. But most of all, I hoped he knew how much I loved him.

I hesitated. What else should I say? Was there anything else *to* say?

Yes. Lots. But I would keep it simple.

Samira: I'm going to miss you.

A vintage Hakeem pause.

Hakeem: Ditto.

A moment later he started typing again.

Hakeem: I'm sorry for ruining things.
Samira: You didn't. It's OK. Honestly.

He paused again.

Hakeem: "I no doubt deserved my enemies, but I don't
     believe I deserved my friends."

Now I took a moment.

> Samira: George Clooney?
> Hakeem: Funny.
> Samira: Wrong?
> Hakeem: It's Walt Whitman.
> Samira: :)
> Hakeem: You watch too many movies.
> Samira: I know.

It was a while before he wrote again.

> Hakeem: You're probably feeling a bit afraid right now. But
> you'll be fine.

I thought so too.

Later that night, after I'd confirmed my parents were properly asleep, I texted Menem. A few minutes later, I saw a flash of headlights from the street through my window. That was my cue.

I smiled, a little giddy that I was about to do this. It was something I'd always wanted to do—sneak out of my bedroom window to meet a boy.

It might have been the effects of too many romantic comedies. But while those stories were simplistic and fanciful, I finally understood their popularity. Falling in love was an intoxicating experience.

Our house was a one-story, so exiting via the window didn't require much athleticism or courage. But my heart was

313

hammering in my chest as I carefully made my way out, lowering the window slowly to minimize noise.

I had joked about a midnight rendezvous, but Menem had suggested we truly make it happen.

Twenty minutes later, just short of 2 a.m., we arrived at a hidden spot overlooking the harbor. Despite a sprinkling of nerves, I felt at ease with Menem, and perhaps because of the darkness and quiet, it seemed like for the first time we were truly alone.

We took a stone staircase down to a patch of grass by the water. Behind us were mid-rise residential flats, the windows mostly dark; in front of us was the cityscape, its multicolored lights winking back at us.

"Are you warm enough?" Menem said.

I tightened my jacket around me. "Yep."

"I can't believe you snuck out. What will the neighbors say?"

I smiled. "Very funny."

"For my lady," Menem said, presenting me with a box of chocolate hearts.

"You really know the way to a girl's heart."

"I'm *smooth* as."

We grinned a little stupidly, but then Menem's face softened. "You must know I love you, right?" he said, holding my gaze. "Right?"

I cocked my head to the side. "And I like you a lot."

The effect was instant. Menem feigned being stabbed in the heart as I laughed.

"Brutal," he said.

I placed the box of hearts to the side, then inched toward Menem. Soon our bodies were close enough for Menem to wrap an arm around me.

"I wish there was a more creative way to say it, but I love you too." I felt Menem exhale.

He pulled me in a bit closer. "Any thoughts on a honeymoon? Maybe somewhere we can do some abseiling?"

I mock-slapped him on the stomach and he shook with laughter. But then he took my hand and kissed the back of it.

I pulled away and turned to face him.

"You okay?" he said.

I reached out to take his hands in mine. My eyes traveled up to meet his, and we stayed like that for a few seconds before he understood. He waited, still watching me, and I nodded.

Menem extricated his hands from mine, then reached up to touch my face. He leaned in and I could barely breathe. Then his lips softly touched mine.

I felt a quickening of emotion, surprising and exciting. He moved away to check in, but I pulled him back. He kissed me again, deeper, longer, and his hands moved down to my neck and my shoulders.

Eventually we separated and I felt breathless. Then we looked at each other and burst out laughing.

"We should do that again," he said.

"We should do that a lot."

We stayed there for another hour, out in the open but in our own constructed bubble.

I knew this wasn't a happy ending to my story.

No. If anything, it was a happy beginning.

Glossary

As this story includes several Arabic words and phrases, a glossary has been included for the reader's reference.

abu—father of (Arabs generally address one another as "father of" or "mother of")

alhamdulillah—praise Allah (used in relation to giving thanks)

Allahu akbar—God is great

a'mmi—paternal uncle

a'mou—uncle (non-relative)

a'mti—paternal aunt

assalamu alaykum—peace be upon you (the standard Islamic greeting)

bismillah—in the name of God

dawah—invitation to Islam (it's the expression used to describe sharing Islam with others and inviting them to the religion)

habibti—my darling, my sweetheart (feminine)

hadith—an oral tradition of the Prophet

halal—permissible

haram—forbidden

im—mother of (see "abu")

inshallah/insha'Allah—God willing

istikhara—the Islamic prayer for guidance

khayr inshallah/inshallah khayr—may there be good,
    God willing

khalee—maternal uncle

khaltee—maternal aunt

khaltou—aunt (non-relative)

marhaba—hello

mashallah/masha'Allah—praise Allah

naseeb—fate; lot in life

nikah—Islamic marriage ceremony

o'balik—may it be your turn next (said to someone as
    a wish for the same event/achievement to happen—
    e.g., marriage, engagement, graduation, pregnancy)

wa'alaykum assalam—and unto you be peace (the standard
    response to the Islamic greeting)

wala himmik—not to worry

yallah—come on; let's go

zaghrouta—celebratory ululation

zakat—almsgiving

About the Author

AMAL AWAD is a writer, director, and performer who lives in Sydney, Australia. She has written for *ELLE, The Sydney Morning Herald,* and *The Guardian,* among others, and has held senior editorial roles at a number of trade media publications. Awad has spoken at schools, universities, and writers' festivals throughout Australia. In 2019, she was a TEDx Macquarie speaker, presenting a talk called "Moving Beyond the Token Minority" in film and television.

In recent years, Awad has also pursued directing and acting in addition to her screenwriting work for film and television. She is the author of eight books, including four novels—*Courting Samira, This Is How You Get Better, The Things We See in the Light,* and *Bitter & Sweet*—and four nonfiction books—*The Incidental Muslim, Beyond Veiled Clichés, Fridays with My Folks,* and *In My Past Life I Was Cleopatra. Courting Samira* is the first of her books to be published in America.

Here ends Amal Awad's
Courting Samira.

The first edition of this book was printed
and bound at Lakeside Book Company
in Harrisonburg, Virginia, in October 2023.

A NOTE ON THE TYPE

The text of this novel was set in Sabon, an old-style serif typeface created by Jan Tschichold between 1964 and 1967. He drew inspiration for it from the elegant and highly legible designs of the famed sixteenth century Parisian typographer and publisher Claude Garamond and named it after Jacques Sabon, one of Garamond's close collaborators. Sabon has remained a popular typeface in book design for its quintessential smooth and clean look.

HarperVia

An imprint dedicated to publishing international voices,
offering readers a chance to encounter other lives and other
points of view via the language of the imagination.